PRIMMY'S DAUGHTER

The Fifth in the Cornish Clay Series

PRIMMY'S DAUGHTER

The Fifth in the Cornish Clay Series

Rowena Summers

The countless links are strong
that bind us to our clay.
The loving spirit lingers long
and would not pass away.

Emily Brontë

This first world edition published in Great Britain 1998 by
SEVERN HOUSE PUBLISHERS LTD of
9–15 High Street, Sutton, Surrey SM1 1DF.
First published in the U.S.A. 1998 by
SEVERN HOUSE PUBLISHERS INC of
595 Madison Avenue, New York, N.Y. 10022.

British Library Cataloguing in Publication Data

Summers, Rowena, 1932-
    Primmy's daughter
    1.   Cornwall (England) – Fiction
    I.   Title

    823.9'14 [F]

    ISBN 0 7278 5326 0

Typeset by Hewer Text Composition Services Ltd,
Edinburgh, Scotland.
Printed and bound in Great Britain by
MPG Books Ltd, Bodmin, Cornwall.

Chapter One

The old woman's mind was drifting again. It happened more and more often these days – but as folk said, if you weren't entitled to spend a bit of time dreaming when you were in your eightieth year, when could you?

Until the landmark birthday had come and gone, Morwen had always bridled at such remarks, still commenting smartly that she still had her wits and senses, thank you very much, and she'd mind and have proper respect from her young 'uns . . .

Young 'uns! Her face softened as she sat in the window seat of her bedroom at the house known as New World, contemplating the sweetly-scented moors stretching away as far as the eye could see, and breathing in the familiar aromas of yarrow and bracken and gorse. *Young* 'uns indeed, and not one of her own under forty years old themselves now. And her contemporaries were all as ancient as she was herself . . .

But she didn't feel ancient in her heart and soul – except when the rheumatics reminded her that she was no spring chicken any more. And the annoying stiffening in her joints was a legacy of the years when she'd scampered barefoot, hither and thither on the moors in all weathers in the service of old Charles Killigrew and his clayworks, as lithe and eager as a young gazelle.

They were *her* clayworks now, she reminded herself. Or, at least, that part of them that belonged to her. Truth to tell, the whole muddling inheritance thing was beyond her thinking these days. Since Ran died five years ago, she had little heart for the doings of the clay business. Losing her second husband

1

had taken all her spark for a long while, and as long as her son Walter said the dividends were healthy, she cared little for any financial dealings.

But their standard of living had long been a world away from her own humble beginnings in a moorland cottage where you could see the stars between the slates. It was so long ago, but Morwen still remembered the way it was . . . and she remembered so well the people whose lives had been intertwined with her own. Some still here, some gone . . . and sometimes she could still hear their voices in her head . . .

"Should we visit the old witchwoman on the moors and beg for a love potion, Morwen? Do 'ee dare to come wi' me?" *Celia . . . oh, my poor, foolish, drowned Celia . . .*

"My name is Ben. We have no need to be formal . . ." *Ben, darling Ben . . .*

"You do me a power of good, young Morwen Tremayne. I like having you around me. So I want you to be my housekeeper." *Old Charles Killigrew, owner of the great clayworks, Killigrew Clay*, who saw more than anyone else that she and his son Ben were destined to be wed.

And the memory of her own voice, young and breathless, newly-married and so much in love . . .

"You and I have always belonged, Ben. I've known it in the heart of me, even if I haven't always admitted it. We can't deny what's destined for us."

Morwen's eyes flickered, brought reluctantly back to the present by the chiming of a clock somewhere in the house, and knowing her companion would be bringing her afternoon tea very soon. At her age, she admitted, she was happiest in reminiscing and she certainly had no truck with listening to tales of threatened strikes at the clay works, or wranglings between pit captains and clayworkers for tuppences and dues.

That was for younger folk to deal with, and nobody expected her to be involved in any of it any more. It was one of the benefits of growing old, and of being a woman in a man's world.

2

Her eyelids drooped again, as they so often did without warning these days. Dreaming about the old days when she had been a beautiful young girl, black-haired and blue-eyed, and the darling of Ben Killigrew's heart . . . and of Ran Wainwright's too, the dream always reminded her . . . and of all the children they had nurtured and cherished between them in her two marriages.

The children they had kept close to home in their beloved Cornwall, and those they had lost to other shores. It was so easy to let her dreaming take her anywhere it chose, to good times and bad, and to moments far too special to forget.

Her daughter, Primmy, had had a series of miscarriages since her marriage to her cousin Cresswell in California. And living so far away from home, each time a letter arrived from Primmy telling Morwen of the latest searing disappointment, it simply tore at her mother's heart.

She knew her girl. She knew the Cornish heart of her, and the way her superstitious reasoning would say that she didn't deserve a child. Not after the brief wickedness of her adolescence when she had dabbled in the forbidden narcotics and led the Bohemian life with her brother Albie and their progressive, arty friends. And unwittingly almost caused a scandal in the family when the news had leaked out to newspapers. Smearing the innocent relationship of a brother and sister, and almost bringing shame and disgrace on the family name. Primmy had finally confessed it all to Morwen, and, loyally, Morwen had believed her story.

Oh yes, they had survived all the storms, yet the one thing Primmy and Cresswell longed for most seemed to be denied them. It was not until they had been wed for a number of years that the joyful news had arrived in Cornwall that little Sinclair Tremayne had been safely delivered. And four years later, their much-wanted daughter . . .

The gilt-edged card announcing the birth had accompanied a personal letter for Morwen, but the name of the child

3

had provoked varying reactions, notably from Morwen's son, Luke.

He had read the card aloud, his one-time thoughts of crossing the Atlantic himself completely forgotten now that he was a fully-fledged university student, and his set were much given to making sneering comments on all things American.

'Cresswell and Primrose Tremayne are delighted to announce the birth of their daughter, Skye, at The Appletrees, Mainstown, New Jersey, June 16th 1891. A sister for Sinclair.'

"*Skye!*" Luke had almost exploded on reading the name of the new child. "What kind of a name is that to give anybody! This is the American influence, Mother. I told you it would happen. Primmy's not seeing sense any more."

"You'd best be careful, Luke. You'll upset your father if he hears you being scathing about Americans—"

"Oh, Father's lived among us for too long for such remarks to bother him. He's almost British by now."

British? Not *Cornish*? *And when did you turn into such a pompous ass*? Morwen thought, eyeing her son in annoyance, who was then a pretentious twenty-two years old and down from university for part of the summer vacation before he went off to stay in Oxford with some of his more obnoxious chums.

Chums, for glory's sake. Morwen squirmed at the term, knowing her lusty daddy would have turned over in his grave had he heard such a namby-pamby word used in their family.

"Anyway, I think Skye is a perfectly beautiful name," she said, not letting Luke's disparaging remarks take away one iota of her pleasure. And how could she, when she had read and re-read Primmy's private and euphoric words to herself so many times, and laughed and cried for joy with her in spirit?

4

'I still can't quite take it all in, Mammie,' Primmy had written. 'After all the previous disappointments we hadn't even dared to think of a name for her until she was safely born. I keep looking at her all day long, and I have to pinch myself to believe that she's really here, and that she's really mine. And the moment I saw her, so beautiful, with such black hair and true blue Tremayne eyes, and looking exactly like *you*, Mammie, it was as if a little bit of heaven had fallen out of the sky and straight into my heart. And right away, I knew there could be no other name for her. She had to be Skye. Cress thinks it's perfect, and so do Aunt Louisa and Uncle Matt, so I hope you and Ran approve.'

Morwen hadn't shown the letter to anyone else but Ran. It was too personal and just too *Primmy* to share. And she tried to squash a small unreasoning jealousy because Cress's parents had obviously been told the news first. She certainly mustn't begrudge them their joy. And they were all family, for goodness' sake. Louisa was her own husband's cousin, and Matt was Morwen's brother, and you couldn't get much closer family ties than that! And they lived in the same continent as the new parents, even if it was thousands of miles apart, by all accounts. Morwen wasn't too bright about geography, and America was America to her.

It didn't matter who was told about the baby first. Primmy was still her darling, if only because she had been the one with spirit, the wild child who had dared to follow her heart as Morwen herself had once done – Primmy, her adopted daughter, yet the one who was more her own than any of the others in so many ways.

Amazingly, Ran had understood how she felt. He wasn't Cornish, as she was, but sometimes she felt that he had a Cornishman's understanding for knowing the things that were important to her. They had grown together over the

5

years, and they had toasted their new grand-daughter Skye together.

"To our beautiful Skye," he had said. "And may the stars always shine on her, honey, as they have always shone on us."

Morwen's heart had warmed to his simple words, said in the American accent he had never lost, nor tried to lose in all the years he had lived in Cornwall. And even if the stars certainly hadn't always shone on them, and the fortunes of the clay empire had sometimes fluctuated to the point of disaster, she wasn't going to comment on that now, when they were both jubilant with Primmy's news.

"I wish I could have been with her," she said wistfully. "To see a new life brought into the world is truly a magical experience, Ran."

"And best left to womenfolk," he said smartly.

"I must admit it's a time that brings women together more than any other," she said, remembering how she had helped at a birthing on more than one occasion and never lost the awesome feeling of privilege at the sight. Births and deaths and all the joys and traumas in between were what drew people together – even one-time rivals.

How little jealousy mattered now, yet how devastating it had once been when she was a young girl, thinking that her darling Ben was paying court to Jane Askhew – Miss 'Finelady' Jane, as she had dubbed her. And years later, a flamboyant woman clay boss had tried to steal Ran from her. Oh yes, jealousy had always been her own personal devil.

"What foolishness is going through your head now, honey?" Ran asked lazily, pouring himself a second glass of brandy, watching her face.

"You wouldn't want to know. Just women's thoughts."

"Then how about if I offer some men's thoughts? How about if you and I take a trip to visit this fine young grand-daughter of ours?" he said, knocking all other thoughts out of her head.

6

Morwen gasped. "You don't mean it! Go to America? Oh, I'd be far too terrified—"

"Why would you? Your daughter did it, and so did your own brother all those years ago. Are you less of a woman than your own daughter, and less spunky that the rest of the spirited Tremaynes? I'm sadly disappointed in you, Morwen."

But he was only teasing her, and as he saw her indignant face, he laughed, and told her pointedly that it was time for bed, so he could see if there was still some spirit in the lovely Tremayne girl he'd married.

She had been a Killigrew widow by then, she'd thought silently, but to Ran Wainwright and to half the young bucks in the county, she was still the lovely Tremayne girl.

But the very thought of going to America, that vast, unknown country, had totally unnerved her. It sent her straight back to the vulnerable young girl she had been, with that proud, straight back and the dramatically beautiful face, when she felt like curling up with embarrassment when one of the gentry looked at her.

Her initial reaction to Ran had been to refuse the idea of this trip absolutely. But then she had second thoughts, knowing how much she would be disappointing him. He was offering her a chance to see the country of his birth; to see her daughter and her new grand-daughter, and her grandson, Sinclair; and hopefully to see her brother, Matt. He and Louisa seemed to see no problem in travelling clear across the continent from California to the New Jersey seaside town where Primmy and Cresswell had made their home.

So in the end she went, with as much trepidation as if she was going to the moon. And just about resisting taking all sorts of good luck charms with her, to keep her safe on the sea voyage, something an old witchwoman of the moors might have once prescribed to ensure good fortune and protection from all harm.

And it had all been worth it. The baby was a treasure, and

7

even Morwen could see herself in the wide-eyed, blue stare and the dimpled chin, and the abundant mop of hair, as black as jet. She wouldn't have missed the experience of seeing Skye for anything, and Sinclair too, even though she found him an odd and serious child. But home was still Cornwall, and once the month was over, she was thankful in her heart to be safely setting foot back on Cornish soil again.

It was strange to think that neither family had crossed the Atlantic again, and yet perhaps not so strange. The New Jersey family had been in California when Ran died, visiting the other grandparents, so there was no question of them reaching Cornwall in time for the funeral, and people had their own lives to live.

But through the years there had been much correspondence, and many photographs of the children and their parents, until Morwen had an album stuffed with them.

She had seen how Sinclair had grown as tall as Cress, and was now dabbling seriously in politics. And how Skye was turning into a real beauty, with the fey Cornish looks that warmed her grandmother's heart. The letters and the photos made it almost as good as having them here. Almost.

"What sorrows me most," she once confided to her artist son, Albie, "is missing the important milestones of their lives. The college graduations, the birthdays, the eventual coming-of-age parties for them both."

Matt and Louisa had shared all of that, while she had learned it all at secondhand, even though Skye had turned into a wonderful and expressive letter-writer. Her writing skills were such that now she actually worked as a freelance for a magazine, so that her words were read by hundreds of people. "*Thousands*," Albie had corrected her, "if not millions."

But Morwen's brain hadn't been able to cope with such quantities of folk. And as her companion entered her room with her tea tray on that early summer afternoon, she told herself severely now that she she mustn't get maudlin with an

8

old woman's selfish thoughts in wishing her family was still all around her like a warm and protective cloak. She would just indulge herself in dreams, and imagine they were here instead.

Skye Tremayne was studying the beautiful oil painting on the wall of her parents' bedroom. Her mother had always insisted on keeping it in her private domain, and Skye had seen the painting almost every day of her life, but she never tired of looking at it. And right now she had a very special reason for imprinting every detail of it in her heart. When she saw the scene for real, she would know it instantly.

"You'll wear that painting out," Primmy said mildly, eyeing her daughter with an indulgent smile. Her beautiful Skye, who had turned out exactly as every mother hoped a daughter would be. And she had been more precious than most, since Primmy had almost given up hope of ever having her.

And now . . . she forced a bright smile, trying not to behave stupidly over Skye's decision. Knowing, somehow, that this had always been destined to happen. And knowing too, how her own Mammie must have felt, all those years ago, when they had waved good-bye to herself and Cress and Cress's parents, on the Falmouth quay. It was natural to wonder fearfully if you would ever meet again . . . and it was foolish to think that Skye's sabbatical would be anything more than the year away that Cress had paid for so generously. Even if she would be so far away, they had the special links that bound them all together. Skye wouldn't be alone.

"Is it really as beautiful as this, Mom?" her daughter said now, smiling her quick, intelligent smile, and tracing the shape of the artist's studio and the clear blue water of the quaintly-named Lemon River with an elegant finger. You could almost see its ripples; almost smell its wafting scent of the sea beyond Truro; and Primmy felt a ridiculous urge to snatch Skye's finger away so that she didn't

9

defile the painting her beloved Albie had given her as a leaving gift.

"It's just as beautiful," she said steadily. "And even more so in reality."

"But the building looks so small. I imagined an artist's studio to be far more spacious. It must have been pretty cramped for you and Uncle Albie to live above the shop, so to speak, after you left home to set up your own place."

"It wasn't cramped at all! Compared with many Cornish homes, it was quite large. Wait until you see some of the cottages on the moors above the clayworks, and then you'll know what small is, my love!"

For a moment, the memory almost overcame her, and she pushed it away. Primmy hadn't yearned for the smells and sights of the clay-working community for years, if ever, but her daughter's enthusiasm was bringing it all back. You could never completely ignore such a troubled background of family heritage, not while the rest of them were all still involved, if not embroiled, in it, she guessed. But she didn't want to think of any of it now.

She saw Skye straighten up, flicking back her long black hair from her shoulders. She kept threatening to have it cut, now that she was a happily unmarried old doll of twenty-three, as she gleefully called it, but they all thought it would be a crime to cut that glorious hair. Besides, it marked her out as somebody independent and unconformist. And Skye liked that.

"Well, I can't wait to meet them all," she declared. "Granny Morwen sounds such a darling, and if the rest of them are like her, I shall have a wonderful time."

"They're certainly not all like her," Primmy warned. "But you wouldn't expect them to be, would you?"

"Well, the young ones will be fun, I'm sure," Skye said breezily, refusing to be dampened. "There are so many cousins I've hardly heard of that I can't keep track of them all."

But it was a pretty sure bet that they wouldn't miss *her*,

Primmy thought. Not for the first time, she wondered how they would react to her daughter. Cornish folk were insular in their location and their outlook, and nothing had changed that much over the centuries. They viewed strangers with suspicion, and she remembered when Cresswell had arrived on the scene, just as open and determined to be friendly as their daughter.

And Primmy had almost shut the door in his face, remembering how he had been the catalyst to turn her feeling of family security and belonging upside down in one childish remark. Revealing that she and her brothers weren't Morwen's children after all, but her nephews and niece. It had been a huge shock to discover it so brutally, a shock from which Primmy had thought she would never recover. And then the adult Cresswell had marched back into her life and into her heart . . .

"You must give me a list of all their names and who belongs to whom, Mom," Skye was saying now. "I'll never remember them all."

"They won't expect you to. Just don't try to do everything at once, that's all."

Skye laughed. "In other words, take it slowly, and don't rush in like the proverbial bull at a gate, in my usual fashion, is that it?"

"It's just that they live at a slower pace of life, lamb, that's all. Don't overwhelm them all at once."

"My Lord, they're not all hayseeds, are they?"

Primmy felt a sliver of anger at this assumption.

"That they are not!"

Skye's father came into the bedroom before Primmy could elaborate on this. Cresswell Tremayne had prospered over the years and his real estate company was thriving, set to become even bigger. He was astute and aggressive in business, but he grinned now as he heard his daughter's remark.

"Careful, honey, your mother bites whenever her family is criticised."

"I do not!" Primmy said at once, and then laughed, knowing

11

she had taken the bait. "Well, maybe I do. They're a rare bunch, and I wish I could be a fly on the wall when they first get a look at you, love."

"Then come with me!" Skye said at once, just as Primmy had known she would. Just as predictably, she shook her head.

"We both know that's not a likelihood. You'll have your work, and I have my music. Besides, what would your father do without me? And Sinclair, too."

Skye snorted. "Why Sinclair wants to bother with all that political stuff I can't imagine. And now he's moved into that Washington DC apartment, he wouldn't even notice you'd gone."

"But your daddy would," Primmy said softly, as Cress's hand reached out and squeezed hers for a moment.

Seeing it, Skye turned away. Those two! Sometimes they acted more like kids than respectable people nearing sixty years old! One of her college friends had thought they were her grandparents, until they saw how they sometimes canoodled and didn't care who saw it. It was sweet and it was slushy, but she admitted she wouldn't have them any other way.

"So are you all ready for the great adventure?" Cress asked her now. "We're driving you to New York to see you off, of course."

"Daddy, I told you it's not necessary!" she said with a laugh. "And it's not such a great adventure to cross the Atlantic any more, though it might have been in your day, of course," she added cheekily.

"Tell that to the poor devils who never survived the Titanic a couple of years ago," Cress said smartly, and Primmy turned on him at once.

"Oh, why did you have to say that, Cress? You know how such things play on my mind."

"Well, if that old Cornish superstition of yours hasn't put you off allowing Skye to travel before now, I reckon she's still got her lucky star overhead."

"Excuse me, Daddy dear," Skye put in teasingly. "But nobody

has to allow me to do anything, remember? I'm twenty-three years old and not exactly an infant any more."

"And I'm still your daddy, and you'll show proper respect for your mother and her family when you get to Cornwall," he said, just as mildly, but with an edge to his voice now.

Skye gave him a quick hug, knowing she had gone too far. It would be her downfall one of these days, Primmy thought keenly. Blundering in without thinking, and apologising for it afterwards. And didn't she know the truth of that!

But they certainly didn't want to send her off to Cornwall on a sour note, and the time was almost here for her to leave. Primmy determinedly kept up a bright facade on the day they drove Skye to New York, even though she hated goodbyes of any description. She had hated it when Sinclair went off to Washington DC and took up with those damn politicians, and she hated losing her bright star now.

If Primmy had her way, she would keep all families neatly together in close communication – and that was the daftest idea she had had in a long time. People had to move on. It was the way things were, and you couldn't stop it.

And she was luckier than most. They were the respected Tremaynes, she reminded herself. They had a beautiful home; Cress was a successful businessman; she had her music. She gave piano concerts, both locally and farther afield, and was acclaimed for her talent. She had a good life, and a husband she still adored. Many women would envy her.

"Now you'll be sure to write the minute you get there and settle in, won't you?" she said, knowing she was acting like a mother hen now, and unable to stop herself.

"Oh Mom, stop fussing. I'll be fine, really!"

But Skye's eyes were as tearfully bright as her own as they hugged one another on the quayside, finally unable to say what was in their hearts. It wasn't going to be forever, thought Primmy, but it damn well felt like it right now.

*   *   *

13

"I watched you come aboard. Are you travelling alone and unchaperoned?"

Skye heard the male voice speak alongside her when she finally had to stop waving to the miniscule figures on shore. She tried to disguise the thickness in her throat as she answered, not wanting any company right now, and angry with this jerk who had invaded her privacy. And who the blazes needed a chaperone at her age!

"I'm travelling on business," she mumbled, hoping it would discourage him. It was partly true, anyway. She had promised to send batches of features to her magazine editor on the Cornish way of life. She hadn't looked at the man beside her, but she realised he was pushing something into her hand.

"Here. I know what it's like. No matter how many times you take leave of your family, it's always hard, isn't it? I'm Philip Norwood, by the way."

In the midst of the acute misery that she hadn't expected to feel on departure, Skye registered three things. One was that the guy had real sympathy in his voice. Two, he was pressing a folded handkerchief into her hand for her to dry her tears. And three, his accent was British.

So now she glanced at him. He wasn't young, but he wasn't old either. He was probably around forty. Since Skye had been brought up by older-than-average parents, she considered this a perfectly normal and interesting age-group for a twenty-three year old to converse with. She was more comfortable and confident with older people than many young women of her age.

"Thank you," she said, dabbing her eyes with the handkerchief. "It's stupid, isn't it? It's the trip of a lifetime, or so they tell me, and here I am, weeping like an idiot."

"It's not stupid at all. Everyone feels the same when they have to leave friends and family. It's normal, and you shouldn't be ashamed to let your feelings out."

14

"Well, thank you again for the pep talk. No, I mean it," she added, in case he thought she was being sarcastic. "I guess I needed to know that other folk feel the same way I do right now."

"So now that we've got that out of the way, why don't we take a stroll around the deck and you can tell me all about yourself," he encouraged.

Skye laughed. "Don't you know that's the very thing that makes a person clam up immediately? Besides, what's there to tell? I'm just an ordinary person doing an ordinary job—"

"Somehow I doubt that. You have a striking beauty that makes you stand out from the crowd, and I'd guess there's a matching personality. Besides, no one's ordinary. Everyone's unique. Didn't your college tutors impress that on you?"

"Yes, they did," she said, so startled by his swift assessment and clarity of thinking that she ignored the compliments. "But how come you know so much about it?"

"I'm one of those dreaded college tutors."

"Oh! Well, now I *am* tongue-tied."

"Please don't be. Actually, I don't usually reveal my credentials on so short an acquaintance. But since we have five days to spend on board, and nowhere to go to avoid one another, why not!"

It was the hammiest sort of chat-up line Skye had ever heard. On a ship of this size, there were probably plenty of ways she could avoid Mr Philip Norwood if she had a mind to do so! But she was surprised to know how much she was enjoying this brief and heady conversation, and saw no reason to curtail it here and now.

"I'm Skye Tremayne," she said simply, stretching out her arm and putting her slim hand in his.

"I'm very pleased to know you, Skye Tremayne. And where is your destination when we reach Falmouth? Incidentally, with a name like that, you're going to feel right at home."

"I hope so. I have a large family living in Cornwall, mostly

15

around St Austell and Truro." Just saying the magical names sent the old excitement surging back through her veins. "My grandparents came to New Jersey to visit soon after I was born, but I don't remember it, of course, so it will all be completely new to me."

And yet not unfamiliar, with all the family history she had begged her mother to tell her over the years, even if she had been strangely reticent over some matters. And Skye had avariciously absorbed the various paintings and water-colours of Cornwall and their heritage that her Uncle Albie had sent as birthday and Christmas gifts.

"Do you know Cornwall at all?" she asked her new companion as they leaned on the ship's rail for a breather, watching the skyline of New York fade into nothingness.

"A little," he said.

"Have you ever heard of an important clayworks near St Austell, called Killigrew Clay . . . ?"

Chapter Two

Walter Tremayne glowered at his handsome son, Theo, across the breakfast table. It was high time the boy found himself a wife to tame him, and moved out. Not that he was a boy any more. He was nearing his thirty-seventh birthday, and the thought of how time was moving on always gave his father a minor shock.

Theo had inherited old Hal Tremayne's salty ways, Walter thought now, but none of his tact. He had taken on his grandfather's old mantle at the clayworks, but he dealt with the clayworkers as if they were scum, in a way his grandaddy never had. It was a pity he hadn't taken account of the name he and Cathy had bestowed on him and turned pious and churchified, like his Uncle Luke, Walter thought sourly.

"I don't care what you say, Father," Theo snapped now, throwing down his newspaper. "The bloody workers have got to be kept in line."

"And you'll be heading 'em straight for strike action if you don't handle 'em with due care."

"Oh, and is that how it happened in the past?" Theo said sarcastically. "I don't think so, from all I've been brought up to believe. And who are the bloody bosses, anyway?"

"Well, not you, my son, and don't you forget it."

Walter spoke now with the mildness that always infuriated his hot-headed son. He'd been hot-headed himself once. Still was, in many ways. He still thought of the clay with a passion, but that passion burned less fervently now that he was getting on in years.

17

But not yet past it, he reminded himself. And not likely to be, not intending to be, while there was breath in his body to keep Killigrew Clay alive.

"You don't need to keep reminding me that the clayworks are in the hands of you and Granny Morwen. Though what she knows or cares about it now could be written on a postcard—"

Walter lunged forward across the breakfast table so fast he knocked over the cruets and rocked his wife's obligatory vase of spring flowers. He cared nothing for that. He only wished he'd been near enough to grab Theo by the throat instead of digging his heavy hand into his shoulder.

"The day you know more than your granny about the workings of the clay is when you can hold your head up high, boy, so don't insult her—"

"Oh aye, we all know how she worked as a bal maiden in her youth," Theo went on recklessly, not yet ready to give up, but his words were becoming desperate, due to the squeezing pain his father was inflicting in his shoulder. "But she's in her dotage now, and not much use to man nor beast as far as business is concerned—"

From somewhere behind him, he felt a stinging blow strike the side of his cheek, and he bellowed out loud. He swung around to see his mother glaring down at him, arriving downstairs later than usual after a restless night, her normally gentle voice brimming with anger.

"How dare you, Theo! That lovely old lady is worth ten of you, and you'll apologise to your father at once for insulting his mother in that way."

"She's not even his real mother," he scowled, rubbing his bruised cheek. Cathy was slight in stature, but she had what Walter always called a backbone of steel when it came to getting her own way.

"Mebbe not, but we're all family," Walter whipped out. "And you just think on this, boy. If Hal Tremayne hadn't made me his sole beneficiary to inherit his part of Killigrew Clay, and made me a partner along wi' Morwen and Ran Wainwright, then you and your brother wouldn't have had the fine education you did. And you wouldn't have been lording it over those poor bastards still toiling in the clay in all weathers, in order to put food in your belly and clothes on your back."

"Can we stop this, please?" Cathy said, having heard it all too many times before. "It's too early in the day to be squabbling, and I hope you're not going to carry on like this when Primmy's daughter comes to visit."

Theo got up from his chair, pushing it back with a scrape, unheeding of his bad manners. Walter hid a small grin, despite his anger with his son. Because such pithy outspokenness was only to be expected, both in the headstrong Tremaynes, and the brusque Yorkshire side of the family.

Walter himself had had to fight tooth and nail to prise his Cathy away from her uncouth father, and marry her. Tom Askhew had never been his favourite person, but Walter had raised no objections when his second son, Jordan, had begged to live with the Askhews in York to learn the journalists' trade on his grandfather's newspaper, *The Northern Informer*.

There had been too many uproars between them all in the past to deal with that one. In any case, Jordan was a man, not a boy, and he couldn't have stopped him, anyway. Walter felt a brief sadness for the days when a man guided his sons' destiny through all the days of their lives – though some might say it was manipulating it rather than guiding it.

And he had never allowed himself to be manipulated by anyone in the whole of his life. Nor dissuaded from working with the clay. It was in his blood.

After Theo had stamped out of the house, Cathy let out her breath in a deep sigh, and handed Walter another cup of tea.

"Your family were always hotheads, Walter," she observed.

"And yours weren't?" he countered.

She laughed, not taking offence. It was all too true, anyway.

19

"Oh, I grant you my father and yours never got on, even though they managed a fine sort of subterfuge between them at one time, didn't they?"

Her face tinged red, even now, after all these years, remembering how Morwen had once revealed how Cathy's prissy mother Jane had had clandestine meetings with the brash young newspaperman, Tom Askhew. When all the time, Jane's family had believed she was meeting the highly approved Ben Killigrew.

It had shocked Cathy at the time. And she had to admit that somehow she couldn't imagine her own mother having a passionate relationship with anyone. Morwen yes . . . oh yes! Even now, at eighty years of age, Morwen still had a sensual quality about her . . . But Jane was far too genteel and fussy and so different in every way from her husband.

"And so did *we*, my love," Walter said, in answer to her question. Reminding her of how they had once made a sweetheart pact, hiding in the little turret room at Ran Wainwright's house, New World, wanting only to be together, against every kind of parental disapproval.

Walter Tremayne had been so determined to have her, and it had been such a sweet and innocent need that drove them to hide away, but it had almost caused a scandal. They had been forced to separate for a long while, but in the end they had won. It said much for the tenacity of them both.

Cathy squeezed his hand in silent agreement.

"It's strange how so many folk want the very ones their families are most against, isn't it? It's almost as if we're driven to it."

"Like our Primmy and Cresswell, you mean? That was a turn-up, if ever there was," said Walter. "I never did fathom out quite why there was such a to-do about it."

"Objections to cousins marrying, wasn't it?" Cathy said, but Walter shook his head.

"There was more to it than that. Anyway, there's nothing unusual in that in our family, nor in any large rural families. No, there were too many discussions behind closed doors that we weren't allowed to hear. It had summat to do with Albie, I think."

He shrugged. It was a puzzle that had no relevance any more, and Cathy put down her cup with a clatter, unconsciously underlining his thought.

"There's no point in worrying about it any more," she said briskly. "It's Primmy's daughter we should be thinking about, and how we're going to welcome her. You know what your grandmother would have done, don't you?"

"Given her a party," Walter stated uneasily, knowing it was *exactly* what Bess Tremayne would have wanted to do. Gathering her clan around her like a comfort blanket, the way womenfolk did, had always been one of Bess's simple pleasures. "If that's what you think, I suppose we should do it here."

"Of course we should! Where else would the girl feel most at home but at Killigrew House? It's where the whole family began, after all. I'll arrange it with Morwen, but I'm sure there'll be no objection. At her age, she wouldn't want to be bothered with having a noisy crowd of people at New World."

Walter ignored the comment about his mother's advanced age. Knowing her as he did, she wouldn't want to be left out of things either.

"Then take my advice and keep it small," he told his wife. "The girl will be overwhelmed enough at meeting all these folk who are family, but still strangers. We don't want to make her feel out of her depth the minute she sees us all, so if any of 'em make excuses and say they can't come, don't force 'em."

Cathy was laughing by the time he'd finished, dropping a light kiss on his balding pate as she passed his chair.

"You're so transparent, my 'andsome!" she said, lapsing into the Cornish for a moment. "You'd far rather be tramping the moors and catching your death of cold by grubbing about in a clay pit, than being a party host, wouldn't you?"

"Well, o' course," Walter agreed, his blue eyes twinkling back at her. "There's no comparison, is there?"

She ran her hands down his broad chest, loving him, still seeing him as the virile young boy he had been, and the still virile man that he was.

"Just be gentle with Primmy's girl, that's all," she said, with a smile that remembered . . .

Philip Norwood smiled at the delightful young woman who had been his fairly constant companion on board ship for the past two days now. They were playing deck quoits, and Skye was winning, as usual.

"So how do you think you'll take to these relatives of yours? They sound a formidable bunch, from all that you've been telling me. Are you very nervous of meeting them?"

Skye tossed her head, sending her glossy black hair swirling around her shoulders and across her face. She flicked it back with a laugh and a tilt of her chin. Her blue eyes had dancing lights in them, and Philip drew in his breath. She was truly glorious, he thought, and if he had been uncommitted . . .

They had found an incredible rapport with one another. They had discussed so many things by now, exchanging family details, hopes and ambitions, in the way of brief companions hugely in accord with one another's company, but who would probably never meet again. Like the proverbial ships that passed in the night . . . But he had never mentioned Ruth.

"Why on earth should I be nervous?" Skye said now, in the quick, light voice he enjoyed hearing so much. "They're only people, and my daddy always said that if I was nervous of meeting big-wigs – or small-wigs, come to that – I should just imagine them in their underwear, and that would surely cut them down to size."

It wasn't an original saying, but it had tickled Skye and Sinclair enormously when Cress had first told it to them so solemnly. And the whole family had convulsed at the time, imagining one of Sinclair's new-found pompous Washington cronies, sitting on their beach-house porch in his underwear and suspenders, and trying to sort out the fate of the nation.

"That's rather a daring thing to say, Miss Tremayne," Philip said, laughing, and revelling in such frankness. "And have you imagined *me* in my underwear, I wonder?"

She shot her quoit across the deck with such fervour that it went out of play, and the game was instantly null and void. She had spoken unthinkingly, as she too often did, just to get a reaction. Philip had a rich, hearty laugh, and she liked that in a man. But despite his laughter, she had registered the deeper, more personal tone in his voice, whether he was aware of it or not. And she knew she had gone too far.

"I wouldn't dream of doing any such thing, Mr Norwood," she said. "It was a silly family joke, and it wasn't meant to be taken seriously! Please forget that I said it at all."

The moment passed, but Skye had the most extraordinary and disturbing thought that although she may not have imagined *him* in his underwear – and what respectable young woman actually did such a thing – Philip Norwood might very definitely have imagined her in *hers*.

"I'm tired of this game, anyway," she said now. "And it's getting very hot this afternoon. Shall we have some lemonade?"

"A good idea. And then you can tell me more about this large clayworks that belongs to your family."

He followed her trim figure across the deck, admiring the cool blue day frock she wore with such aplomb, and the glimpse of her slim ankles above the sensible cream button shoes. Many of the other women passengers dressed up to the nines even for the day-time sporting and other activities. But Skye Tremayne had style and an unerring dress-sense, and when she appeared in a more sophisticated creation for the evening's dinner, she always looked a sensation.

And Philip told himself he had better keep a firm hold on his emotions, for they were already in danger of running away with him. He should definitely mention Ruth, knowing it would create the required barrier between them. But when you left out a vital piece of information for too long, it became more and more difficult to find the right moment to reveal it.

"And *you* can tell me more about your lecturing," she went on. "I've never heard of exchange semesters before."

"It's not that new," Philip said, when they had settled themselves on canvas deck-chairs, and a steward had appeared as if by magic with two glasses of cool lemonade.

"I always liked the idea of travel," he went on, "and I applied to be available for any exchange positions that might occur. I've been in New York for a year, and now I'll be tutoring at Madron College in Truro for about six months—"

Skye sat up. "*Truro!* Then we'll be almost neighbours. Why haven't you told me this before?"

"I wanted to surprise you," he said with a smile. "You don't expect me to reveal all my secrets at once, do you?"

"You'll be telling me next that you have a wife and six children waiting at home," Skye said with a laugh.

"I don't," Philip said briefly.

She hardly realised she had been holding in her breath until he answered. It would make no difference to her if he *did* have a wife and six children – though it would probably make quite a difference to the wife if he was such a travel-bug. Skye wasn't looking for a husband or any kind of attachment, not for years yet. But she *did* enjoy this man's company, more than any other man she had ever met, and it was refreshing that his conversation wasn't peppered with details of children's ailments and domestic doings.

And dear Lord, how shallow and *awful* that made her sound, she chided herself. Such a bigoted attitude would all change when the right man came along, of course, and she cheerfully expected it to happen one day. Just not yet.

"Well then," she leaned back in her deck chair, half-closing her eyes against the fierce glare of the afternoon sun. They were almost halfway across the Atlantic and there was hardly a breath of a breeze today. Early summer was already upon them, the way her mother said it always suddenly arrived in Cornwall. Though, listening to her lyrical reminiscences, a person would think it was *always* springtime and summer there.

"Well then – you first," Philip encouraged, breathing in the light floral scent she always wore.

If he went into a roomful of people blindfolded and she was there, he would know it by her scent, he thought.

"You wanted to know a bit more about Killigrew Clay," Skye said. And then she turned her head to look at him and spoke more slowly, with a note of amazement in her voice.

"Do you know, I've only just realised that every time I say those words, my heart beats a little faster? Isn't that extraordinary? I've never been there. I know next to nothing about how china clay comes out of the ground and ends up as pots and plates on people's dining-tables – and medicines – and yet the very name has that weird effect on me."

She gave a shaky laugh as she continued without waiting for a reply. "Of course, my Mom always says it's the Cornish in me. She calls it fey, and it proves that I'm a true daughter of Cornwall, no matter where I was born."

She stopped abruptly. She was the cool and sophisticated Miss Skye Tremayne of Mainstown, New Jersey; self-sufficient and utterly self-confident, with rich and doting parents; she didn't need to lift a finger to work if she wanted to lead the indolent life; but she knew exactly where she was going with her freelance magazine work that she loved.

And yet right at that moment, she felt as if the weight of all those past years, all those past generations, was crowding in on her. Crushing her, mocking her, and telling her that however modern she thought she was, she was still the product of all those who had gone before, who had been as strong as she, and could be just as vulnerable too.

"Are you all right, Skye?" she heard Philip Norwood's concerned voice say.

His face came into focus in front of her, intense, rugged, a distinguished lecturer's face, and she nodded.

"Do you believe in omens – premonitions, precognitions – and all that hokum?" she murmured.

"I don't know that I do, but then I don't have a Celtic background. I know it's supposed to be part of the Celtic heritage, with the Welsh and the Irish – and most definitely the Cornish, of course," he said, watching her. "It's that kind of sixth sense that says you've been to a place before, or met someone before, or even had a particular conversation before, so that you know what someone is about to say before they say it. It's not necessarily a phenomenon, in my opinion, because too many people experience something of the same at various times of their lives."

"And there speaks the objective college lecturer," Skye observed, recognising the lengthy debating technique immediately, and knowing that he was trying to calm the sudden irrational fear he must have seen in her face. But what did she have to fear, for pity's sake?

"I'm sure your mother must have mentioned such things to you in the past, but we all have to choose whether or not we believe in them, Skye."

"Her own mother is reputed to have healing hands."

Skye hadn't thought about that for years, but it had charmed her so much when she was a child, to think of Granny Morwen being able to put her hands on another person and cure them of a headache or a sore tooth. Whether or not that was how it actually happened, she didn't know. At the time, she had tried it out herself on an unwilling Sinclair, but he had teased her so much she never knew if it had worked or not. And most likely not.

"Is Granny Morwen her real mother, or her adopted one?" Philip said, having heard some of the story by now, and encouraging her to go on talking until the colour returned to her pale cheeks.

"Her real mother died when she was very young, and Morwen

26

and Ben Killigrew took in the three children of Morwen's dead brother, Sam. But Morwen was just as real a mother to her, and to my uncles, Walter and Albie."

"And then they had children of their own."

Skye began to smile. "When I think how tangled it all got, I'm thankful that my mom and daddy only had Sinclair and me! Yes, Morwen and Ben Killigrew had two children, Justin and Charlotte. Justin never married, and he died from consumption years ago. Charlotte married and has two daughters who I'm really looking forward to meeting. And I think I'll leave the story of the Wainwrights until another time," she added. "It can't be of any real interest to you, and you're being very kind in letting me talk like this, Philip."

"Nonsense. I'm not being kind at all. I've always been fascinated to know how dynasties begin."

"My goodness," Skye said, starting to laugh. "I'm not sure we're important enough to be called a dynasty!"

"Well, I wouldn't be so certain about that," he said in all seriousness. "As a historian it sounds to me as if you have a very colourful and intriguing family background. I hope somebody is going to record it all for posterity."

Skye stared out to sea, watching the small, curling waves that hardly stirred the surface of the sunlit blue ocean. Thinking, not for the first time in her life, how a small snippet in a conversation could suddenly assume gigantic proportions in the mind. It was like tossing a pebble into that ocean, and seeing how far-reaching the ripples would spread. And sometimes it took someone else to see what was right under your nose, and had always been there, waiting for the right moment, and the right person, to bring it to the surface.

"Somebody probably should," she said slowly, trying not to admit how sickeningly fast her heart was beating with excitement, yet mixed with an inexplicable sense of foreboding too. Of touching something that shouldn't be touched . . . of reviving ghosts who should be left to their silent world . . . impatiently Skye pushed the feeling out of her mind.

For who better to record it all than someone who was at the heart of the family, who loved it, and had been raised on tales of the old days, even if she had only half-listened with childish impatience to them at the time? They were still imprinted in her mind and her soul. The memories were as much hers as anyone's. She had inherited them, and therefore they belonged to her.

"A party?" Morwen asked her daughter-in-law dubiously, when Cathy had driven herself carefully to New World in the new motor car she had persuaded Walter to buy her, and then been almost too nervous to drive except at a snail's pace.

Morwen accepted that motor-cars were useful things to get folk more quickly from one place to another, but they were still nasty, noisy machines, compared with the horse-driven vehicles of her youth. And she didn't altogether trust them, even though Walter had said that you had to move along with progress, or you would stagnate.

Cathy was removing her driving gloves now, and also the bonnet tied with a chiffon ribbon from her greying fair hair, and clearly preparing to stay for a while, though she stated that she didn't want any tea, thankyou, before she was even asked. Morwen gave a small sigh, not really in the mood for company. But Cathy wasn't *company*, she reminded herself. Cathy was family.

"Walter and I thought a party would be a nice thing to do for Skye, Mother, the way we've always done it to celebrate important occasions in the family."

She spoke blithely, since Morwen would know very well that Walter had little say in such women's doings, and even less interest. "We ought to make Primmy's girl as welcome as possible, didn't we?" she added, when Morwen didn't respond immediately.

"She'll be staying here, of course," Morwen said finally, in case Cathy had any other ideas in mind.

"Oh, of course!"

Morwen Tremayne Killigrew Wainwright was the matriarch of the family now, and they all still consulted her and deferred to her, and knew better than not to do so. Even Cathy, née Askhew.

"Although she may have a mind to stay with Albie and Rose in Truro, rather than in this rambling great house with only an old woman for company," Morwen ruminated, as if the thought had just occurred to her. "But the maid has to make up her own mind on that. Just as long as she knows there are plenty of folk ready to welcome her."

"She can be assured of that, Mother," Cathy said, a little tartly. "Now then, about this party."

Morwen sighed again. Why should she bother her head with parties and being polite to folk dolled up to look like stuffed shirts? Besides, when someone like Cathy got that determined glint in their eyes, it was a foregone conclusion that she was going to organise everything her way.

And she would do it as beautifully and efficiently as ever, the way her own mother would have done. Jane Askhew had been full of the social niceties in the days when Morwen Tremayne was all fingers and thumbs, and as gauche and tortured at a party as a fish out of water.

"You see to it all, my dear," Morwen said now. "Just let me know what the cost of it all is, and I'll see to it—"

"Good heavens, Mother, there's no need for that! I hope you don't think I was hinting at any such thing, and if Walter can't provide a party for his sister's girl, then I don't know what the world's coming to. It's not as if we're paupers, and I understand the business is doing well, despite Theo's constant grumblings."

Unconsciously, she patted her hair as she spoke, and Morwen didn't miss the way she elevated the clayworks to 'the business' in her genteel way, and glossed over the irritations of her menfolk. Cathy truly hated any unpleasantness among them, believing there should be sweetness and light and harmony in all things. It took a more down-to-earth body to know that it

29

could never be like that. Such healthy verbal sorting out of problems had never bothered Morwen, nor even the occasional fisticuffs to clear the air.

On the contrary, she had grown up on it and thrived on it, and a bit of hustle and tussle never hurt anyone. At least it made you feel *alive*. It was a pity this miss – this *matron*, she corrected herself – couldn't see it in the same way.

"What's to do with Theo now, anyway?" Morwen asked. "Putting the cat among the clay pigeons again, is he?"

Cathy pursed her lips, not seeing the joke. "I don't know why you always belittle his efforts to keep control of the business, Mother. You can't allow the workers to dictate to the management, can you?"

"Oh, *management* now, is it?" Morwen said, her blue eyes beginning to sparkle. "You should leave the men's doings to the men, my dear. Theo's got his head screwed on properly, but you have to let the workers know where they stand, and he'll know the right words to say when the time comes, no matter what the trouble is. He takes after his father and his grand-daddy in that respect."

"More than anyone in my family, you mean."

"Cathy, I don't want to fight with you," Morwen said gently. "Life's too short, especially when you don't have too much of it left to you. Go home and plan your party, and let's all aim to give Skye a happy time while she's here."

"You're right," Cathy said, standing up, clearly relieved that this visit could be cut short. She gave Morwen a quick peck on the cheek, and remembered to ask after her health a mite late.

"I'm eighty years old, and my joints are stiff," Morwen said drily. "So don't expect me to be leaping about on the moors, or dancing at parties. But I'm well enough, so you can report back the same to anybody who's a mind to be interested."

Minutes after Cathy had gone, the homely companion that Walter had insisted lived in at the house after Ran died, came into the room with their tea, her head on one side like an inquisitive bird. In fact, with a name like Miss Hawkes, Morwen had christened her Birdie, and the name had stuck.

"You torment that one, you wicked 'un," she remarked.

"You were listening as usual then. Thought you might be. One of these days, you'll hear summat you don't like, you old crone," Morwen said smartly, reverting to their own special way of talking. Sometimes it was such a relief to revert back to the old moorland ways that she felt more akin to Birdie than any of her large family, Morwen thought sadly.

"What's to do that you wouldn't want me to hear that I don't know already?" Birdie challenged her. "There's few fam'ly secrets I don't know about."

And that was what *she* thought . . .

"Never mind all that. Tell me your verdict. Is Mrs Cathy Askhew Tremayne getting to be as pompous as my son, Luke, or is she not?"

"'Tis not for me to say, me dear. I'm only the hired help." Then, after a pause: "But since you ask, I'd say there's not much to choose between 'em. Now then, what'll it be? A buttered scone or a tea cake?"

"Tea cake. And get that self-satisfied look off your face and come and tell me what gossip you've learned in St Austell today. I can always tell when there's something."

They both enjoyed the game of baiting one another. It was different in public, or when any of the family was around, but in private, they suited one another very well. And for someone around her daughter-in-law Cathy's own age, thought Morwen, Birdie was a sight more lively and earthy.

When they were both seated with their refreshments, the companion leaned forward, her round face a touch more serious than usual.

"'Tis no more than rumours, I'm sure, and no reason for you to concern yourself with it."

31

"With *what*, you irritating emmet?"

Birdie grinned at the abuse and then the grin faded. "There's folk who say that war's coming. That it's been too many years of peace, and that we allus have to pay for it."

"Is that all?" Morwen said.

"Ain't it enough?"

"Well, it would be if it was true, but such dire predictions are always being bandied about. You know well enough that Cornish folk are superstitious about anything, and if there's no superstition to suit the occasion, they'll invent one. Where did you hear it, anyway? I'll bet it was in the Blue Boar, and not from any reliable source."

She scoffed, knowing very well that Birdie wasn't above sharing a jug of ale with any farmer or sea-faring man who would pay for it.

"Don't you feel none o' that famous shivering in your bones then, just hearing me tell it?" Birdie challenged her.

"I do not. And I've got more important things to think about than a lot of stuff and nonsense about a war that's never likely to happen."

Without warning, she shivered all the same, but she knew it had less to do with Birdie's wildly speculating informants, than with the fact that she had already lost a grandson and a nephew to a war. Albie's young son had died at Mafeking in 1899, and then her brother Jack's officer son, Sammie, whom they were all so proud of, had been killed soon after.

Two tragedies coming so fast after one another other had almost destroyed them at the time. So whatever gossip Birdie had to tell her, she wanted no more talk of wars.

"'Twasn't no kiddley-wink talk, neither," Birdie added slyly now. "I ran into that fortune-telling woman in the town, and she reckons she can see war clouds gatherin', and there ain't no stoppin' 'em, so you mind and remember what I'm sayin' to 'ee, missus."

Chapter Three

The two men leaned on the fence rail, checking the speed of their newly-acquired Arab horse as the young lad raced him around the track. The older man banged down the timer on the clock with a bellow of satisfaction.

"He's a bloody marvel, and so are you for spotting him, and bidding for him, Bradley," Freddie told him, his moon-face alight with pleasure as he beamed at his nephew. "We should do bloody well out of this nag."

"It's a knack I have, Freddie," Bradley said, not averse to preening himself. He'd always had a high opinion of himself, and he'd long since stopped referring to Freddie as Uncle. "And he's going to bring in a few bob all right. We should enter him in some local derbys to begin with, to put him through his paces, and then go for the big stuff in England once he's proved himself. It'll put up his odds for the punters with a few wins on record."

"That sounds a good move," Freddie said, nodding.

Venetia would really have approved of the way Bradley had shaped up, he thought suddenly, her name returning to his consciousness as it so often did without warning, even after all this time. And the childless couple had made a smarter move than they could have known, when they'd begged Morwen to let her wayward young son come and live with them in Ireland, as he so badly wanted to do.

It was also destined to be Freddie's salvation, as he freely admitted. It was more than twenty years ago when his adored Venetia had broken her neck in a riding accident, and it had all but turned Freddie's brain to think of life without her. He had been the one to need Bradley's company then. Needed it, and had it in full measure.

He pushed the painful memories out of his mind now, as the two men tramped back across the fields to the house, leaving the stable-hands to see to the horses. Freddie, with his gammy leg, was not as agile as the younger man, but rarely complained except in the worst of Irish weather when it played up so cruelly. But life was good for the Cornish exiles. They had a valuable stud now, and their name was well-respected in breeding and racing circles.

But the mention of England had stirred something else in Freddie's brain.

"Have you had any thoughts about meeting this American cousin when she comes to Cornwall, Bradley? We could always invite her here for a spell, of course, and your mother might even stir herself out of that great mausoleum of a house and come with her. But if the girl's to be staying for a year, there's no need for urgency," Freddie added, knowing he should probably make the gesture, but none too enthusiastic about it.

"Mother won't come," Bradley said abruptly. "She and I never had much time for one another, and she's no sweeter to me now than she was when I was a boy."

"You can hardly blame her for that, with all the strife you caused her," Freddie said mildly.

"I don't blame her. I just always seemed to be the whipping-boy among the three younger ones. Brought it on myself, of course. I never could keep my mouth shut, could I?" he added with a grin. "Not that anybody could rival Cresswell in that respect."

"Well, you're all settled now, and you all made good lives for yourselves." Freddie didn't care to waste time dwelling on old scores and upheavals. Life was too short, and memories were best kept where they belonged – even good ones.

Bradley gave a raucous laugh. "So we did. But God knows

we never expected Luke to become a preacher. Still, in a rumbustious family like ours, it can't do much harm to have a stake in heaven, one way or another. But Emma ending up a farmer's wife was summat to turn Mammie's stomach. She always did think of Emma as her precious little peach. Somehow I can't see my sister trudging happily among the cow-shit, either. I thought she'd turn out to be airy-fairy and arty-farty – more like Primmy and Albert, in fact."

"You always did have a fine turn of phrase, Bradley. That fine school we sent you to in Dublin obviously did you a power of good," Freddie said. He was still mild-mannered, but he didn't particularly like these caustic remarks. He could cuss with the best of them, but he was of a generation that respected the family, no matter what they did.

"So what do you think this girl of Primmy's will be like?" Bradley went on. He never noticed sarcasm in others, even while he was adept at using it himself.

"She'll be beautiful, for certain sure, if she's anything like her mother and grandmother," Freddie remarked. "How could a Tremayne woman be anything else?"

He saw Bradley give a dark scowl, and sighed, knowing that the deep-seated resentment of his origins still hadn't left him. Freddie thought he should have outgrown it long ago, but he had taken his boyhood resentments with him. And there was no reason why it should be so. They had a successful business partnership; they were richer than they had ever dreamed they would be; they had all they ever wanted, except for women to share their lives, and that didn't seem to bother Bradley at all. But he still couldn't seem to bypass the seething inner conflict that he had been born a Wainwright.

He didn't even have the respected name of Tremayne, like Freddie and the rest of his mother's family, nor the much more priviliged and esteemed one of Killigrew that he'd always envied so much. He had told himself a thousand times that it was futile and foolish to resent a lovely woman like Morwen Tremayne

35

for having had two husbands and reared a brood of children, some of whom weren't even her own.

But he did, damn it to hell and back. He had always done so, and he always would.

"I wonder if she had anything to do with these bloody suffragette women," Bradley said, his mind going off at a tangent as the men entered the fine house.

They dutifully left their boots in the porch, and put on house-shoes before going into the drawing-room to sink the first brandy of the day.

"Who are we talking about now?" Freddie asked, swirling the golden liquid around his glass and breathing in the fine aroma. They could afford the best, and they revelled in it.

"Primmy's daughter. Skye. And what a poncey name that is to go to bed with!"

"Why do you think she'd have had anything to do with women's suffrage?"

"Think about it! You read the last letter Mammie sent. She writes stuff for a magazine, which ain't your normal occupation for a well-bred young woman, is it? So I reckon she's bound to be forthright and strident, marching and screeching with the rest of 'em. You mark my words. She'll be a dead cert for one of the wretched baggages."

He scowled. He had never been able to forget the horrific incident the previous year, when Emily Davidson had thrown herself under the king's horse at the Derby. Freddie and Bradley had both witnessed it, and couldn't forget it. They had still been in England doing some horse-trading ten days later, when the vast funeral procession in London had made such a martyr of the suffragette, before the coffin had been transported from King's Cross to Morpeth and burial in the family vault. Every last detail had been widely reported in all the newspapers, and proclaimed as a tragedy at the time, but there were folk who had other ideas on that.

It was an avoidable farce, in Bradley Wainwright's opinion.

36

It may have promoted the women's movement more acutely than all the imprisonments and hunger-strikes and force-feedings that the principals had endured, but in his opinion, women should keep to their proper place in the world. And that didn't include marching about like lunatics and behaving disgracefully in public. That was a man's role, he thought, without ever seeing the irony of it.

"You shouldn't prejudge your cousin, Bradley," Freddie said shortly. "Her mother was a lovely girl, if occasionally led astray by her feelings. And if Cresswell was anything like our Matt, well, you never knew him in the old days, when he had an almost poetic nature, according to our Morwen."

Bradley spluttered into his brandy glass. "*Poetic*! I thought he made it rich in the gold mines of California. I can't imagine the roughnecks he came in contact with having much truck with a *poet*. They'd be seeing him as a very different kind of proposition."

He sniggered nastily, not seeing the dark and painful stain on Freddie's face. Freddie might be all of sixty-seven years of age now, and a man of the world. But he could remember as if it was yesterday, how he'd felt as a young boy, when he'd come across his tutor and his friend, buggering one another. He hadn't known the word then, nor what it meant. But he knew it now, and it still sickened him every time he remembered how his innocence had been shattered on that day.

"Our Matt was no bum-boy, and I'll not have that kind of talk in this house, Bradley," he snapped, chastising him as if he was a child instead of the well-built man he was now.

"I never meant anything by it," Bradley said lazily. "But you know what they say about poets and artists and—"

"You'd best stop right there if you know what's good for you, boy," Freddie said warningly. His blue eyes glinted. They didn't often fall out, but there was a danger of it now. Such sniggering was wholly undeserved, in any case, because his nephew Albert Tremayne was a respected Truro artist, with a wife and family,

37

who didn't credit any whiff of scandal from the lips of this braggard.

Freddie was the youngest of the older generation of Tremaynes, and nearer in age to the children of his brother Sam. And as such, he was always ready to defend them, even if there had been an odd kind of whispering going around regarding Albie and Primmy at one time. But then she had upped and got engaged to Cresswell and been whisked off to America. Love's young dream had had nothing on the two of them then, he recalled, a smile softening his rounded features.

"Oh, let's forget the lot of them and have a game of checkers. Do you fancy a wager?" Bradley asked, realising he had gone too far yet again.

"Why not? Providing you're prepared to lose a packet."

There were those who thought it was a queer set-up for the two men to be living in such close harmony, and never a hint of a woman between them. Those who still recalled the horse-mad Lady Venetia Hocking Tremayne remembered her as more masculine in appearance and manners than many men, and drew their own conclusions about the relationship between Freddie and his male companion. But they lived in a relaxed and tolerant rural community, and whatever they did, as long as they harmed no one, it was nobody's business but their own.

Walter kept his finger on the pulse of all that went on at Killigrew Clay, despite the fact that his son, Theo, considered himself in charge now. Walter had been entrenched in all its doings for far too long to let go of the reins so easily.

Besides, Theo's hot temper was more likely to stir up a hornet's nest among the clayers than to appease them when their grumbles reached the boss's ears. And right now, they were complaining about the shifts, and wanting the hours cut so they could spend more time with their families.

"But still wanting the same wages, of course," Theo told his father angrily as they drove up to the works high on the moors. "Who do they think they are, giving ultimatums to us? They don't rule the pits. We do."

"What ultimatums are these?" Walter said sharply, having heard nothing of any such thing, and clinging to the side of Theo's prized Austin motor that he drove at reckless and unnecessary speed through the narrow moorland lanes.

"Oh, there's no need for you to bother your head about 'em, Father. They don't amount to anything—"

"And don't you treat me like an imbecile or a yester-man! What ultimatums are you talking about?"

Theo shrugged. He hadn't wanted Walter here today, but as usual, he'd had no choice. If he'd gone on ahead, Walter would have turned up on horseback anyway.

"What do you think? It's nothing but talk. Puffs of wind, that's all. And it's the usual thing. Strikes. Marches to the offices in St Austell to bargain with us. Sending a spokesman to *The Informer* with their complaints and having 'em made public in that scandal rag. Bloody stupid threats, and I'm damn sure I'm not telling you anything new."

"You haven't told me any of this before," Walter snapped.

"I didn't see the need to worry you—"

"Well, in future you'd better see the need."

Theo stared ahead, wishing he'd kept his mouth shut. He could handle this perfectly well, and it was high time his father stopped meddling. But he knew better than to say so.

His grandad Hal had gone on controlling the clayworks long after Walter's age. Once a clayworker, always a clayworker, it seemed, whether you were boss, or humble kiddley-boy fetching the tea, or bal maidens like Granny Morwen and grandmother Bess had once been.

He grudgingly admitted that with a heritage like that, it was hardly surprising that Walter wouldn't let go. It would take an earthquake or a fatal illness to shift him, and he didn't wish that on anybody.

He drew the car to a halt above the vast sprawling works, looking down on the hive of industry that still formed the heart of Killigrew Clay. The four pits were spread out, but Clay One was the biggest and had always been Walter's favourite. The huge milky green clay pool where a bal maiden had drowned years ago was as deep and mysterious as ever. That part of its history meant nothing to Theo, but Walter always liked to pause here and ponder for a few moments.

"What do you see when you look down there, boy?" Walter said suddenly. They scanned the glittering sky-tips of minerals and other waste thrown out of the china clay, so high now from all the clay that had been gouged out of the ground over the years that they were truly mountainous spoil heaps.

"I see industry and success," Theo said. "And I aim to keep it that way. Why? What do you see?"

"I see the past and the future. 'Tis all there for me, Theo, more than you'll ever know. Everything here represents part of my life, and your life too. Even these cottages—"

"I know all about them, and I thank God I never had to live in 'em, so don't start telling me to count my blessings. I leave that to Uncle Luke. How Granny Morwen and her parents and brothers were all crammed into one of these hovels, I'll never know, but you have to move on, Father. You've said it often enough yourself. We're a huge business concern now, and not a little tin-pot affair—"

Walter snorted at his derisory words, ever mindful of the fact that he too had started life in one of these small cottages, and been glad of the family that loved him.

"Killigrew Clay was never that. When so many smaller clayworks were bought out and swallowed up by larger concerns, we were one of the few able to stand firm. I still remember the time when a flashy woman clay boss thought

40

she could lord it over we Cornish folk, and buy us out. But she failed, like all on 'em failed."

"She turned up at a town meeting, didn't she?" Theo said, having heard the tale and read the newspaper accounts many times before. Clay meetings were for men, not for the likes of women, especially women coming down from London with their quick city ways and thinking to mystify the simple folk.

"That she did," Walter said. "Harriet Pendragon was her name. She was a fine figure of a woman and no mistake. And 'twas plain to see she'd set her sights on Ran Wainwright. She wanted him as much as she wanted control of the clayworks."

"Oh, ah?" This was something new to Theo. "And what did Granny Morwen have to say about that!"

Walter laughed. "Your granny was certainly no backwoods maid when it came to fighting for her own, Theo. Let's just say that the Pendragon woman was the one to back down in the end, and leave it at that. But if we're not to be seen idling here all day, we'd best get down to see what's to do."

Theo started up the motor again, wondering for a moment just what this new American relative was going to make of them all. This cousin with the impossible name . . . Skye . . . she could almost have been named after the Killigrew sky tips, he thought mockingly.

Then he forgot all about her as the motor neared Clay One, and he hooted his horn to let the men know of his approach as always. He spared a glance for the newly mechanised carts taking the waste up to the top of each tip, and coming down again empty with trundling efficiency.

Yes, progress was the thing, he told himself. You had to go with it, or go under.

In the end, it was a storm in a tea-cup, Walter reported to Cathy that evening. They were dining alone in the huge dining room at Killigrew House that could house a large family, and which

41

he always felt they rattled around in now. Perhaps Theo was right in one way, he thought fleetingly. He was more suited to life in a cottage than life in a mansion . . .

"So nothing much happened, did it?" Cathy said, not over-concerned with what went on up on the moors. It had never been part of her early life, and she couldn't feel the same way about it as the clayfolk did. She didn't mean to belittle them, but it was so different from her own upbringing that she couldn't see why Walter should get so het up about it any more. It was time he left it to younger folk.

"Theo could do with a lesson in compromise," Walter stated in reply. "The long hours didn't suit half the men, so we've come to a solution for a try-out period. We're simply staggering the shifts, so that those who want to do two short shifts instead of one long one, can do so. That way, we don't have to pay 'em the same wage for doing less work, and everybody's satisfied."

"My word, I didn't know my husband was such a tactician!" she said.

"You thought I was just good for grubbing about in the clay, did you, woman?"

Cathy laughed. "No, dar, I didn't think you were only good for that," she said teasingly. "But who's to sort out all these different shifts? It sounds a mite complicated."

Walter started to laugh as well. "Your educated son soon began to dig himself into a hole, insisting that it all had to be done properly, and with lists posted up so that each man knew exactly where he was and when. Before he knew what was happening, he'd landed himself with the job, so we won't see hide nor hair of him for a few days. He'll be busy at the offices with his paperwork.

"All the same," Walter went on, more soberly. "I'm glad the spring despatches are well behind us now. 'Twill give us a bit of a breathing-space if the war rumours are right. Not that anybody really knows, despite what your father's printing in his newspaper now. He were always a scare-monger."

Cathy was indignant. "He never shied away from the truth, if that's what you mean. If something was deserving of public attention, then he was prepared to print it. And Jordan's the same," she added, knowing that in Walter's eyes, the claying son was worth ten of the other, even though he tried to love them both in equal measure. But taking up with Tom Askhew in the newspaper world was not Walter's idea of men's work.

"Jordan's becoming northernised," Walter said.

"Oh, and is that so bad? The world doesn't begin and end in Cornwall, Walter!"

"Yours did, same as mine. I don't recall your being rushed off to Yorkshire with your parents with any great glee. I remember tears and—"

"And so do I," Cathy said softly, remembering how their youthful parting had been such a painful and heartbreaking time for them both. But that was long ago . . .

"Anyway, you were going to tell me something else, weren't you? Why should these vague rumours of war, which I don't believe any more than you do, affect us? It's not as though our boys would be eager to fight. Thank goodness they're past such mistaken thoughts of glory."

"You were always a pacifist, weren't you, dar? Just like your mother."

But before she could react to that, he went on. "And how it would affect us, my dear head-in-the-sand woman, is that our biggest markets are in Europe. If war did happen, those markets would be instantly closed to us, and we're not yet fully established in the American market to make it highly profitable. We couldn't rely on the medical outlets to keep us rich, either, though I daresay the demand for medicinal supplies would grow once the casualties began—"

"Walter, stop it. You're frightening me!" Cathy burst out, her eyes wide. "For somebody who thinks it will never happen, you've thought it all out pretty well! But it's just tittle-tattle, and there's no reason to believe it at all."

43

"Your father seems to do so," Walter said drily. "Haven't you read Jordan's latest report? Tom wouldn't have let that pass his editorial eye unless he approved of it."

"Of course I've read it, and it was purely a speculative article written by a boy with too much imagination. All Jordan was saying was what *might* happen, not what was going to. And I don't want to talk about it any more. It makes my head ache, and I've more important things to think about."

"Oh, and what're they?"

"Skye's welcome party, of course. And I can't think why that should make you smile in that silly fashion."

Skye's exact date of arrival in Falmouth hadn't been widely advertised to her Cornish family. It wasn't that she wanted to sneak up on them, but she was more unconventional than most, and she had had the unconventional notion of taking a good look around before she made her presence known.

It was one reason why she had told no one the name of the ship she would be travelling on, nor the actual date and time of her arrival.

It would be nice to be met, but far more exciting to find her own way around this county of which she had heard so much. Besides, she intended spending a couple of days in the sea-port of Falmouth first of all, before going farther west. She had lived for twenty-three years without meeting these relatives, so a few days more weren't going to hurt anyone.

And not for all the tea in Asia was she going to admit for one moment that a sense of nervousness was starting to creep in. It wasn't that she was afraid of meeting new people. It was just that there were so many of them, and they would all want to inspect her like a specimen under a microscope. They would all have their own expectations of what Primmy's daughter was going to be like.

"You look as if you're laying ghosts," Philip Norwood

44

remarked on their last evening at sea. "Don't tell me the great excitement in the adventure has waned?"

Skye pulled a face. "You see far too much, but no, it hasn't exactly *waned* . . ."

"Wavered then?" he suggested. "Cracked a little? Deflated like a spent balloon?"

"Stop it!" she laughed. "It's just a faint touch of cold feet, if you must know, and I didn't think I'd be admitting that to anyone."

"Why not? You're human, like the rest of us. So just remember the underwear trick."

"I really wish I'd never mentioned that to you!" Skye said. "I'm embarrassed every time I think about it."

"I didn't think anything would ever embarrass you. You always seem in such perfect control of yourself."

"Do I?" she said in surprise. "I'm not sure that makes me sound a very attractive person. It sounds far too cold and unemotional."

"And if you're fishing for compliments—"

"I'm not—"

"Then let me assure you that you're the loveliest young woman I've ever met, and I'm perfectly sure that beneath that sophisticated exterior there beats a heart that is going to be full of emotion the moment you set eyes on your ancestral home and family."

Skye said nothing, but the heart of which he spoke was beating much faster than usual at that moment. She nodded.

"I'm sure you're right," she murmured. "And do you think I've done the right thing, in not letting them know when I'll be arriving?"

"That's up to you. But a list of ships' arrivals is always announced in local newspapers, anyway, so they'll have a pretty good idea when a ship from New York is arriving!"

"So I'm asking for your advice."

But she had begun to realise that he rarely gave it. It was the

45

tutor in him, of course, offering suggestions and choices, but allowing the students to decide for themselves which course to take.

She wasn't one of his students, though . . . and it would have been so wonderful if he'd said he had a few days to spare, and that he'd be happy to escort her around the county that was so new to her. Seeing it all through his eyes . . . seeing it together . . .

Skye stared unseeingly across the elegant ship's dining room, to where the band was playing, and the dancers were taking to the floor, and she knew she was in danger of reading too much into their instant friendship. Such empathy wasn't love. It wasn't even lust, though Skye knew enough of the world to know that there were times when Philip was aroused by her nearness. In the waltz, and the sensual closeness of the foxtrot, and the passion of the tango . . .

"May I have this dance?" Philip asked her quietly now. "There's so little time left for me to hold you in my arms so legitimately."

From his voice, and the intensity of his dark eyes, she knew at once that the feelings weren't all on her side, and she felt a small, rising panic. This hadn't been meant to happen. It wasn't part of her plan. It wasn't happening . . .

She threaded her way through the dining tables ahead of him, her heart thudding now, and turned into his arms. The lights had been lowered, and the band was playing a dreamy waltz as the ship ploughed gently through the summer night.

It was a night made for lovers, and there was no way on earth that Skye could resist leaning her head against Philip's shoulder, nor miss the way his hand above her waist caressed the silkiness of her long hair.

"You know what I want more than anything, don't you?" he said against her cheek.

"Yes. Something I can't give you," she whispered, unable to spoil the magic of the moment by pretending to misunderstand.

46

"Can't, or won't?"

They were jostled by another couple then, and their smiling apologies saved Skye from having to give an immediate reply, but she was very aware that she had just encountered the biggest decision of her life.

"Will you take a last turn around the deck with me in the moonlight?" Philip asked gravely, when the dance ended.

"I'm not sure if I should. Will my honour be safe?"

But she spoke lightly now, trying not to betray how very emotional she was finding the situation. She had never met anyone she liked so well. But shipboard romances were not to be trusted. They never lasted. They were not the Real Thing. Even if she had been looking for the Real Thing.

"You'll always be safe with me, Skye," he said, tucking her arm in his.

They left the dining-room, aware that some of the older passengers watched them leave with fond glances. Whatever Skye's own opinion, it was clear that their association *was* being seen as more than just friendship. But while she was no prude, she wasn't fast either, and she had no wish to get that kind of reputation.

But Philip had never even *kissed* her, for pity's sake, so what was she getting so all-fired uppity about!

The ocean had never seemed so balmy and beautiful as it did tonight, she thought. The path of golden moonlight on the tranquil water seemed to stretch away to infinity, as if there was no beginning to it, and no end. The way she wished this night could be.

She shivered, and at once Philip placed her gossamer wrap more securely around her shoulders. As he did so, he bent his head, running his fingers beneath the fall of her hair and kissing the soft white skin of her neck.

"Don't – please, don't—"

"Why not? Isn't it what we both want?" he said, in a strained tone that was unlike his normal one.

47

"Yes. It is." She couldn't deny it. "But I don't want this lovely voyage to end with recriminations or regrets, Philip. I would far rather remember it as a few days out of time, if you like, that I shall always treasure."

"Good God, if that's not enough to dampen a man's ardour, I don't know what is," he said. "Don't you know that I would never have spoken to you like this if I didn't think there was something very special between us?"

She didn't answer, but the fragile, magical spell of the night had been broken now. She wanted him so much, but she had never felt this way before, and it scared her.

And she knew what the consequences of making love out of wedlock could be. Some of the desperate letters sent to the magazine had made her more aware than most young women of what could happen through a moment of reckless passion.

Not to mention the disgrace to the family . . . and how could she descend on them all here in Cornwall with that kind of anxiety at the back of her mind!

"Then perhaps it's time for us to say good night, my sweet and lovely Skye," Philip was saying more gently now. "Because if we stand here much longer, I swear that I won't be able to resist kissing you."

"Then don't resist it," she said in a strangled voice. Because if one kiss was all they could have, what harm could it do?

He pulled her slowly into his arms, and she was held as tightly as though she had melted into him. She could feel his heartbeat, so close to hers that they merged into one. His mouth was cool on hers from the slight evening breeze, and she could taste an erotic saltiness on his lips.

And then she was kissing him back with all the passion in her soul, wishing that this night would never end, and that there was no tomorrow. For who knew what tomorrow might bring?

Chapter Four

There was a restraint between them the following morning. It shouldn't have been there, and Skye couldn't understand why it was. Nothing terrible had happened – but perhaps that was it. Perhaps Philip had thought it would happen, and was disappointed in her. She didn't want to think that of him. She had thought him a man of integrity, and still did.

But now, this morning, dressed formally for disembarking, and with the coastline of Cornwall beckoning them, there was no magic between them. Other passengers were chattering excitedly now that the long voyage was almost over, but for Philip Norwood and Skye Tremayne, the conversation was stilted and brusque. And she couldn't bear it.

"Philip, what's wrong?" she said quietly. "I know there's something bothering you, and I don't want us to part like this. Can't you tell me what it is?"

He didn't look at her as they watched the huge, natural harbour of Falmouth coming ever nearer. He had already pointed out the two great fortresses on either side of the vast stretch of water – Pendennis Castle and St. Mawes Castle – the sentinels of past battles and reminders of a turbulent and bloody history.

"I should have told you before now," he said abruptly. "I never intended to hide it, but somehow it just happened."

"Goodness, it can't be so dreadful, can it?" she said, trying not to show her alarm. Surely he wasn't suffering from some ghastly illness that was going to cut his life short . . . ?

"It's not dreadful at all. But you told me so much about yourself and your family and your life—"

"Well, so did you!"

She knew that he had taught at various universities. And from the honours he had received, that he had mentioned so modestly, she guessed he was well respected. She knew he had an aged mother in a Ladies' Rest Home in London, where he originated. She knew there were few other relatives, except distant cousins he never met. She knew he wasn't married.

"I didn't tell you everything," he said abruptly.

His voice made her ridiculously nervous. "Well, you didn't have to. Really, Philip. I'm sure there were some things that were none of my business—"

"I have a fiancée. Her name is Ruth, and she'll be on the quayside to meet me."

"Oh. Oh, I see."

He turned away with a frustrated gesture. "No, you don't see. Any normal young woman whose delightful company I've so enjoyed on this voyage has a right to be angry at my keeping such a vital piece of information to myself."

"Then perhaps I'm not normal. I'm certainly not angry."

A different emotion from anger surged around in her heart. She was unaccountably upset . . . shocked . . . feeling suddenly as if the bottom had just dropped out of her world as all the best penny-dreadfuls would have the jilted lover feel. But she wasn't the jilted lover, and they had only shared one kiss. And she was damned if she was going to let him see how she felt. She had too much pride for that.

He still didn't look at her. "May I tell you a little more, while there's still time?"

"If you like. If you must."

They looked at one another then, and if ever expressions spoke far louder than words, Skye thought this was the time. Philip's eyes were darker than usual, and she knew that hers must be as tortured as she felt deep inside. It was madness to

50

feel this sense of betrayal because he hadn't told her about his fiancée until the last moment. It didn't matter. It *shouldn't* matter. But it did.

"Ruth and I practically grew up together. Our parents were very close friends, but I hadn't seen her for some years until she turned up at the university where I was teaching several years ago. We sort of drifted together–"

"You don't have to tell me this–"

"It was because we shared a common background, and always had a lot to talk about, that people seemed to link us together. Before we knew it, we had suddenly become engaged."

"Nobody *suddenly* becomes engaged," Skye snapped, anger overtaking all other emotions at last. "You make it sound as if you didn't have a mind of your own."

She had to hit out to cover her misery. She tried to tell herself he was spineless to have drifted into an engagement in this way, but she just couldn't believe that of him. There had to be something else, but right now she preferred to keep the anger uppermost.

"I did and I do. But Ruth needed me."

Something in his voice made her contain her anger.

"Is there something wrong with her?"

The moment of confession, if that was what it was about to be, was lost, as various shipboard acquaintances crowded around them to say goodbye. If he'd really been going to tell her anything more about Ruth, Skye knew he'd be too loyal to say the engagement had been a mistake. Even if it had. And what right did *she* have to even think such a thing? Unless it was that fey, Cornish sixth sense her mother always spoke about. The sense that was telling her – no, *shrieking* at her – that this was not destined to be a marriage made in heaven.

But there was no more time for discussions or questions, because the ship was docking at the Falmouth quayside to a fanfare of hooters and noise. And Philip Norwood was pressing her fingers tightly in a brief hand-shake of goodbye.

"Be happy, Skye. Perhaps our paths will cross again one day. I certainly hope so."

"It's possible," she said, as lightly as she could. "I'll be visiting relatives in Truro sometime. If I see you across the street I'll be sure to say hello."

She knew it was practically a snub, but somehow she couldn't stop herself. Short of saying how much she longed to see him again, it was better that they should part like this. Still friends, and no harm done, even if he had virtually told her he'd wanted to make love to her last night.

She had wanted it too . . . no matter how wicked it might have been, she had felt a passion for him that was as new and exciting as being reborn. And if she had the slightest smidgin of common sense about her now, she'd forget it. And him.

She had slipped away from him long before the passengers began crowding off the ship, and she didn't see him leave, nor the woman meeting him. She couldn't have borne that, even though she was still asking herself how it was possible to feel so intense about someone she had only known for five days!

But you could know some people for a lifetime, and yet you still didn't really know them at all. And there were others, who just walked into your life, and seemed to have always been a part of you . . .

"*Stop* it," she told herself severely. "He doesn't belong to you and never did, so just be thankful you had the sense not to do anything stupid."

Though from all she had heard about some of her Cornish family's reckless escapades, she doubted that any of them would be so surprised if she had. But maybe that didn't include making love with a man who was already promised to somebody else. She didn't want that on her conscience.

And since her Uncle Luke was a man of the cloth, she supposed she had best try to curb her natural high spirits to a certain degree, at least until she knew how these Cornish folk were going to receive her.

But even as she thought of it, she rebelled against it. It wasn't in her nature to pretend to be something she was not. If the family couldn't take her as she was, then she would simply move on somewhere else. She had a whole year to enjoy here, and she was going to make the most of it.

The first thing she was going to do was to find a small hotel where she could stay for a few days and acclimatise herself with Falmouth and the surrounding area. She was finding it extremely disturbing, as well as interesting, if she thought about it objectively, how you could look forward to something for so long, then when the moment arrived, you wanted to delay it a little longer. It was almost as if you were afraid the reality wouldn't live up to the dream.

She stepped onto the quayside, her baggage being set down at her side by a ship's steward, and looked around her uncertainly for a moment. Her hat was skewered on to her head with a silver hat-pin, but in the breeze from the shore, it felt perilously near to flying off, and she clutched at it involuntarily.

"Miss Tremayne, I believe," she heard a male voice say. "Miss Skye Tremayne, newly arrived from New Jersey."

She whirled around and looked right into a pair of eyes that could only belong to a family member. None of the Tremaynes were exact doubles of one other, but it was always the eyes that gave the connection away. A smile began to curve around Skye's lips as she saw the man beam down at her.

"Well, yes, I'm Skye Tremayne, but how did you know . . . ?" she said unnecessarily. He knew, the way she knew, but it was spooky, because they were still strangers.

The next second she was clasped in his embrace, and she knew a second's panic at being hugged so fiercely by this large man. Then she heard a woman's voice close by, amused, and slightly impatient.

"For pity's sake, Albie, let the poor girl breathe or she'll think you're accosting her and call the constables."

Skye struggled out of the embrace, her face alight with pleasure now as she registered the name.

"*Albie*? You're Uncle Albie?"

Her breath caught with excitement. But of course, he had to be, and her heartbeat settled down. The family likeness was evident, and Albert Tremayne was so like her mother.

The woman laughed, answering for him.

"We're your Aunt Rose and Uncle Albie, my lamb," she said. "We've been watching the newspaper items for news of ships' arrivals from America for days now, and we guessed this would be the one. And a fine summer morning it is to welcome you to Cornwall."

She was buxom and asthmatic, but as she paused for breath, Skye knew at once that she could abandon her planned few days alone. It didn't matter. After the awkward conversation with Philip that morning, she had begun to realise that time alone might be spent brooding, which would do her equilibrium no good at all.

She needed company, and this friendly couple were just the right people to take away the first strangeness of being here. She rarely suffered from nerves, but for the first time, she decided it might be as well, too, not to have to meet the entire family all at once.

"It's lovely of you both to meet me like this," she said. "I had planned to spend a few days here in Falmouth to get my bearings before travelling on, but I'll fall in with whatever you have in mind." Then she paused, for perhaps they didn't have anything in mind for her at all.

Rose ushered her along with them, while Albert carried Skye's baggage to their waiting motor along the quay.

"If 'tis Falmouth you want to see, then 'tis Falmouth you shall see," Rose said in her deeply rural accent. "'Twill be no hardship for Albie to drive back home to pick up a few things for the two of us, and we'll all stay in a hotel for a coupla days. 'Twill be a little holiday for we as well."

"Oh, but it sounds like a good deal of trouble–"

"Course it's not," Albert said. "If Primmy's girl wanted to go to Timbuktu, I'd take her, and be glad to do it."

Skye glanced at Rose at this declaration of loyalty to his sister, and didn't miss the slight pursing of Rose's lips.

"I'm sure I won't want any such thing," she said quickly. "It was just an idea to look around the town, and one night will probably be enough. I'm dying to see St Austell and the clayworks, and Granny Morwen, of course. And Truro."

Her natural enthusiasm came bubbling to the surface again as she spoke, right up until she mentioned the word Truro.

Truro was where Philip Norwood was going to be working for six months, and where a woman called Ruth had arranged to meet him after they had spent a year apart. Not just *any* woman, she reminded herself. His fiancée. The woman he was going to marry.

Albert Tremayne drove off at a leisurely pace from the quay. There was no hurrying in a town like Falmouth, with its quaint cobbled streets and steep, narrow steps between the crowded buildings. On the harbour, fishermen were mending their nets and loudly discussing their catch, and the air was heavy with a pungent mixture of salty smells. Skye had never seen anything quite like it, and she pushed everything else from her mind save the delight of absorbing new sights and sounds.

"We'll stay one night then," Albert said. "'Twould probably be best, for your granny will be impatient to see you, and she'll start thinking we'm hogging your company."

"You don't think it will be too much for her, my being here, then?" Skye said anxiously.

Rose hooted. "The day any of us young 'uns tire Morwen Tremayne out will be a red letter day indeed!"

Skye hid a smile. These particular 'young 'uns' were around sixty years of age, but what really struck her was how Rose

55

referred to Morwen as Morwen Tremayne. Not Morwen Killigrew, as she had once been when she'd become the wife of the heir to Killigrew Clay; not Morwen Wainwright, as she had become when she wed her handsome American husband.

Rose had referred to her as Morwen Tremayne still, bearing the same proud moorland name as theirs, and hers. Curious. And Skye was sure it said something for the esteem in which they still all held Morwen Tremayne.

She put the intriguing snippet to the back of her mind, becoming more interested in the congested traffic now, a hotch-potch of raucously hooting motors, horse-drawn vehicles and bell-ringing bicycles, as Albie steered his own car away from the harbour and through the town.

"It's so busy, and so *old*!" Skye exclaimed. "I've never seen such tiny buildings all cramped together as if they're trying to reach the sunlight."

"You wait 'til you see the moorland cottages above St Austell, my dear, then you'll know what small is." Albie said the name of the town as if it was all one word.

"Falmouth has always been an important shipping place, Skye," Rose told her. "And it has some connection with the old Killigrews, of course—"

"Now don't be filling the maid's head with nonsense, Rose," Albie said lazily. "The Killigrews of them far-off days had nothing to do with we St Austell folk. Killigrew's a well-known Cornish name, see, girl, and you'll find plenty of folk sharing it. Just like the Tremaynes."

"All the same," Rose said, glowering at the back of his neck from where she and Skye occupied the rear seats of the motor, "I daresay Skye's interested in more of our history than just that of the clayworkers."

"Oh yes—"

"Well then," Rose rushed on. "'Twas Sir Walter Raleigh himself who came to the town and persuaded them in authority to develop it. Until then, there was only one other dwelling here besides the Killigrew mansion, as it was then."

"My goodness," Skye said, trying to be impressed.

But she was starting to find Rose's constant chatter irritating, and was thankful they had decided to stay just one night in the town after all. Everything had changed, anyway.

Her plan had been to spend a little preliminary time on her own, to find her bearings and acquaint herself with this strange new country in a relaxed and casual way. But plans could still be altered, and Rose had inadvertently given her a different idea.

"You did say Uncle Albie would have to drive to Truro and back to fetch your things for a night's stay, didn't you?"

"Oh, don't trouble your head about that, my dear."

She was good at directing Albie, thought Skye. And he seemed ready enough to let her do it. After all that her Mom had told her about him and their early days, she was sure he was no milksop, but Rose certainly liked to wear the trousers.

"But now that we've driven through here at such a snail's pace, and I've seen something of the place," Skye went on doggedly, "I believe I'd prefer to go straight to Granny Morwen's house as soon as possible after all. Am I being an awful pest? I shall see if I can arrange for a hire vehicle to take me."

She left the words hanging in the air, knowing they would be picked up at once.

"You'll do no such thing, and I confess I shan't be sorry to get away from Falmouth. The port's always too full of foreign seamen for my liking," Albie said now. "You'll stay with us in Truro tonight. Then we'll take you on to New World tomorrow. You'll want to see the studio where your mother and I lived, I'm sure."

"Oh, yes! And I shall know it right away. Mom has always kept the painting you gave her as a going-away gift on the bedroom wall above her bed, and I never tired of looking at it. I always knew I'd get to see the real thing one day."

57

She was the one to prattle on now, suddenly aware of a chill in the air. Once, Aunt Rose's face must have been very pretty, Skye thought, but when she frowned, as now, there was a definite look of discontent about her thin mouth.

But what had she said, for pity's sake? Just that remark about her Mom keeping Albie's painting above her bed. And what was so wrong with that, when the brother and sister had been as close as two peas in a pod?

And how could a middle-aged wife and mother be jealous of a closeness that had ended so many years ago, when Primmy sailed away to America to become Cresswell's wife?

Thank goodness she had, Skye thought practically now. Because if it hadn't happened, then she wouldn't have been here at all. Nor Sinclair.

Thinking of her own brother for a brief moment before she forgot him again, she remembered just in time not to ask about her Truro cousins. Albert and Rose's son had died at Mafeking. It was a long time ago, but it was best not to mention it unless they did.

And perhaps it was that loss that had changed Rose Tremayne from the laughing girl whose image she had seen in one of the family portraits Albert had sent them, to the easily-irritated woman she sensed her to be now.

"So we'll go on to Truro," Albie said comfortably, clearly not as aware of Rose's displeasure as his niece.

Which was odd, reflected Skye, since he was a true child of Cornwall, and she was only an imported one.

"And how was the voyage, my love? Did you meet any interesting travelling companions?" he went on, sending her instantly and momentarily dumb.

Truro had long been home to Albert Tremayne, and Skye would be staying in the same room her mother had occupied when she and Albie had shared the accommodation above the studio. And Truro was where Philip Norwood was. She wished she could stop thinking about it, but the thought seemed determined to stay in her head, no matter how much she tried to kick it out.

What would he be doing right now, she wondered? She hadn't even had the chance to ask any more about Ruth. Did she live in Truro permanently, or was she just visiting, and staying in an hotel to be near Philip for a while? Or was she a university person too, so that they would be together on the campus, sharing their days . . . sharing their nights . . .

Skye was furious at her own thoughts. It wasn't seemly to let such wanton, reckless thoughts enter her mind. But she was a passionate woman with passionate ideas and a vivid imagination, and it was impossible not to visualise them together. Philip, and the shadowy woman who loved him . . .

She tried to dismiss those thoughts the minute she set foot inside the studio. This place had been so real to her for years, that she felt she already knew every room, every corner of it. She knew how it would smell, with that mixture of turpentine and paint and oils that made up an artist's creative world. Even the undefinable scent of the new canvases were evocative to her nostrils, and she simply stood and breathed it all in.

Being a part of it at last. Being Skye. Being Primmy. In that moment she had the extraordinary feeling that they were one and the same.

"Welcome home," Albie said softly.

And she opened her eyes, startled, without being aware that she had even closed them.

He was standing, watching her, while Rose had gone on upstairs to the living quarters to make some tea. She saw him shake his head slightly as if he was looking at a ghost.

"What is it?" Skye asked nervously. She might have felt an almost mystical sense of continuity moments before, but she wasn't sure she wanted to sense what she saw in Albie's face.

"You're so like her," he said at last. "You have the same mixture of spirit and serenity that she had. The same as my mother, Morwen, had – still has. And that glorious hair . . .

I never expected . . . most young women these days wear their hair up, and it gives a certain hardness to their features. Primmy never did that. Primmy was always so beautiful, so natural."

As he rambled on, unable to stop, Albie was horrified at hearing his own voice becoming clumsy and embarrassed. Knowing he must sound now like an awkward adolescent to this sophisticated girl from New Jersey, instead of the middle-aged and acclaimed artist that he was.

"Please don't go on so," Skye said with a shaky laugh. "I assure you Mom wears her hair in a very sophsticated style nowadays, and the good dames of Mainstown who go to hear her piano recitals wouldn't have her any other way."

"And she still plays just as sensitively as ever, I'll bet," Albie said.

This was safer ground, but he turned away before Primmy's beautiful daughter could guess at the torment he had gone through when she left for America with Cress. It was right and proper that it had happened the way it did. They had been so much in love, and he had been glad for them both that things had turned out well for them. And he had found Rose, and fallen in love himself.

But some things never diminished, never died. Love was like that, and the artist and the poet in him knew that neither time nor distance could change it. And he had loved Primmy in a way not even he had understood until it was too late. By the time he did, he had thanked God that it *was* too late. Because not for the world would he have destroyed her innocence.

But now here was Skye. Here was Primmy. And it was a cruel God who could do this to a man, Albie thought savagely. Testing him once, and now testing him twice.

"Are you two going to poke about down there all day?" came Rose's prosaic voice. "Bring Skye's things upstairs, Albie, and let her get settled in. She can see all your arty stuff when she's had a cup of tea and one of my fruit scones."

60

The uncle and the niece smiled at one another, and the fey moment passed.

Later, having had her fill of fruit scones, rich with thick Cornish cream and Rose's blackberry and apple jam, Skye felt as though the studio was stifling her, and she knew she had to breathe some fresh air. She told her hosts she would just love to take a stroll during the evening, since Primmy had told her how she and her father had once gone on a tripping boat all the way down the river, and then spent the afternoon lying in the grass and discovering their love for one another.

"I hope I'm not being indiscreet and breaking a confidence, but Mom said you and she always shared everything, Uncle Albie, so you probably know all about it anyway," Skye said apologetically.

"Well, sometimes it's good to be reminded," he said without expression. "But we'll take a stroll after tea if you've got your land-legs back. Rose won't come. She doesn't care for walking. But you'll be interested in seeing our cathedral and the new college, I'm sure, being a bit of an academic yourself."

Skye laughed a little shrilly. "Oh, just because I send my work to a busy magazine office, I wouldn't give myself such a grand title. And anyway, I'd far rather see the river."

But in the end, Rose did decide to come with them. Skye wasn't sure whether to be glad or not. She felt a great and unquestioning affinity with Albie, feeling as if she had always known him. But Rose . . . Rose was an outsider. She wasn't a true Tremayne, nor a Killigrew, nor a Wainwright . . .

She registered her thoughts with something like panic. *She* was the outsider, for glory's sake! She was the one who had to establish her identity with this large family, who didn't know her at all.

But she dutifully took a great interest in everything she was shown, knowing now why her mother had loved this town so much. This *city*, she reminded herself. Knowing just how

61

a renegade brother and sister who didn't have the remotest interest in the family clayworks business, could set up their own establishment well away from St. Austell. Knowing exactly that feeling of wanting to be independent, and not tied to the past, because it was just why she had insisted on striking out on her own in the commercial writing world.

So why on earth was she here? She suddenly asked herself. Here, where the past was all around her, and there was no way she was going to escape it.

By the time they had done the riverside walk, then retraced their steps to stroll around the town in the evening air, like so many others were doing on this mellow evening, Skye was beginning to feel very tired. The very air here was soft and somehow draining. And she *had* been travelling for a long time.

And now she had seen Boscawen Street and the impressive frontage of the Red Lion Hotel that her mother thought such a landmark; the Lemon Quay where the river boats departed from; the lovely light-grey stonework of the cathedral that made a town a city; and glimpsed the university.

And despite her resolve, Skye knew that all the time they walked, and the many times they were stopped while she was introduced to various folk as Primmy Tremayne's daughter from America, her eyes were searching for a tall figure with rugged, intelligent features, who belonged to somebody else.

"Have you seen enough yet, Skye?" Rose asked her.

"I think I have for the time being," she told her aunt gratefully. "I pooh-poohed Uncle Albie's remark about getting back my land-legs, but now and then I feel as though the motion of the ship is still beneath my feet, and it makes my head a little dizzy. Is it normal, do you think?"

She was talking quickly, to cover her momentary gloom. There was no changing fate, and if fate had thrown Philip Norwood her way and then decided to take him away from her, so be it. And *that* was the craziest thought she had had yet!

"It's quite normal, and a well-known phenomenon," Albie said, tucking her hand in his arm. "A good night's sleep will set you right, my love, and we don't want to tire you out on your first night here."

As they walked back to the studio, Skye spoke determinedly.

"Look, you've both been wonderful to me, and I do thank you, but I feel I should go and pay my respects to Granny Morwen as soon as possible now. Tomorrow, I think."

It was odd how she had so wanted to see this place above all, since it was where her mother and Albie had shared such a Bohemian life, by all accounts – and she was sure she had never learned the half of it – but now she couldn't wait to get away. And Rose wasn't urging her to stay.

"Quite right, my dear. Morwen will be anxious to know you've arrived safe and sound, and we'll take you to New World whenever you say. You'll know that they have the telephone installed there now, and so do we, of course, for business purposes. Not that you can ever hear anything properly on the scratchy thing. But I think Albie should speak to his mother this evening to let her know you've arrived."

"Naturally I will," Albie said. "You don't need to remind me of my duty, Rose."

Not for the first time, Skye sensed the small feeling of animosity between them, and yes, it was time she left. At one time she had thought she might stay here for days, perhaps weeks, absorbing her mother's past. Now, somehow, she knew she never would. You couldn't live someone else's past.

But the mention of the telephone had directed her thoughts elsewhere. She knew where Philip Norwood would be. The college would surely have such modern methods of communication, and if she ever needed him she only had to pick up a telephone and ask to be connected with him.

If she ever needed him . . . she felt her heart miss a beat and then race on at the thought. Needing him was something she knew she must never do, but it was a poignant sort of comfort to know she could contact him if she was desperate.

What in pity's name was *wrong* with her? she thought later, as Albert asked the operator for his mother's telephone number, and waited for them to be connected.

She had had gentlemen friends before, and her parents had seen nothing wrong in her enjoying the company of both sexes. But never had she felt so gauche and out of sorts as she did now. And the sooner she got away from Truro and all its past memories and futile longings, the better.

Albert handed the telephone to her with a smile.

"Your grandmother wants to speak to you, Skye," he said.

She took the instrument, aware that her hands were shaking. Aware that this piece of crackling, mechanical equipment was about to bridge the generations. They had written to one another many times; exchanged photographs; learned much about one another; but they had never heard one another's voice.

"Granny Morwen?" Skye said, oddly husky.

Chapter Five

Morwen put the telephone receiver back on its hook, her hands shaking slightly. Silly old fool to get so het up over hearing a voice, she told herself. It didn't even have the remotest touch of a Cornish accent. The accent was quick and bright – after the initial huskiness – an accent that was similar to Ran's. But, that apart, the voice still had more than a touch of Primmy in it, her darling Primmy . . .

She gazed into space, looking somewhere where Birdie couldn't follow, and the pragmatic companion gave a loud sniff. For all that she was Cornish-born, Birdie didn't have a fey bone in her body, but she could respect the fact that other folk did, providing it didn't send 'em off into the realms of fantasy.

And seeing Morwen's pale face now, she decided there was no time like the present for a drop of brandy. Knowing there would be no objection, she went to the decanter on the side table, to pour them both a tot.

"She's come, then," she stated, rather than asked.

Morwen started. "Yes, she's come, and she'll be here tomorrow, so tell Mrs Arden to make sure her room's ready."

"What's to do? The room's been ready for days, as you very well know, and no amount of fussing and fretting over it will make it look any cleaner," Birdie said tartly.

Morwen gave a slight smile. "You're a hard-hearted woman, aren't you, Birdie?"

The woman gave a grimace that was meant to be a smile,

not taking offence. "That's as mebbe, But I'm also a practical body, missus, and not so soppy as some."

"Yes, well there's times when a bit of soppiness never hurt anyone. And if you can't feel a bit of a heart-tugging over seeing a grand-daughter you've never seen since she was a babby, then when can you? I just wish—"

She stopped abruptly. For one wild, impossible moment she had been going to say she wished Skye's natural grandparents could have been here to see this day.

Sam, her adored brother Sam, and Dora, his wife – and the two of them having been dead for nearly half a century now . . . Morwen's face whitened still more at her own stupid thoughts, and she gave an unconscious shiver as if she was looking at her own mortality.

"Hand me that brandy, you old goat," she went on roughly to Birdie. "I'm in dire need of a warming. And this is a celebration, so let's look cheerful and not as though the world was falling in on us."

"You won't be saying that if all the rumours be true," Birdie muttered, turning away. But not before Morwen had heard her. She may be old, but there was nothing wrong with her hearing, nor her senses.

"You're not going on with these scare-mongering war stories, are you?" she said in exasperation. "I tell you, 'twon't happen, and don't you go alarming Skye with your nonsense. I want no such idle talk while she's here."

"Oh? And I thought you were meant to be the one wi' the second sight," Birdie mocked her.

"I never professed to have it, nor wanted it, and if I did, I'd be sure and keep such thoughts to myself, and not scare everyone in sight with such talk," Morwen snapped.

Sometimes, just *sometimes*, she thought, she could wish Birdie Hawkes back where she came from, on the borders of Cornwall and Devon, which was practically upcountry. But she immediately retracted the thought, just in case wishing

66

could make it come true. Her friend Celia had always believed that it did . . . and she didn't really want to lose Birdie.

They frequently rubbed each other up the wrong way, and her stuffy preacher son Luke thought it appalling the way Morwen allowed the other woman to bait her. But they suited one another, and that was all that mattered. And they sometimes behaved particularly badly whenever Luke was around, just out of cussedness.

Morwen switched her thoughts. She supposed she had best let the rest of the family know that Skye had actually arrived in Cornwall now. They would all want to meet her – well, probably not her brother Jack and Annie and their girls, who lived somewhere on the Sussex coast now, and never came home to Cornwall.

They had moved as far away as possible after the death of their son, transferring their thriving boat-building business, just as though a different location could take away any of the hurt and the memories. Morwen could have told them all about the futility of that, if they'd cared to listen.

But they were hardly family any more, she thought, with a sense of sadness. They didn't keep in touch, except for sending an obligatory card at Christmas. So she could discount them. But the rest . . .

She was glad Skye had gone to Truro first of all, knowing how Albie had been dying to meet Primmy's girl. Rose might not have been so keen, she thought, knowing how possessive Rose had always been over Albie, even to the extent of being pointlessly jealous of all the years Albie and Primmy had shared at the studio.

But now they had already met Skye, and would be bringing her to New World tomorrow. She mentally ticked off the other names in her head, knowing she couldn't put it off any longer.

"Find me my book of telephone numbers, please, Birdie, and then you can ask for the numbers so I can let the family know she's here."

67

She began the calls, knowing she would be exhausted by the end of them. Walter and Cathy were naturally delighted at the news, and promised to be here after supper the following evening. The welcome party was as good as planned, Cathy told her, exhausting her immediately . . . Theo would surely come with them tomorrow evening, Cathy added, providing he didn't have anything else planned, and giving the neatest excuse on Theo's behalf.

"I knew Cathy wouldn't waste any time over this party," Morwen said drily to Birdie. "She was always an organiser of the social graces, just like her mother."

Preacher Luke Wainwright was unavailable at the present time, his housekeeper said grandly, giving him his full title, even though she knew very well who was calling. He was out giving comfort to a dying parishioner, but she would be glad to pass on the joyful message when he returned home.

"Pompous loon," Morwen muttered when she put the receiver back. "The pair of them would make good bedfellows – or at least, they would do so if Luke was that way inclined."

Birdie laughed, and Morwen laughed with her. There was no one else in the world that she could make such outrageous remarks to now, but sometimes it was good to forget that you were the part-owner of one of the biggest china clay works in the county, and remember that you were once a young bal maiden, running wild and barefoot across the moors, and as cheeky and free with your words as any kiddley-boy.

God, how she sometimes wished you could go back, she thought, with a sudden ferocity that shook her bones. To be young again, and full of the spirit and vivacity that everyone knew was in Morwen Tremayne.

"All right, so who's next?" Birdie's voice broke into her useless dreaming.

"Charlotte and her brood. I doubt that they'll want to visit until the party, but we'll let them know in advance what Cathy's

arranging. Skye will be glad to meet Charlotte's girls. The rest
of us will seem like ancients to her."

She hadn't thought of it like that before, and she didn't want
to think of it now. But true to expectations, Charlotte said she
would be in touch with Cathy and they would all certainly want
to be at the reunion.

"'Tis hardly a reunion, since none of 'em have ever met the
maid before, is it?" Birdie said, pedantic as ever.

But by then, Morwen was tiring. She didn't like the telephone
and never had. It was alien to her, even though she often thought
you could sense folks' feelings from their voices, even when you
couldn't see their faces. Sometimes their words said one thing,
while their tone said another.

"Just one more call," she said. "I'll write to Bradley and
Freddie, because I don't suppose we'd prise them away from
their beloved horses. But I want to speak to Emma."

She waited with fond anticipation while Birdie asked the
operator for the number of the farm. Emma was the youngest
of the Wainwright brood, and living over Wadebridge way.
Morwen's sweet, ethereal Emma. As a child she had always
seemed only on loan to her.

But she couldn't have been more wrong. And now Emma was
a strapping, red-faced farmer's wife, and devoted to her pigs and
sheep in place of the children the couple never had. And another
surprise was that the brawny farmer husband, Will, was quite
besotted with his flower-beds and glass houses.

At the spring shows where they sold their livestock for a
pretty penny they also displayed their daffodils and herbs, and
made a handsome profit on them.

Morwen still found it incongruous that two country folk with
such fat, sausage-fingers, could tend such delicate flowers and
produce such glorious blooms.

"Emma, 'tis me, Mammie." No matter what the rest of them
called her, to Emma, at forty-three, she was still Mammie. The
world might change for the worse or the better, but in that

respect, Emma remained the same. It cheered Morwen's heart to know it.

"Mammie! We were just talking about you, and wondering when you were going to give us the news. Is she here yet?"

"Tomorrow. Albie and Rose are bringing her—"

"Oh ah, they'd have wanted the first look-see," Emma said amiably. "So what's the plan?"

"We'll be having a party here at New World once Cathy's arranged it all, so I'll let you know the date as soon as I can. You'll both be sure to come, won't you? There's no lambing or pig-squealing to stop you, is there?"

Emma gave a shrieking laugh. "Oh Mammie, lambing's well and truly over by now. But Will says 'tis a pity the daffy season's over, or we'd have made a right display for the maid, and filled the house with blooms. Though I know where they'd have ended up," she added.

"You just keep the date free as soon as I let you know, then, and you know there's plenty of room for you to stay the night," Morwen said.

"That depends on what Will says."

Morwen sighed as the conversation ended. Where had her little girl gone – the one who always ran to her, and wanted her Mammie to the exclusion of everyone else? The one who had nearly died from the measles, and Jane Askhew had been the one to keep vigil with herself and Ran, when the two of them had nearly collapsed from sheer exhaustion. Now, all Emma wanted was Will, and her lambs and her pigs.

Her mouth twitched at the nonsense of the thought. Because of course it was right and proper that folk moved on.

But her flowers . . . Morwen's face sobered. Emma knew her too well. She might not know the whole of it, but she knew that once a year her mother made a special pilgrimage to Killigrew Clay, just to gaze down into the clay pool where her friend Celia had drowned herself, rather than face the shame of what she had suffered.

70

An illegitimate child would have been shameful enough, but to deal with it in the way she had – *they* had – Morwen added, was the wickedest of all. Taking a witchwoman's potion, and burying the thing, the waste – no, the *child* – she made herself think brutally. Celia hadn't been able to cope with any of it.

It was decades ago now, and yet sometimes it was all so real to Morwen, as if she could still hear Celia's terrified weeping as Ben Killigrew's cousin had seduced her up on the moors near the standing stone.

And Morwen's annual pilgrimage always ended at Penwithick Church, not the moorland parish where Luke was now all puffed-up in importance as resident preacher at remote Prazeby, but where Celia was buried in the old churchyard, along with so many Killigrews and Tremaynes and Wainwrights.

And she always lay a sheaf of wild flowers on Celia's grave, the way she had done on the day she was married to Ben Killigrew in that very church, a lifetime ago.

"You're drifting again, and 'tis time you were in your bed," she heard Birdie say. "You'll want to be sprightly to greet the maid tomorrow."

"*Sprightly*, is it! I'll leave that to the young 'uns," she said, as tartly as she could, considering that there was still such a heartache inside her, every time she thought of Celia Penry. It didn't happen so often nowadays, but when it did, it could still catch her unawares.

But Birdie was right. It was high time she was in bed, and she'd be glad to shut everything out of her mind until tomorrow.

Skye was on her way. At last she was going to meet the matriarch of the family, whom her Mom and Dad held in such esteem. What would she be like? She had heard such tales, and she had always imagined she had a weird affinity with the spirited girl that Morwen Tremayne had once been.

But she wasn't about to meet a wildcat young girl of seventeen who had fallen in love with the son and heir of Killigrew Clay and eventually married him against all the odds. She was going to meet an old lady. Her grandmother.

"Nervous, Skye?" Albie asked her, glancing back in the car.

"No!" she lied. "Should I be?"

Rose laughed. "Some folk might say you should, my dear. Your Granny can be a formidable woman."

For Skye, at that moment, the sudden memory of herself and Philip Norwood laughing like conspirators over reducing folk to size by imagining them in their underwear, surged into her mind. Making her heart leap . . . not with the shame of imagining an old lady in that way, but in bringing Philip's image so vividly alive.

She concentrated on watching the passing scenery, and glorying in the wildness of the countryside as they crossed the lanes and byways and headed towards St. Austell.

They would reach New World before they reached the town, so the sight of the clay works and the sky tips must wait awhile longer. But by then the excitement in her heart had overcome all other thoughts. It wasn't so much a feeling of coming home, as a sense of having been here before in some other life, some other time. Spooky, but oddly reassuring.

And the moment she was enveloped in Morwen's arms, she knew why she had made this journey.

As for Morwen, she had to stop telling herself she was seeing ghosts. This was Skye. Not herself or Primmy, nor all of them. Skye was unique. Herself. A fact that became perfectly obvious when she declared her intention to stay here at New World for as long as Morwen would have her.

"That's what I hoped you'd say, dar," Morwen said, using the quaint endearment Skye's parents used to one another. And if she thought it surprising that Albie looked almost relieved that Primmy's daughter seemed not to want to spend more time with him and Rose, she ignored it.

"I want to see everything, Granny Morwen!" Skye said,

after they had gone, and she and Morwen had spent a glorious couple of hours looking through the masses of photographs in the albums. "I'm longing to see the clay works and the cottage where you used to live – and you do know I'm planning to write some articles for my magazine about Cornish life, past and present, don't you? I'd love to send some of these photographs as well, but I guess most of them are too precious for you to part with."

She rushed on hopefully, her words almost tripping over themselves in her excitement now.

"If there's any similar to one another, you can have 'em," Morwen said. "But you're right. Some are far too precious to part with."

"But perhaps I can get copies of them. I could try taking them to a photographer, or perhaps to the newspaper offices. I'm sure they could do them without damaging the originals," Skye persisted.

Morwen laughed. "You're a Tremayne all right and no mistake, my lamb!"

"What does that mean?" Skye said, but pleased at the comment.

"You don't give up, do you? Once you see something you want, you'll go to the ends of the earth to get it."

"Like you did, you mean?" Skye said daringly, and not allowing herself to apply such thoughts to wanting Philip Norwood.

She wasn't selfish enough to try to steal another woman's man . . . but she was honest enough to admit to herself that she *did* want him, in every sense of the word.

And Morwen was laughing now, and telling her to mind her manners when she spoke to her elders. But her blue eyes sparkled, giving Skye more than a glimpse of how strong-willed Morwen Tremayne had once been . . . wanting Ben Killigrew . . . and wanting Ran Wainwright.

But it was clear that Morwen was getting tired, and Skye knew they had better leave any more discussions until tomorrow. After all, they had plenty of time to get to know one another.

"Is there any chance of my hiring a bicycle while I'm here?" she asked, as they prepared to go to bed. "I'd like to explore on my own, and not be a bother to anyone."

"You'll never be that, Skye, but I'm sure it can be arranged. I'll ask Birdie to see to it, if you're sure that's what you want." And didn't she understand the need to be independent, and to form her own ideas? And this intelligent girl would want to see everything for herself, if she was going to write things about them all for her magazine.

For the first time, Morwen felt a tiny doubt. There were too many things that should never be written about for all to see. Private things, personal things . . . but she was sure Skye had integrity too, and wouldn't want to expose anything that was best kept buried for all eternity.

Glory be, but what was she making such a fuss about! Who would be interested in Celia's drowning but those who loved her? And there were precious few of those left now . . . only herself, in fact, she thought, with a huge shock.

And who would be concerned about Sam Tremayne's dying in a mine shaft when Ben Killigrew's little rail-tracks collapsed with the weight of clayfolk going on an outing to the seaside? But even as she thought it, she knew Skye would be *very* interested in that particular happening.

For Sam had been her natural grandfather, and if things hadn't taken the turn that they did, with Dora dying so soon after from the measles, and leaving three orphaned children, then Primmy's life would have taken a very different turn, along with her brothers, Walter and Albert. And there would probably have been no Skye.

"Are you all right, Granny Morwen?" she heard the girl's voice say now.

"Just sensing a goose stepping over my grave," she replied,

a little laboured. "And hoping you'll not uncover too many old secrets that are best kept where they belong."

"I'm sure there are none," Skye said, just as sure that there were. What family didn't have secrets? And this one was hers. She belonged to it, and therefore it belonged to her.

She wrote to her parents that evening, as she had promised to do the minute she reached New World. There was so much to say, about Albie and the studio and the extraordinary feelings she had at just being here at all.

But there was one topic she hardly mentioned at all, and that was Philip Norwood. She had already told them of their meeting on the voyage, so she merely said they had parted company at Falmouth, and naturally she didn't expect to see him again.

When she had finished her letter, she put out her bedroom light, half wishing she hadn't brought his name into the letter. It was the way lovers always wanted to speak the beloved's name at every opportunity . . . the way they so often gave themselves away. And she was all kinds of a fool for believing in love at first sight. Or in a shipboard romance that hadn't happened, anyway – however much the two people concerned had wanted it to happen.

She shivered, snuggling down in the unfamiliar bed, determined to put him right out of her mind, and tried to think of nothing at all.

Philip Norwood had already come to the sad conclusion that his engagement had been a big mistake. It had been a comfortable inevitability, but now that it had happened, he wasn't the kind of man to jilt a girl he'd known for so long, and who had always looked up to him and depended on him. He couldn't be the one to break Ruth's heart.

But re-entering her silent world made him even more aware of his frustration, and all the more so every time he recalled the quick, light voice of the vivacious girl he had met on the voyage

75

back to England. The girl with the unlikely name, and the wide, unconsciously voluptuous smile. And the expressive blue eyes that would have made poets wax lyrical about cornflowers and the colour of the sea, and which made even a prosaic lecturer like himself go weak at the knees, just picturing them gazing into his.

God, how he had wanted her, and how he had censured himself for almost revealing the feelings he had found so hard to control. It would have been disastrous, knowing that he had a duty to Ruth. He was no cad. But the hell of it was that he *still* wanted Skye Tremayne more than he had ever wanted anyone, and certainly more than he had ever wanted the pale-haired girl he'd known all his life.

He watched her skimming her hand in the water now, as they rowed gently down the river in the boat he had hired for the day before he settled into his college duties. Ruth had been living for some time with an elderly aunt just outside Truro, and it had seemed so fortuitous when the college post there had been offered to him.

Now, shamefully, he wished it had never happened, and they could perhaps have drifted apart as simply as they had drifted into the engagement. But if he hadn't been on that particular ship, he would never have met Skye Tremayne . . .

He felt the touch of Ruth's hand on his knee, and he started, thanking God that at least she wasn't a thought-reader. He looked at her intently as she made the quick, expressive hand movements and exaggerated mouthings he had long since taught himself to follow, to be able to communicate with her.

"Philip, what's wrong?" the gestures said. "I know something is bothering you."

Thankfully, she could lip-read, so that he didn't have to take his hands off the oars to use the sign language that was so natural to her, and so difficult for him.

"It just feels strange coming back here after the bustle of New York, that's all," he said with a forced smile. "In a few days everything will seem more normal, especially when I begin work."

"And then I'll hardly see you at all."

Her eyes were large and unblinking, and at that moment they seemed to Philip to be all-seeing. As if she knew very well he welcomed the very thing she looked so mournful about.

They said that people with disabilities developed other senses, and deafness didn't exclude a strong sense of awareness when something was wrong. Or when someone didn't feel the same way about you as they had once done.

He reached out a hand and squeezed hers.

"We'll find time to be together, Ruth. We'll make time."

It wasn't said with any great enthusiasm, and guiltily, he knew it didn't matter. Because she couldn't hear the words.

"You're a blessed miracle worker, Birdie," Skye told her delightedly, eyeing the splendid bicycle that had been delivered to New World by mid-morning the following day.

It had been one of her favourite pastimes to bicycle around the New Jersey coast, free as a bird and beholden to no one. And she anticipated the same pleasure here, with added enjoyment, because every fold in the hills or turn of the road would be a new adventure.

"I know a few folk," Birdie said modestly. "Though you wouldn't be catching me on one of them machines myself."

Skye laughed, itching to be out of here now, and finding her own way around the countryside. She reported to Morwen before she did so, asking how far it was to Killigrew Clay, and if she could bicycle there.

"Time was when we all walked to Truro Fair from St Austell, there and back again, so if you've the heart and legs for it, you should manage it well enough. 'Tis uphill most of the way, o' course, but 'tis downhill coming back."

Skye laughed, loving the moments when Morwen lapsed into the old way of speaking. She was a grand lady now, but there must have been a time, thought Skye, when she spoke the way all the local folk did, lilting and soft, and catching every young man's eye . . .

"I'll be sure and be back in good time for meeting the folks this evening," she said now.

"You'll want summat to eat afore then," Birdie said, not approving of this way of behaving.

Morwen was less fussy. "Go and ask Cook to pack up a pie and a bottle of lemonade for you, Skye. The kiddley-boys and bal maidens survived on far less in a day."

Skye gave her a hug, already feeling that they understood each other very well. And she had learned plenty of those days from her Mom. Primmy hadn't had much time for claying, but when Primmy had charmed her litle daughter with tales of the old days, Skye had thought that she might well have been a bal maiden herself, given the chance.

She had pictured herself scraping the clay blocks and setting them out to dry in the linhay, stacking them pyramid-high on their carts and sending them careering down the steep hills from the moors to Charlestown Port at St. Austell for shipping to far-off destinations. And making Killigrew Clay prosperous in the process.

And now she was going to see it all for herself at last.

By the time she had toiled up the last bit of moorland track, and glimpsed the huddle of cottages ranged like a row of soldiers along the top of the moors, she was hot and drained. The sky-tips were ahead of her now, vast white mountains that glinted in the sunlight with their mineral and waste deposits.

She paused to catch her breath, drinking in the scene, and then had to scramble to the edge of the track with her bicycle as a dark green motor-car swept past her.

"Pig!" she yelled after it, but it vanished in a cloud of dust, leaving her choking, brushing the dirt from her skirts, and furiously straightening her hat. Some way she was going to arrive at the clayworks, looking like a hoyden! Not that she intended making her presence known, she had decided. This was just a preliminary look.

"Be 'ee lost, pretty maid?" she heard a voice say.

She whirled around to see a wispy-haired, dishevelled old woman with an armful of sticks, who seemed to have appeared from nowhere. She wasn't a frightening spectacle, and Skye wasn't easily unnerved, though the toothless grin left something to be desired for dental hygiene, she thought.

"No thank you," she said. "Just finding my way around."

"A stranger, be 'ee?" the woman nodded sagely. "And one o' they Tremaynes, I'll wager, come from across the sea. I heard one of 'em was coming back."

Skye didn't particularly want to get into conversation with such a disreputable old crone, but this was local colour, she reminded herself, and she was a journalist, and this was what she had come for. Besides which, she could do with a breather from the stiff uphill ride.

"Well, hardly coming *back*, since I've never been here before," Skye told her. "But my name *is* Tremayne, and I daresay the news got around that I was coming."

The woman shook her head. "Didn't need no news reports, my pretty. I seen it coming long ago. 'Twas certain sure that one of 'ee 'ould come back. They allus do, see? The one that went off wi' that other 'un after the wrecking years ago – *he* came back. Then there was the one that caused all the fussing – *he* came back and took your mammie with 'un. Now you."

Skye stood as if transfixed as all this detail into the Tremayne family life emerged from such an unlikely source. There were some bits that she knew, and some she simply didn't understand. And she was suddenly angry at this crowing female.

"You should be careful what you say about folk," she snapped. "Spreading lies about them is called slander, and you could be made to pay heavily—"

The old woman gave a sudden cackle that made Skye's heart stop for a moment and then race madly on.

"*Pay*? What would I pay with, my pretty? The likes of me don't have money to squander, 'cept for they who want a special potion or a bit o' special advice. And you'd best come down off your high horse if 'ee knows what's good for 'ee. I'll say one thing for 'ee, though."

Skye knew she shouldn't ask. She should peddle away as far as possible from this disturbing old crone. But almost against her will she found herself snapping out the question.

"And what's that?"

"I heard tell of Morwen Tremayne and her doings from a sister long since gone, and you'm a spit of her, by all accounts. Same looks, same hoity-toity manner, and same nature. 'Twill be the ruin of 'ee if 'ee don't watch out."

"Why should it be? It wasn't the ruin of Granny Morwen!"

Dear Lord, why was she even *continuing* this conversation and defending herself? thought Skye. She got back on her bicycle without another word, and pedalled onwards without glancing back. But she didn't need to do so to sense that the old crone was standing motionless, watching her go.

As she reached Clay One she was telling herself to forget it. At least, the last part. She didn't intend forgetting the snippets of family history that had come her way so oddly, and which tantalised her so.

And then she saw the stationary dark green motor car that had almost knocked her off her bicycle. Without thinking, she marched up to the man getting back into the driving seat now, and rapped on the window to attract his attention.

"Where I come from, we have a name for people like you who have no consideration for others on the road," she snapped, before she could stop to think.

Theo Tremayne looked up in annoyance. He had been far too occupied with juggling with the new work rosters to waste time on flippety young women who spent their time idling about the countryside just to take a look at the quaint clayworkers.

But now he registered the flashing eyes and the sharp accent. And he knew at once who she was. He opened the car window a fraction, as if it was all he could spare, and he drawled back at her, exaggerating his Cornishness in a welter of sarcasm.

"I'm real mortified if our rusticated ways offend you, Ma'am, and you'll understand that we country folk are only just getting used to these new-fangled mechanical machines."

Skye glared at him, knowing he was mocking her, and thinking that if this was a sample of her granny's clayworking folk, then she didn't care for their manners.

"You could at least apologise!"

"What for? For driving on my own bit of moorland at my own pace? You're the one who's trespassing, girl, not me."

Skye looked at him silently. "Who are you?"

"Now why should I tell you that? It's no business of yours, and I see no reason to pander to your nosiness."

Before she could think what he was going to do, he had shot off in a downhill direction, leaving her seething at his rudeness. *Pig*, she thought again, finding great satisfaction in the word, while thinking she did the lovely pink creatures a disservice by even comparing them with that oaf.

She became aware of a few curious onlookers. She smiled at the clayworkers, only to have them retreat into whatever part of the works they were involved in. So much for trying to be friendly, she fumed. It was obviously true what they said. Cornish folk were wary of strangers.

Chapter Six

Theo Tremayne acknowledged that his cousin Skye was a corker, but too young for his taste, despite her spirited manner. He preferred more worldly women, and had little interest in flighty younger things – especially colonial cousins. There had been enough of those in the family already.

But he was hugely looking forward to visiting his grandmother with his parents that evening, and showing Miss High-and-Mighty Skye Tremayne just who he was.

His mother didn't tell them his Uncle Luke would probably be there as well, until they were nearing New World in Theo's motor. Just in case it persuaded them to turn back . . .

"Well, that'll put a damper on proceedings for sure," Walter grunted. "It'll be grace before supper, and grace after supper, and giving thanks to the Lord every which way he can think of for the girl's safe delivery here."

"It's called celestial insurance, Father," Theo grinned. "Didn't you know he's preparing his place in heaven?"

"Stop it, the pair of you," Cathy scolded them. "Anyway, Luke's not a socialising man, and it's more than likely he won't stay long, nor want to come to her welcome party."

"Hallelujah to that!" said Theo.

Cathy clamped her lips together, privately agreeing with the sentiments, but too dignified to say so. Besides, while the men conversed privately with Morwen it would give her a chance to let Skye know the party was arranged for two weeks' time. Subject to Morwen's agreement, of course, she amended.

Luke's sedate horse-driven carriage was already at the house when they arrived. He scorned all modern transport, believing that the old and trusted gave him a certain prestige and solidity in the church and his flock at Prazeby and the surrounding moorland area.

Theo groaned, seeing it. To his mind, the old goat was as stuffy as a horse-hair sofa, and he wondered just what he would make of their volatile cousin.

He felt a quickening of interest, remembering those flashing blue eyes and pithy tongue – and contrasting them with Luke's ponderous and sermonising ways. If ever two related folk were at opposite ends of a personality scale, it was those two, he thought.

"I'm glad to see you've cheered up, Theo," his mother said severely, "Now be on your best behaviour, both of you."

Walter glanced at his son, privately wondering how the hell his sweet and lovely Cathy had turned into this waspish monster . . .

Three people awaited them in the drawing room. Luke greeted them as grandly as if he owned the place, while Skye looked at Theo and felt her face flood with colour.

"It's *you*!" she stuttered.

"I do believe it is, dear cuz," he said mockingly, enjoying her discomfiture.

"Have you two met already?" Morwen exclaimed.

"I wouldn't say we had *met* exactly, Granny Morwen," Skye snapped, before Theo could add his own piece. "If you mean was I almost knocked down by a thoughtless oaf driving a motor far too fast on a country lane, then yes, I suppose we've met."

She was suddenly aware of the silence in the room and knew how tactless she had been in bursting out with her feelings. She should have been serene and dignified, like Aunt Cathy, but that had never been Skye Tremayne's way. If a thing had to be said, then it had to be said.

Luke cleared his throat in the irritating way he had. "Strong words, my dear young lady—"

"Oh, I can use far stronger ones if the need arises," she said, seemingly unable to stop herself retaliating. And then she chewed her lip, knowing how badly she must appear to these fine folk. She looked directly at Morwen, her eyes appealing.

"I'm sorry. Mom always says I've a miserable habit of speaking before I think. May we begin again, do you think?"

To her amazement, she heard Theo laugh.

"Of course. And I promise to go slower the next time I see a pretty girl on a bicycle."

He was half-mocking, but she had the grace to smile and to accept his apology, by which time everyone was making noisy conversation. But she knew her quick temper had to be curbed. Especially here, where she was the outsider.

Theo's final peace offering was to suggest taking her to a theatre in Truro one evening the following week.

"There's a mime party touring the towns, and I think you'd enjoy it. Although it's nothing as grand as you'd see in New York or one of your big cities, of course."

"I don't come from a big city, and I hate New York," she told him. "Mainstown is very small-fry. But thank you for the invitation, and I accept."

If he was prepared to offer her friendship, she'd be foolish to refuse it. Just because they had got off to a bad start, they were still kin, and remembering the suspicious looks she had got from the clayworkers, she wasn't turning her back on friendship.

Luke stayed long enough for supper, and to say the obligatory prayers of thanks for Skye's safe arrival. He told them importantly he had other folk to visit on the way back to the parish, or he would gladly have stayed longer. They all heaved a sigh of relief when he had gone.

"How did you ever come to have such a son, Mother?" Walter asked mildly. Before she could reply, he turned to Skye.

"You'll have already discovered, my dear, what a diverse bunch we are."

"Was he always so pious?" she asked carefully, knowing there were plenty of less complimentary thoughts in her mind. Luke Tremayne might be a stalwart of Prazeby parish, but there was no warmth in him, and Skye guessed he would show no mercy to one of his flock who fell by the wayside.

"He used to be a gentle soul, overshadowed by his brother Bradley," Morwen told her. "He once had ambitions of following Walter and Ran into the clayworks. Then, when Bradley left for Ireland with your Uncle Freddie, and your mother went to America, Luke changed completely. It was as if he had to wait until his brother and sister left him space to breathe."

"Good God, Mother, you're turning quite poetic in your old age," Walter said with a grin. "Anyway, we were such a large brood, we all needed a bit of space to breathe, not just brother Luke."

"You didn't lack for space up on the moors," Morwen said tartly. "And you always knew just what you wanted."

As Skye listened to them, the journalist in her was piecing together the revealing fragments of their relationships as if it was a giant jigsaw puzzle. Which was just what it was, she thought. Every family was unique, and with such a large one as this, there must be so many untold stories . . .

"So what do you make of us all, Skye?" Cathy asked, smiling, the perfect lady.

Why did people ask such inane questions? Skye thought at once. *And how was anyone ever supposed to answer them?*

"Give her time, Mother. She's hardly stepped off the boat, and she's not met the hay-seeds yet," Theo drawled.

"Thankyou, Theo," Morwen said. "Now, do you boys have business to discuss wi' me or not? Cathy and Skye can amuse themselves while we go into Ran's study."

She never called it anything else. The wood-panelled walls and leather chairs, the family photos and sketches that had belonged to Ran, still evoked his aura in her mind in that room, and she would have nothing changed in it. She sat behind Ran's big oak desk and waited.

"We've sorted out the shift work rosters, Mother – at least, Theo's done it, and the men are satisfied with it."

"They've got no choice," Theo put in arrogantly.

"There's always choices," Morwen said. "Your daddy and granddad Hal never needed to lord it over 'em, and nor do you. And if the clayers chose not to work and had to tighten their belts for a few weeks, then we'd be the poorer for it as much as them, so don't give me any of that pompous boss nonsense. You're as bad as your Uncle Luke sometimes," she added, knowing it would rile him.

"God preserve me from that," Theo muttered, but realising he'd gone too far.

"As I was saying," Walter said heavily, when there was a pause. "The shift work's taken care of, but we should seriously look towards getting the autumn loads on the move before time this year. 'Twould mean paying overtime, but the weather's fine and the clay settles quickly now with the new air-dries, and there's no shortage o' workers."

"Why such haste?" Morwen said, suspicious at any hint of change. "We've never brought the dispatches forward before, and Stokes and Keighley may not agree to send their wagons at an earlier time from the usual."

"Yes they will, Mother." Walter sounded more urgent now. "Young Enoch Stokes is more progressive than his father ever was, and they're keen to expand their chemical and medical supply depot. But 'tis only because we've been in business for a good many years now that they'll take all the clay we can get ready by the middle of August—"

"*What*? A month before time? It can't be done!"

And she hadn't worked at the linhay, scraping and stacking for all those years, without knowing the truth of it. But even as she spoke, she knew that those days were long past. Things had become more streamlined, production was speedier, and far fewer women clayworkers were needed now.

"Yes it can, Gran," Theo assured her. "In fact, I'd strongly advise it."

In the small silence then, Morwen felt her stomach clench and go cold. She recognised the feeling. It was not so much a presentiment of something that *might* happen, but more a certainty that events were about to shape all their lives, and there was nothing anyone could do to stop it. It was a feeling that she hated, and which had frequently proved to be as certain as the sun rising each morning. She spoke angrily.

"Will you two emmets tell me what all this is about, or do I have to play guessing games about my own clayworks?"

"It's not just the northern dispatches that we need to think about, Mother. You'd best read this letter," Walter said. "I can't pretend that things don't look black."

She took the envelope he held out to her. She knew the name on the back of it. Hans Kauffmann was one of their best European customers, and had become a friend over the years. She read his words quickly, skimming the usual platitudes until she came to the part that Walter indicated.

'I have no wish to alarm you, my friend, but despite the way the sun shines and the people are enjoying the hot summer, there are storm clouds gathering over Germany. There are rumours everywhere, and it would be a foolish man who does not heed them. We have been friends and business colleagues for many years, but if our two countries were at loggerheads, for want of a more sinister word, I fear for us all. Both our businesses would suffer, and communication between us would cease. I cannot make my anxieties any clearer than that, and nor do I wish to put into words what I so strongly dread.'

Walter watched his mother, feeling additional alarm. She had always seemed invincible, but right now she looked the old woman that she was; still with the remnants of a long-ago beauty in her face that time would never destroy, but with parchment-like cheeks and sunken eyes.

"I'm sorry, Mother," he said roughly. "I didn't want to worry you, but you had to know."

"Not worry me? I'm still a partner in Killigrew Clay, and anything that concerns it, concerns me, and I'm not ready to be put out to grass yet."

But the spark quickly faded, and she spoke more thoughtfully. "Hans Kauffmann is a cautious man, and not one to speak out unless he strongly suspects something. I've heard war-mongering tales from Birdie, but I've not repeated 'em, since such gossip can produce wildfire panic. But you're thinking 'tis not all nonsense, aren't you?"

"I am. And I agree that Hans is not a man to write such things unnecessarily, however guarded."

Yes, that was the word for it. It *was* a guarded letter, thought Morwen. As if the likeable German who had come here several times to visit the clayworks was looking over his shoulder even as he penned the words, for fear of repercussions.

"Then if you think 'tis wise to get the clayers working double shifts or overtime to get the clay dispatched as soon as possible," she said carefully, "see to it right away."

Walter spoke quietly. "I think 'tis a very wise move, Mammie. We may have to be payin' out bonuses as well, but 'twill benefit us in the long run."

The unspoken words were all there, and Morwen wasn't stupid. If war came ... *if war came* ... then the European markets would be closed to them, and they would have to rely on the few American markets they had – and the reliable northern firm of Stokes and Keighley. At least they would want as much raw clay as they could acquire, she thought,

89

echoing Birdie's words in her mind, since there would be a huge demand for extra medicinal supplies . . .

She shivered, not wanting to think in those terms for one moment. She had already lost a son and a grandson to a war, and although there were no young boys of military age in the family now, she had no doubt that patriotic pride wouldn't stop those who had a mind to enlist.

And since Charlotte's girls had always taken after their mother's caring and child-minding ways, they would almost certainly want to go off and be nurses . . . Morwen could see it all happening as clear as daylight.

Theo was adding his piece now. "Now we've got your blessing, Gran, you can leave it all to us. We'll explain everything to the clayers tomorrow. And my rosters have made allowances for extra shifts where necessary."

He eyed her warily as he spoke, knowing she would see that this had been planned before they came here tonight.

Had she actually *given* any blessing, Morwen thought? In any case, wasn't that more in Luke's line of business than hers? Her thoughts were becoming muddled, because what was she giving her blessing *for*, exactly?

To get their autumn dispatches off to Europe earlier than usual to Kauffmann's Fine China Factory, to steal a march on a country that might or might not be going to war with themselves; and to provide a chemical and medical supplies company with the wherewithal to patch up the multitude of young men who would be wounded or dying in such an event.

She experienced one of those moments when everything in her mind seemed to be slipping sideways, sending her imagination to places where she didn't want to go, and seeing horrors she couldn't even begin to contemplate.

She felt Walter press a glass in her hand, and his voice was urging her to sip the golden liquid it contained.

"Take a drop of brandy, Mother, and then we'll join the

others. And please don't fret yourself. It may all come to nothing, and we must all pray that it does."

But she knew her son, and if Walter thought there was a risk of anything impeding the progress and prosperity of Killigrew Clay, he would fight tooth and nail to prevent it.

But you couldn't ward off the inevitable, said a small voice inside her head. National and world events were larger than the doings of one small Cornish company, however successful. They could swamp them, and crush them . . .

"I'm well enough," she said. "You'll report back to me directly after your meeting tomorrow, and for tonight we'll say no more about it. Skye will think we're an odd set of relatives to be closeted in here all evening. Is it agreed?"

They rejoined the women, and it was clear they were both relieved to see them. It didn't altogether surprise Morwen, for they were like chalk and cheese. Cathy strove so hard to preserve the gentility she had inherited from her mother, while Skye was a modern American girl, with all the exuberence of a young puppy. And there was no denying which of the two Morwen was drawn to the most.

"Skye has been telling me how shocked she was to see the extent of the clayworks," Cathy said, in an obvious attempt to show a dutiful interest in a world that didn't interest her in the least, beyond the material comforts it gave her.

"Shocked?" Morwen said.

Skye grimaced. "Aunt Cathy exaggerates my meaning. I was awed at how vast it all was, and how the deep pits had gauged out so much of the hills and moorland. And I was surprised to see how all the workers were covered in the china clay dust."

Walter laughed. "The fine folk of St Austell can tell you all about that. The clayers never had a good name for us when the loaded wagons careered down the steep hills, scattering clay-dust everywhere. Even though it's mostly transported by rail to the port now, they're always complaining about turning the streets into a ghost town."

"I'm sure Skye must be getting tired of all this clay talk by now," Cathy said pointedly.

"Actually, no. I find it fascinating!" Skye was quick to say, and meaning it.

"Oh ah. Townsfolk and upcountry grockles allus find we quaint clayfolk fascinating," drawled Theo, putting on a rich Cornish accent.

"Stop it, Theo," his grandmother chided him. "Take no notice, Skye. He's just teasing."

"I think I'm beginning to understand that," she grinned.

But she was glad when the evening came to an end. Since the discussions in the study, there was an air of tension in the house that was never explained. But it was there all the same, and Skye could feel it as surely as if it was tangible.

The following week she dressed with some excitement for her outing to the theatre with Theo. A mime concert sounded, well, *fascinating*, and she reminded herself to keep the word confined to her thoughts.

She hid a smile as she climbed into Theo's motor. The last time she had seen it he had nearly run her off the track, but since then she had been more cautious in her bicycling visits up to the clayworks, as drawn to it as if it was a magnet. The Pit Captain of Clay One had shown her around, explaining the workings in great detail, and acting as proud as a bantam cock as he did so.

"I'll never understand it all properly," she told Theo as they sped along towards Truro. "But I can see how important an industry it is by the great number of works in the area."

"There's fewer now, but they've become more streamlined," he told her. "Even we've shut down two pits. Now there's just Clay One and Clay Two, since we sold out the others to a china stone works, but production is faster and more efficient."

"Didn't Grandad Ran own a claystone works?"

92

"That he did. Prosper Barrows. It was sold some years ago when it was all played out. But that's enough clay talk for this evening, though I suppose you're taking it all in for your lady magazine readers."

Skye bristled at once.

"How patronising you are! The magazine is a general one, not just for lady readers, and we cover all kinds of features, both domestic and and those of world interest."

"Really? Then a war in a far-off country would also be of interest, would it?"

He spoke with idle amusement, but he hadn't made allowances for her journalist's instinct.

"Of course. If there was one about to happen, I'd be only too pleased to hear about it and report back."

"Oh, I was just speaking generally, of course."

But Skye had the surest feeling that he was not.

The theatre was small and old-fashioned, well suited to a performance by a mime troupe that was widely advertised as the Cornish Mime Players by colourful posters and placards outside the entrance.

Skye had seen mime artistes performing *al fresco* in the squares in New York on her few visits there, and had always been impressed by how versatile they were, and how much could be said without a word being spoken. A bit like life, really, she had always thought.

They had the best seats in one of the little boxes at the elevated sides of the stage. She looked across the small, gaslit auditorium to where a group of people were settling in their seats moments before the lights were lowered, and the performance was about to begin.

"Someone you know?" Theo whispered, as he heard her audible gasp.

"I'm not sure . . . possibly . . ." she tried to be casual, even though her heart was beating so wildly now.

"Well, you'll have another chance to take a look and see if you know the ladies in the interval," he said.

She didn't know who the elderly woman, and the younger, pale-haired one were. But she would know the man anywhere . . .

She concentrated on the performance, knowing her grand-mother would want to know all about it when she returned to New World. And searingly aware all the while that across the auditorium, no more than a stone's-throw away from her, was Philip Norwood. And he wasn't alone.

"Do you know that lady, Philip?" Ruth's elderly aunt said. "You've been staring at her for an uncommonly long time."

"I apologise, Miss Dobson," he said hastily. "But I believe it's Miss Tremayne, whom I mentioned to you before."

"The young American woman, you mean? How interesting. Perhaps we may meet her later. I'm sure Ruth would like to meet the lady who made such an impression on you."

"Perhaps," he agreed, though it was the last thing he wanted to do. Nor did he realise he had made quite so much of Miss Skye Tremayne as the lady seemed to suggest.

He was uneasy. He wouldn't want to hurt Ruth's feelings, but she had an unerring way of knowing what he was thinking. She could almost be Cornish in that respect, if their sixth senses were anything as accurate as they were reputed to be. He felt her tug at his sleeve, and turned to her at once.

"I'm sorry, was I neglecting you?" he said with a smile.

He read her quick hand signals. "Is she the one?"

He realised her aunt had been facing Ruth, so she would have read her lips easily enough. He also registered that there had been only one question in Ruth's mind at that moment. He also registered the way she had queried it.

Is she the one?

He knew he could never answer Ruth with the honesty she deserved. Because ever since the day he had met her, thoughts of Skye Tremayne had filled his mind, and he no longer denied

94

it. But he would never dishonour the lady who wore his ring . . . though even that was a lie, because he knew he dishonoured her with every passionate longing he felt for someone else.

"Yes, it's Miss Skye Tremayne from New Jersey, and I daresay it's one of her relatives with her," he told Ruth.

"Can I meet her?"

"Of course. I'll arrange it."

What else could he say? And how could he truly deny the chance to speak to her, and breathe in her scent, and gaze into her eyes?

He beckoned one of the theatre stewards, and asked him to convey a message to the lady and gentleman in the opposite box, requesting that they join him and his companions for drinks in the theatre lounge after the performance. The message came back they they would be happy to do so, and from then on, there were two people in the theatre who saw none of the rest of the first part of the performance.

"How nice to meet you again," Skye greeted Philip warmly. "May I introduce my cousin, Theo Tremayne?"

Did she notice a glint of relief in Philip's eyes that the man was a relative and not a beau . . . ?

Skye censured herself for the fleeting thought, for if it were so, then how dare he, when his fiancée was standing so quiet and still by his side? Her thoughts were in turmoil.

Philip introduced his lady companions. The older one was gracious and well-spoken, while Ruth gesticulated quickly, smiling at Skye all the while.

"My fiancée remarks on your beautiful hair," Philip translated. His gaze wandered to the glossy, blue-black hair that hung so straight beneath the fashionable hat she wore, and was so much in defiance of current trends. She had toyed with the idea of pinning it up, like Miss Ruth Dobson's, but now she was glad that she hadn't. Glad, glad, *glad*, because it was Philip's eyes telling her that her hair was beautiful.

95

As the small group took refreshments she was aware of how intently Ruth Dobson concentrated on her. It was natural, she supposed, since the deaf girl was obliged to lip-read the conversation, but although it was her aunt who asked questions, wanting to know all about Skye, it was Ruth whose presence made her feel uncomfortable.

It was nothing to do with her deafness, it was just the feeling that Ruth saw more than the casual meeting of shipboard acquaintances.

At the end of the interval, to her horror Skye heard Theo speak pleasantly to the others.

"My mother and grandmother are holding a party for Skye at the end of next week. I'm sure you would all be most welcome to join us."

"Oh, but shouldn't you ask Granny Morwen first?"

"I'm not sure if we will be free—"

Skye and Philip spoke simultaneously, and then paused together. She saw Ruth touch his arm and signal quickly.

"It seems I am out-voted," he said with a smile. "Though Miss Dobson does not care for such outings, Ruth and I will be delighted to come to the party."

"Please give me the address of your rooms and I'll see that you're sent an official invitation," Skye said, knowing how stuffy she sounded, but unable now to think of anything but that fate had taken a hand, and that she was to spend an evening with Philip Norwood. Albeit in the company of a dozen or more relatives, and his fiancée . . . it was a thought that was both dangerous and delicious.

Morwen made no objection to the extra guests. Nor did she miss the extra glow in the girl's eyes whenever a certain young man was mentioned.

"You say the fiancée is deaf?" she said.

"Yes. I don't know if she can talk at all, but she makes

no attempt to do so, other than by mouthing certain things. I daresay she found the mime performance very enjoyable."

Lord, how condescending that sounded! As if Ruth Dobson's deafness meant she could only take enjoyment in childish things, when she was a grown woman, with all a woman's feelings and emotions. And a man who wanted to marry her.

"Did you like her?" Morwen asked.

"Of course. Why would I not?"

"Why indeed?" Morwen said dryly. She put her hand on Skye's arm. "We don't always choose the people we love, my lamb. Sometimes they're chosen for us."

"I didn't say I *loved* her!"

"I wasn't talking about Miss Ruth Dobson."

Skye said nothing for a moment. And then: "How does anyone know if they're truly in love?"

"Oh, it's not that difficult," Morwen said, as dreamily as if she were a young girl, as vibrant as the one watching her with such troubled eyes now. "You think about him all the time, even when you've no intention of doing so. His image comes between you and whatever you're doing, and his voice is constantly in your head and in your heart. And the memory of his touch is sometimes so real that you feel bitterly betrayed when you turn around and he's not there at all."

She gave a small, self-conscious laugh as Skye's eyes grew more rounded at such revelations.

"Just listen to me going on so! An old woman shouldn't indulge in such fantasies."

Skye spoke softly, unwilling to break the spell. "I don't think they were just fantasies, Granny Morwen. They were too heartfelt – too *real*."

"One day I might prove it to you."

"How will you do that?"

Morwen gave a secret smile. "You're not the only one with literary inclinations. Not that an old woman's rambling diary accounts could be called anything so grand."

97

Diaries? Skye's heart leapt, remembering her casual thought about writing a book based on her family's lives. It would be exciting, but time-consuming, to try to get all the information she would need for such a project.

But Granny Morwen had diaries.

Before the request could brim on her lips, she saw Morwen shake her head.

"You'll have to wait until I'm ready for the telling, dar. And the time's not ripe just yet."

Chapter Seven

The nearer the date of the party, the more nervous Skye became. Walter and his family were the first to arrive at New World, followed swiftly by Albie and Rose. And then Charlotte and Vincent Pollard arrived with their two daughters. Luke put in the briefest appearance, then said he had to be away to his duties. And Emma and Will Roseveare swept in, bringing a faint whiff of the farmyard with them, and an air of vitality that Skye warmed to at once.

All these children and grandchildren belonging to Morwen, she marvelled, and all of them so different in temperament, yet all with a look of the old family about them that both her parents had inherited.

"Once a Tremayne, always a Tremayne," Primmy had once said. "Grandad Hal once told me that no matter how many others might come between, we stick together."

"I wish I'd been able to meet him," Skye had said. "He sounds such a darling."

And Primmy had laughed, and told her he was a darling and a stubborn old stick, and that most of them had inherited that as well – including her ewe-lamb daughter.

Skye remembered the words now, as she took the gift that Emma was handing to her with a cheerful smile.

"Open it, my dear, and then show it to Mammie. She'll be surprised. She thinks all I have time for is the farm, but I've found a new interest of late."

Skye opened the parcel, and smiled with pleasure as she saw

the little jug inside it. The clay hadn't been fired to a gloss, but its earthy matt surface had been painted with glossy yellow flowers around its base. The flowers stood out in sharper relief because of the contrast in textures.

"Oh, it's lovely," Skye exclaimed. "And how clever you are to have done it all."

"Oh ah. We hay-seeds busy ourselves with other things besides the chicks and pigs," Emma said without rancour. "See, Mammie? What do you think?"

Morwen smiled indulgently. "I never fail to be amazed at anything you do. Emma. You know that."

"It's beautiful, Aunt Emma—"

"For the Lord's sake, girl, call me Em, or you'll make me feel a hundred years old."

"Well then, it's beautiful, Em," Skye said with a laugh. "Don't you think so, Granny Morwen?"

Before Morwen could reply, Theo had taken the pot from her hands and was examining it carefully, before handing it over to his grandmother for her inspection.

"It's made well enough, Emma, but it's inferior clay," he said. "You should have come to us for the best quality."

"Why haven't you made your own pots before now then?" Skye asked. "I would have thought it was a natural extension of the clayworks."

"And there speaks a babe in arms," Walter stated.

"Have I said something I shouldn't?" Skye asked, thinking it no more than was usual if she had.

"Take no notice of 'em, my dear," Emma said breezily. "The whole family's been stick-in-the-muds where the clay is concerned. Anybody with half an eye can see there's money to be made in pots and plates. But these clayfolk just keep sending it off for others to profit out of we simpletons."

"I'd thank you not to call Walter and Theo simpletons, Emma," Cathy said frigidly, while Charlotte's two daughters simply sat and giggled at the sudden spat going on between

100

the older ones. "It's a handsome enough pot, I'll grant you, but it's hardly going to rival the big potteries."

"It's not intended to, ninny."

"Well, I think it's perfectly lovely," Rose said, to Skye's surprise. She had sat in the background for so long, seemingly overwhelmed by these forceful relatives, but now her face was pink as she came to Emma's defence.

All the menfolk had drifted to another part of the drawing-room by now, and Skye could see that Morwen was tiring of all the bickering. She wished Philip would come. And just as surely, she wished he would not. It had been a bad idea on Theo's part to invite him, and her nerves were already jumping at knowing he would be here soon.

As the womenfolk prattled on, covering the slight awkwardness of moments ago, her journalist's ear caught a snippet from the far side of the room. Men's conversation was frequently more interesting to her than domestic affairs, but this would seem to concern *her*.

"If there's any hint of danger, her mother will be whisking her back home, if I know anything about Primmy."

"They'll have heard about it by now. All the newspapers here were full of it, and such news travels fast. The poor bastard was murdered in cold blood, and his wife with him."

"Keep your voice down, Walter. You know Mother won't tolerate that kind of language," Albie said sharply.

It was too much for Skye to resist. Without seeming to hurry, she moved across the room to join the men. Protocol or not, this was her party, and she dearly wanted to know what they were talking about.

"Who's been *murdered*?" she asked, loud enough for everyone to hear. Charlotte glanced her way, and Cathy was clearly disapproving. Rose came swiftly to join her.

"I think we should leave men's talk to the men," she said quietly.

101

"Poppycock, Rose!" Emma was suddenly there too. "What's to do, and who's been murdered?"

"It's nothing that need concern you, Em, nor any of the ladies," Albie said shortly.

"It sounds as if it might concern me, though, if you think my mother might want me to return home," Skye told him. "So you may as well tell us, because I surely won't give up until you do, Uncle Albie, dear."

Her voice was light, but her eyes were steely now, with a look that Albert recognised only too well. Primmy's eyes had looked just that way when she demanded the truth, and nothing and no one was going to stop her from getting it.

Walter shrugged. "Well, if you must know, the Austrian Archduke and his wife were shot dead by an assassin as they toured Sarejevo. It's far removed from us, but the newspapers have been creating a fuss about it as usual, and predicting all kinds of outcomes."

"Like war?" Skye said. When they didn't answer, she gave a shrug. "Oh, come on, all of you. Don't treat us women like children! If there's going to be a war, we need to know about it, don't we?"

Morwen's voice was suddenly loud and sharp.

"Skye, my dear, do leave the men to their own discussions. I realise you have a literary interest, but I think we should enjoy your party without any talk of war."

"I'm sorry, Granny Morwen," she muttered.

Morwen had never been averse to a verbal battle or any other kind, but this was one she couldn't fight and couldn't win, and she was finally realising it.

"In any case, your visitors have arrived," Theo told her. "Put on a pretty face, there's a good girl, or they'll wonder what kind of household they've come to."

She glared at him for patronising her, feeling her heart begin to race erratically, knowing that she was about to see Philip once more. And too late, she realised she had said nothing about Ruth to warn them.

She spoke quickly. "I should have told you that Miss Dobson is deaf, but she is remarkably skilled at understanding all that is said, providing you don't turn away from her."

And if that didn't sound like the most awful, patronising remarks, she didn't know what did!

Mrs Arden showed the newcomers into the room, and Skye tried to greet them both with the same amount of enthusiasm, while her eyes saw only Philip. This feeling has to end, she thought, appalled. It's not right.

For a moment, she caught her grandmother watching her, and she could have sworn a *frisson* of understanding flashed between them. Then to her amazement, Charlotte's daughters took Ruth Dobson in hand, talking to her in the expressive sign language that she had seen Philip use.

"Don't look so surprised, Skye," Charlotte said with a smile. "It happens to be part of the girls' training, and they'll be glad to be able to put it into practise."

"I'm so sorry you heard that," Skye murmured to Philip. "The women in my family are not the most tactful."

Including herself . . .

"But you are the most beautiful," he told her quietly. "You shine like a star in this company, and in any other."

"You know you musn't say such things," she said, but it was one of those rare moments in a roomful of people when everyone else was occupied, and it was almost as if they were alone. But not quite. As Skye raised her glass of cordial to her lips with hands that shook, she saw their reflections in the large mirror that took up one side of the drawing-room. Everyone was reflected as if in a little tableau. And across the room, facing them, and no doubt reading their expressions, if not their lips, was Ruth Dobson.

"Tell me how you're liking it in your new college."

"Well enough, when I can keep my mind on the curriculum,

though I'll know more when the next term starts in September," he said. "And how do you like your large family?"

She wondered if she had really heard his first words, but she knew she must have done, because she could see his feelings reflected in his eyes, and they echoed her own, so much . . . and it frightened her.

"I'm having a good time, and bicycling all over the place," she said determinedly. "But you really must come and talk to my grandmother, after showing such an interest in the family background."

She walked away from him, knowing he would follow, before he could give the expected reply that his interest was only in her. *Was she becoming a thought-reader now?* she wondered. Or was she just imagining the things she wanted to hear? If so, it was a dangerous game she was playing, because he belonged to someone else, and she would do well not to forget it.

"I'm afraid Ruth has been taken over by my female relatives," she added. "Should you rescue her?"

"Actually, no. She dislikes meeting too many people, and she much prefers to sit in a corner and observe the world."

And you don't, Skye thought silently. *You prefer to be involved in the world, and not to be just a bystander.*

"So this is your Mr Norwood," Morwen greeted him for the second time. "Sit beside me, young man, and tell me what you think of my grand-daughter."

"Granny Morwen, *please*," she said with an embarrassed laugh, moving swiftly away from the pair of them, but she didn't miss Philip's reply.

"I think she's the most delightful young woman who ever crossed the Atlantic."

"That's what I thought," Morwen told him. "So watch out that you don't break her heart, or anyone else's."

"I aim to do nothing of the sort, Ma'am."

A little later she told him to go and mix with the others then, and she watched him go with a strange sense of sadness. For didn't she know only too well that gnawing ache to be with the one you loved, when you were not free to do so? And it was as plain as a pikestaff to Morwen, that if ever two people were in love, it was her granddaughter, Skye, and Philip Norwood.

Almost to Skye's surprise, she saw how Ruth blossomed by being the centre of attention among Charlotte's girls. She was relieved, not quite knowing what to say to her, nor how to say it. She wasn't accomplished in the art of silent conversations, she thought ruefully, remembering the many spirited discussions she and her parents had enjoyed. And she had always preferred the company of men – not in any sexual way, but in the intelligent ways they conversed with an intelligent female.

"What are you looking so serious about, Skye?" Albie's voice said beside her. "You'd best not let Cathy suspect that you're not enjoying this little gathering. It may be Mother's house, but it'll have been Cathy's organising."

She laughed. "Of course I'm enjoying it. But tell me, do you really think this assassination portends war?"

"Who knows?" he said. "There are hot-heads in every race, and it only needs a spark like this one to light a tinder-box of emotions."

"Well, if anyone thinks I'm going to be sent scuttling home because of it, they can think again! Mom would never send for me as if I'm a child – and if she did, I wouldn't go!"

"And there speaks Primmy's daughter," Albie said dryly. "But I suggest you leave any more thinking and eat something instead, or Cathy will be affronted that we're not doing justice to her catering."

But the next day brought a telegram boy toiling up to the house, with a message from her mother that Skye didn't want to read.

'Newspapers here full of the happening in Sarejevo. Advise that you cut visit short and come home.'

Skye had no intention of doing any such thing. Wars were

horrible, but there was a stimulus about being here on the fringes of Europe where it might all be happening, that Skye knew would be far removed from the comfortable life back home. But she consulted Morwen right away.

"You don't think I should go, do you, Gran? I'm only just getting to know people."

"You must do as your heart dictates," Morwen said. "If events take an ugly turn, your folks will be anxious about you, but you're not a child, Skye."

"And it's not as though I'd be crossing the English Channel to be really in the thick of it, is it!"

But she avoided Morwen's eyes. For of course she would want to be there. She was a journalist, and that very day she intended cycling into Truro to send back a telegram of reassurance to her parents, and to visit the offices of *The Informer* for information. Not to seek a job, for they would almost certainly not want to employ a woman in a man's world – at least, not yet. For who knew what might happen, if war came, and all the young men – and older ones – went away to war? Might not women be seen as useful citizens at last?

She shivered as her thoughts raced on, wondering if she was having one of those old premonitions her mother used to relate, that was part and parcel of the Cornish make-up.

"I liked your Mr Norwood, Skye," Morwen said, and she didn't miss the rush of colour in the girl's cheeks.

"He's not *my* Mr Norwood."

"But you wish that he was," Morwen stated without con-demnation. "Be careful, my lamb."

And who was seeing far too much now?

"He was a very pleasant shipboard companion," Skye said solemnly, and then her composure slipped, and she twisted her hands together. "And as you so rightly suspect, Granny dear, we rather fell for one another, and I had hoped – but you see, I didn't actually know about his fiancée until our last evening. He should have told me before."

106

Her voice was full of pain and resentment now, and the unspoken words were plain for anyone to hear. He should have told her before she fell in love with him, and then perhaps she could have controlled the wild emotions that were racing around her senses now.

"Then think of this as a test, my love, and you'll be all the stronger because of it."

But she didn't want any old test. She wanted Philip Norwood, with a fierce and primitive passion that almost shocked her. She had been mildly in love before, but never like this, never so that she couldn't think of anything else now that she had seen him again.

"I doubt that people of your age were ever tested in such a way," she told Morwen, for want of something to say to cover her turbulent feelings.

Her grandmother's laugh was slightly incredulous.

"Oh, Skye, do you think love was only invented for your generation? Or only for the young?"

"Well, no, of course not," she said, floundering. "But you're such a stable, *family* person, I can't imagine that you would ever have been tempted to do anything wrong."

"Then just go on believing it, for I'm not telling 'ee any more," Morwen said with a chuckle that was almost girlish.

Skye's face broke into an answering smile, recognising the old patois in the older woman's voice.

"Why, Granny Morwen," she said softly. "I do believe you're hinting that you were quite wicked in your youth!"

"Mebbe so, but 'tis in my head and heart and nobody else's," Morwen replied more tartly.

How sadly true that was, she added silently. *There were no husbands or lovers to make her heart beat more wildly, to share her life and fill her body and soul with ecstasy now* . . . she composed her face quickly, before this young 'un could dream at the stupid thoughts going through an old woman's brain.

But she saw more than even Skye imagined. The girl was

107

in love with this Philip Norwood, and he was more in love
with her than ever he was with his pale-haired fiancée. There
was tragedy in the making here, and she knew it. Maybe they
should send Skye to Yorkshire, she mused, to spend time with
the Askhews and her cousin Jordan. She would enjoy their
newspaper world. But she already knew that no one would
send Skye anywhere that she didn't want to go.

"What are you going to do today?" she asked now.

"I'm going into Truro to send a telegram back to Mom,"
she said. "And I may call on Uncle Albie."

Before she left the house, Walter arrived, saying he had
something of importance to say to his mother.

"I'm just leaving," Skye said.

"No, wait, girl, since 'twas summat you said that started the
whole idea stirring in our minds," he said.

"Something *I* said?"

It could only have been something reckless, she thought
uneasily, but for the life of her she couldn't think what.

"Well, you and Emma between you," he went on, and then
looked at his mother. His blue eyes were alight with the kind
of glow a man had for a woman – or a sense of ambition.

"You'd best get to the point, Walter," Morwen said. "Or
'twill take Skye all day to get to Truro."

"I'll drive her there."

"Thank you all the same, but I'd rather cycle and see the
countryside properly." And why didn't he get *on* with it!

"Well then, me and Theo have been up all night thinking
about it, and coming to the same conclusion as Emma. Why
the devil haven't we exploited what we have right under our
noses, and gone into pottery production on our own account?
It's like she said. Folk will always need cups and plates, and
it's acknowledged that Killigrew Clay produces some of the
finest and whitest clay in the district."

"But you know nothing about pottery-making."

"We can learn. If Em can do it, I'm damn sure we can. We'd

start off in a small way, Mother, and we'd bring in skilled craftsmen to do it. We'd want to make it distinctive enough so that everybody knows this is Killigrew pottery made from Killigrew clay. What do you think? We obviously need your say-so before we go any further with the notion."

Morwen didn't say anything for a moment. It was a completely new venture, and one that had clearly caught Walter's imagination. And she could guess why. She had frequently seen potters demonstrating at Truro Fair, inviting children to try their hand at it. The young 'uns hadn't been able to resist, especially Walter, loving the feel of the wet clay in his hands as always. This would be an extension of his boyhood dreams, but perhaps that was *all* it was.

"I'm not sure, and it takes some thinking about."

"Uncle Walter, it's a *marvellous* idea!" Skye burst out. "How clever you are to have thought of it. It surely can't fail to be a success."

"Now, hold on, missy," Morwen told her. "There'll be enough excitement in these two boys without you adding to it and trying to persuade me."

Walter smiled faintly at being called a boy, but he hadn't inherited the Killigrew passion for nothing. Though it was more the *Tremayne* passion in his soul, he thought. The Killigrews and the Wainwrights were afterthoughts, compared with the Tremaynes from the upalong moors above St Austell. And that was something else that needed thrashing out.

With a fierceness he hadn't felt for some time, he knew he wouldn't want their new venture to be called Killigrew Pottery. There had to be some special name for it that was separate from the clayworks, and yet had a special significance with it. But that could come later. For now, he had to convince his mother that this was the way forward.

If there were to be dwindling china clay markets because of any conflict in Europe, they had to look inwardly to other outlets. The paper-making industry took a certain amount of clay to glaze their product; and Stokes and Keighley would always be loyal buyers; there were cosmetic firms showing an interest in the usefulness of the clay; but using it themselves, and seeing their own proud name stamped on every piece of pottery, whatever its name, fired his imagination as brightly as ever his sister Emma fired her humble pots.

"I'll leave you two to discuss it," he heard Skye say now. "But for what my opinion is worth, Granny Morwen, I think it's a wonderful idea."

She left them then, knowing how business folk worked. There would be talks and arguments, backtracking and doubts, discussing the finances and looking at every angle, and allowing themselves time to think.

Nothing would happen quickly. It could hardly do so, since nothing like this had been considered before. But she felt an excitement akin to Walter's, and her business mind soared ahead. Advertising was the way to get any product noticed. *The Informer* newspaper in Truro would be a start, and they had connections with *The Northern Informer*, where her cousin Jordan worked. If the pottery became *really* famous, she could arrange for advertisements in her own magazine in New Jersey, and they could export.

She laughed at her own enthusiasm as she pedalled along the lanes towards Truro, and free-wheeled down the slopes, feeling the sun on her head, and breathing in the sharp tang of the sea, and the scent of wild flowers and bracken growing on verges and moorland all around her.

And remembering that her first mission that day was to send a telegram back to her mother, the thought surged into her head that she felt that she wanted to stay for ever. She hadn't been born here, but this place was already a part of her. It was in her heart. And coming from a modern young woman who thought herself beyond such emotional thoughts was one of the most surprising ways in which her attitude was changing.

That, and being in love.

110

Once she reached Truro, she took a breather on a bench by the river, and then the answering telegram was dispatched before she found the offices of *The Informer* newspaper. Her nostrils twitched at the familiar smells of ink and chemicals, and her ears were instantly assaulted by the clatter of typewriters.

The bored receptionist had been disinterested as she asked to see the editor, but he came forward with a smile at hearing her name. David Kingsley was younger than she had expected, and good-looking in a heavily-set, swarthy way.

"Miss Tremayne, it's always a pleasure to see a member of your illustrious family."

"Why, thankyou, Sir," Skye said, taken aback by his educated voice and manner.

"My predecessor had family connections with them, of course, and your cousin Jordan is well thought of in our northern affiliate. Please come into my office, and I hope you'll take some tea with me?"

"Thankyou, yes," she said, warming to him.

"So what can I do for you?" he asked.

She gave a small laugh. "I don't really know that you can do anything. I'm staying with my grandmother and visiting my relatives, and since I do freelance work for a magazine in New Jersey, I wondered if you could show me any old issues to throw some light on the area, and my family in particular. American readers are intensely interested in anything from this side of the Atlantic. If you could loan me any issues, I'd be enormously grateful, and take great care of them."

Lord knew why she was gabbling, or suddenly so nervous. She wasn't asking for the earth, even though it had been a spontaneous request. But she couldn't think why she hadn't thought of it before.

"I'll be glad to help you in any way I can," he said. "When you've finishd your tea, we'll go into the basement and go through the archives."

"I don't want to take up too much of your time—"

"Nonsense. My time is at your disposal, Miss Tremayne."

She couldn't be unaware of his admiring look. She knew she presented a trim figure in her pale cream suit, the skirt just flared enough to allow for easy cycling, and her long hair kept reasonably tidy beneath the flowered hat. She hadn't missed the pressure of his fingers when he'd taken her gloved hand in his, and she had enough vanity to feel a glow of pleasure at his interest. Even if he didn't interest her in any special way, it did a lot for her woman's self-esteem to know that she was admired.

They spent more than an hour in the basement studying the archive newspaper issues, and by the time they emerged upstairs again, decidedly hotter from the enclosed atmosphere, Skye had a bundle of them to take away with her.

"It was stifling down there," she commented. "But thankyou for being so patient. I know how busy you people are."

"Will you have lunch with me?" he said abruptly. "A new riverside inn has just opened that's proving very popular. I would deem it a great honour, Miss Tremayne."

Skye had other places to go. She had intended calling in on Albie and Rose, she should go back to New World and study the archives and see what she could glean about this clayworking world, and she should say no to an invitation from a man she had only just met.

"That would be lovely. And won't you call me Skye?"

"I will if you'll call me David. Is it a bargain?"

They cut across the formalities as easily as cutting through butter. It had been this way with Philip, thought Skye, but Philip had never been free, and she forced her resentment of his deceit to overcome all other feelings. It was safer that way, knowing nothing could come of their attachment. But here was David Kingsley, who was a pleasant young man with whom to spend an hour or so, and who shared the world that she knew. And that was all she asked of him.

"My cousin told me about the tragic events in Sarejevo.

Do you think there will be a war?" she asked him directly, when they had been served with enormous servings of meat pie and peas.

"Undoubtedly," he replied, to her consternation.

"Oh, I had hoped you were going to scoff at the idea. Do you have any inside information?"

He grinned. "It's easy to see your journalistic background, Skye, and good to talk with an intelligent woman who doesn't have her head in the clouds and think only of marriage and babies."

"I'm not sure that makes me sound very feminine!"

"Then forgive my impertinence when I assure you there could never be any doubt about that."

But she wasn't a journalist for nothing, and she knew well enough that he hadn't answered her question. She also knew enough to hold on to it.

"So what do you know that the rest of us don't?"

David shrugged. "Nothing specific. But it's well known that Germany has a huge, well-trained army, ready to move at one word of command from the Kaiser. They've been restless for years, and once they assert their power over neighbouring countries, we'll have no option but to declare war."

"Why is that?" she said, trying not to become unduly alarmed at his earnestness.

"Because under the Treaty of 1839, Britain had promised to protect Belgium from her foes. If German troops march into Belgium, as the most likely and least-defended target," he shrugged again, while Skye's nerves tingled.

"Can we please talk about something else?" she said swiftly, knowing she had been the one to provoke this change of attitude in him, but wanting to get away from it now.

"Of course," he said, leaning across the table to squeeze her hand for a moment. "And I believe someone is watching you very closely. Is it someone you know?"

*   *.   *

113

It had to have been fate that made Philip Norwood escort his fiancée and her aunt to this very inn, he decided. It was new, and had been highly recommended, and it was full of people enjoying the sunshine. His brief introduction to the summer college term was over, and Ruth had insisted that it was far too hot to stay indoors.

But the unexpected sight of Skye, listening so intently as she looked into the eyes of a very personable young man, twisted his heart. And when the man reached across to touch her hand and she seemed to make no objection, he could hardly bear to sit here a moment longer.

"Shall we go, ladies?" he said abruptly. "If you've both finished your meal, I have to return to my rooms to begin writing my next term's project for the students."

He invented the need for work on the spur of the moment. And if he was unnecessarily curt, the unworthy thought flashed into his head that at least Ruth couldn't hear it. He knew her aunt would be only too pleased to be indoors and away from the river smells. But Ruth's gaze had followed his own, and seen the flowered hat atop the long black hair and the slender figure of Miss Skye Tremayne.

She might be deaf, but she wasn't stupid. Any normal acquaintance of the young lady would have wanted to stop and say hello, and to thank her for last night's party.

The fact that Philip preferred to hustle them all away spoke far more to Ruth than any words could have done. And it needed serious thinking about.

Chapter Eight

For the next couple of weeks, Skye immersed herself in scouring the old newspaper issues and writing articles for inclusion in the magazine back home. The flavour of the past and the present seemed to envelop her. There were interesting reports about strikes and marches, and the fluctuations of china clay fortunes over the years. There was an inclusion of her own parents' departure for America with Cresswell's folks. And an arresting piece of information regarding a lady called Harriet Pendragon, who was apparently refuting all interest in Killigrew Clay in perpetuity.

Skye's nose smelled a story here, but since her grandmother had succumbed to a summer cold and taken to her bed, she felt disinclined to question her about it. But she wasn't so reticent with Theo when he called to enquire about Morwen's health.

"It's past history, but you'd do well not to mention that name to her, nor to my father," Theo warned her.

"Why on earth not, when it's here in the paper for all to see?" But it wasn't for all to see, only for those who had access to old and forgotten events. And those who remembered.

"Do *you* know what it's all about?" she asked Theo.

"I heard tell of it. The woman tried to buy out various pits in the district, but she had her sights set mostly on Killigrew Clay, and especially on its owner."

Skye wondered which of them it could have been. Was it his own father, Walter? But she daren't ask so boldly.

"Do you mean Ben Killigrew?" she said instead.

115

"No. It was long after he was dead that the Pendragon woman came into town dressed like a harlot, by all accounts, and decided to make Ran Wainwright the target for her affections."

"So what happened?"

Theo shrugged. "There was some tale of Morwen saving the Pendragon woman from an accident at Truro Fair. Mebbe that's what turned it all, but I don't rightly know, and nobody's telling. I'd advise you not to pursue it."

And if Harriet Pendragon had set her sights on Morwen's husband, there would have been more than a little jealousy between the two women, thought Skye. She knew all about Morwen having once been wild and strong-willed, but if this Pendragon woman was as sensual and rich as Theo implied, then those things could be a powerful attraction to a man. Even a married one. Or one who was betrothed.

As the thought slid into her mind, Skye determined anew to put all thoughts of Philip Norwood behind her. There was no need for her to visit Truro too often, and she had thwarted any ideas David Kingsley might have of pursuing her by saying she would be busy for the next month, but that she would bring the archive material back when she had finished with it. His admiration had been flattering, but she didn't want any such involvements, and he could hardly mistake her coolness.

But Theo had also come to New World to report that he and Walter were looking into the possibility of using one of the disused linhays at Clay Two as a small pottery, as an initial experiment into costings and production. One of the Pit Captains had a brother who could throw a pot, and his nephew was also learning the craft, and the pair of them were willing to start things off.

It all sounded pretty haphazard to Skye, but even the largest business concerns had to start somewhere, she conceded, and from recent conversations with her grandmother, she knew Morwen wouldn't agree to spending a large outlay on speculation until they were sure it was a viable concern.

Theo said he thought he might drive over to Wadebridge tomorrow to take a proper look at Emma's pots, and Skye asked eagerly if she could go too.

"Why not?" he said lazily. "It's always better to be looking forward than back."

She guessed he was referring to her current interest in their family history, but surely nothing could harm them from that – and looking forward was becoming less and less comfortable. Every newspaper was now predicting that war was imminent. All the talk at the clayworks was of enlisting, and if that happened, there was a real danger of losing half their workforce before the autumn dispatches were sent off.

No amount of overtime and bonus inducements had got them halfway there yet, and a small, unestablished pottery wasn't going to make a ha'porth of difference to the mountains of china clay left waiting to be sold. Even she could see that.

"I'll call for you tomorrow morning, Skye," Theo told her. "Be ready early, for we won't want to stay the night. I can't abide the stink of pigs for too long."

However much she tried, she couldn't really like Theo. There was a nasty side to him that she hadn't found in any of her other relatives. Not that she knew Freddie and Bradley in Ireland, but from what Cathy had scathingly told her, she guessed they would stay firmly entrenched where they were until all thought of hostilities was over.

Emma welcomed the visitors with open arms, glad of a diversion. She loved her life, and she loved her man, but farming could be tedious work, which was why she and Will had taken to flower-growing. But how much time could you give to watching bulbs grow and flowers blossom?

The pots now, that was creative, and something she enjoyed so much, even though she was no expert. She led the visitors out to her little shed and the outside oven, with as much pride as if she exhibited a new-born babe.

117

"So you'm taking up my suggestion, are you?" she said triumphantly. "I knew you'd see the sense in it."

And mine, Skye added silently, but happy enough to let Emma take the credit for it. She admired the makeshift arrangements Will had made for Emma to work in, slightly amazed that such an ungainly person had the skill to produce something of more than passable beauty in such basic surroundings. With Killigrew money, they could surely do far better, and go far.

"I suppose you'm thinking 'tis all poor work," Emma said cheerfully. "But it keeps me happy, and I've even had a shop in Padstow asking to buy a coupla pots to display in their window. I might get rich yet, so you'd all better look out."

"It's not poor work at all, Em," Skye said, before Theo could put the dash on her words. "You've done well, but have you ever thought of getting together with the others for a more commercial arrangement?"

Emma shook her head. "No, I'm happy to potter in a small way. I'll gladly give 'em a few pointers, but there's plenty of folk more expert than me, and anyway, I'm no businesswoman, nor ever wanted to be. If you can make a success of it, Theo, then good luck to 'ee."

It was odd how so many of them reverted to the country way of talking when they got together, Skye thought. But it was also somehow endearing, like clinging to childhood and a way of life that was gone forever.

The August Bank Holiday festivities were not going to be subdued by any crisis in faraway Europe, and people flocked to the beaches and the rivers, or took picnics into the country as usual. The moors, as well as every cottage garden, were in full blossom, and the sun shone brightly, as if the storm clouds of war had never existed.

Everything that was safe and serene came to an end on the fourth day of August, when with the speed of a swooping hawk, the news became rife that Germany had invaded Belgium, and therefore Britain had declared war on Germany.

Barely a week later a rare letter from Skye's brother arrived at New World, and her face was hot with shame at his words as she read it.

'I urge you to come home, Skye. Mother and Dad are worried, and your place is with them, not with these unknown Cornish hicks. I can't give you any confidential details, but I can tell you there are serious thoughts going on here in Washington that if any tin-pot little European country thinks it will draw the United States into its squabbles, it can just think again. I can't make it any plainer than that.'

Dear Lord, was there ever a more pompous prig than her brother, Sinclair! Skye thought. How hateful he sounded, and how ashamed she felt of him. He reminded her of Uncle Luke. The preacher and the politician, they were two of a kind, Skye thought savagely, before screwing up the letter and tossing it into her waste-paper basket.

'If I go anywhere, it will be to see where I can help,' Skye wrote back at once. 'Aunt Charlotte's girls are already busily rolling bandages to help the wounded. Do you think I'm lily-livered enough to desert them all now? I'm writing to Mom and Dad, and I know they'll understand.'

She gave a shiver at her own words. For of course they wouldn't. they'd want her home, safe from harm. But remembering those girls of Charlotte's – what the devil *were* their names? – she knew there would be wounded men, and dead heroes, and horrors that no women had ever encountered before, other than the brave ones who had always been prepared to be nurses and aides. And young girls like . . . like Vera and Lily Pollard, that was it . . . would be ready to do their bit. It should make all of them feel ashamed. She said as much to Morwen, her face troubled.

"Don't let your thoughts dwell on it," Morwen told her. "If you feel the need to work, I'm sure Walter will find a job for you at the clayworks if the men start deserting us. Birdie tells me there are long queues of men rushing to enlist in the towns. We'll soon be a country of twittering women."

Skye started to laugh at her mournful face, and at the thought of grubbing about in the clay as her grandmother and forbears had done! Working as a bal maiden certainly wasn't for her . . . but catching the glint of anger in Morwen's eyes, she hastily re-arranged her features.

"I'd be less than useless, Gran, but I'll have to do something useful. It may be that there'll be an opening for me at *The Informer* if they start to lose their reporters."

And she could always stay with Albert and Rose, but she wasn't sure that would be such a good idea, since she had sensed a withdrawal in Albie at the party that she couldn't explain. And it was only the vaguest notion, anyway.

She hadn't gone through all the archive newspapers yet. But pursuing the details of her own family history seemed of less importance right now than the way everyone was suddenly caught up in a sense of patriotic fervour.

Just as Walter and Theo had feared, a gang of clayworkers from each pit declared themselves a Killigrew Pals Battalion, and went down to St Austell to enlist together.

There was no option but to close Clay Two temporarily, and put all the remaining clayers to work at Clay One. Once the dispatches had gone from there, they would decide what was to be done.

All thoughts of bringing the pottery into operation now had to wait. Everything concentrated on moving the clay to whatever destination they could, because, just as predicted, all their European markets were immediately closed to them.

It alarmed Skye that Morwen had taken to her bed almost permanently now, as if to close her mind to all that was happening, and seemingly took no interest in the war stories that began to circulate, or their own situation. No matter how much Skye tried to stimulate her with snippets of information, she was listless in the continuing hot weather, and Birdie advised the girl to leave her be.

"But I'm worried about her. She's ill—"

"She's *old*," Birdie corrected. "And she's seen enough of life to know when she's coming to the end of it."

"Please don't talk like that! It's bad luck! My Mom used to say so, and she was never wrong."

Once the reduced orders for the autumn dispatches had gone, the Killigrew workforce shrank alarmingly as more men signed on, and were sent to do their inadequate training and then sailed for France with alarming speed.

By mid-October only young boys and old men and a scattering of women workers were left at the idling clay pit that had once been throbbing with activity. Boastful assurances that it would all be over by Christmas were heard less and less, and across the English Channel the battle of the Marne had been fought to a bloody conclusion.

With guarded privileged information, Skye learned from David Kingsley that newspapers were instructed to play down the real horrors, and to make much of the triumphant announcement that a threat to invade Paris had been averted by our brave Tommies and the French soldiers. But it also told those shrewd enough to read between the lines, that the German army was a force to be reckoned with.

Posters depicting Lord Kitchener's stern face and pointing finger were already demanding many thousands more volunteers; and Birdie, the fount of all knowledge, whether true or false, told Skye sourly that the number was to replace the number of dead on both sides of the conflict.

And Queen Mary appealed to women to form knitting circles to knit 300,000 pairs of socks for their brave boys to wear in the winter months to come.

*   *   *

Making an obligatory visit to her Aunt Cathy at Killigrew House in St Austell one afternoon, Skye encountered a group of earnest-faced women knitting furiously, their needles clacking like a thousand cicadas in a forest. The fact that they all sat in a circle in Aunt Cathy's parlour wearing their outdoor hats made the scene even more incongruous.

"If you want to help, Skye, there is more wool and needles in the box," Cathy told her.

"Thank you," she said in a strangled voice. "But I'm sorry. I never learned to knit."

There was the briefest pause in the clacking, and then it continued even more furiously and disapprovingly, as if to make amends for this brash American girl who couldn't even knit a pair of socks for a soldier. And she could have sworn she heard one mutter something about the long hair being so unsuitable for a woman of Skye's age.

Aware of their scorn, she felt appallingly useless, and she left them to cycle on up to the moors to the clayworks. All the workers were at Clay One. But Clay Two was where the old linhay was, that was supposedly going to be turned into a pottery and save the Killigrew fortunes.

"Miss Tremayne!"

She heard her name, and she turned with a start. The Pit Captain, Bert Lock, was coming out of the linhay, and behind him was someone who could only be his brother, and a younger, brawny man. Skye's fleeting thought was to wonder why the younger one wasn't rushing to enlist like all the others, and then she saw the heavy black boot, and the way he limped to compensate for his clubbed foot.

Bert apologised for not shaking her hand. "I 'ouldn't want to mess up your fine gloves, Miss, but perhaps you'd care to see what me and my brother Tom and young Desmond here have been a'doing. 'Twill turn into a going concern, I reckon, with all the raw materials ready for the using."

"You don't mean the pottery? But I thought it was all put on one side for the time being"

"Ah well, since these two misfits have nothing much else to do with their time, the two on 'em thought they might as well move their tackle up here where they've got more room than in town. Poor Desmo can't do nothing in the way of war work, see, on account of his foot, and Tom's only useful with his hands and not his brain."

"Mr Walter made no objections to the plan, Miss," he went on anxiously, in case he expected her to go tale-telling to her uncle. "We'm only using up the clay that's standing around useless, and Mr Theo gave us the say-so an' all."

"Then I'm sure it's all perfectly in order," Skye said. She was surprised no one had told her about this before, but why should they? She was only the American cousin, and Walter and Theo spent more time in Truro with the accountants lately than at the clayworks or visiting New World. And Morwen seemed to have lost interest in anything that went on outside her own four walls.

"So are you going to show me what you've been doing?" she asked, as none of them seemed able to make a move without some direction. Tom Lock definitely looked two cents short of a dollar, thought Skye, and his son was large and oafish in appearance. But she was prepared to be charitable, and anyway, everyone said you couldn't judge a book by its cover, even if she had always thought it was a crazy and short-sighted remark to make.

Inside the linhay her eyes widened. The potters had indeed brought up all their tackle as Bert called it. They had installed two wheels, and buckets of water and all the raw materials they needed was spread around them. On a shelf nearby there was a small range of pots and dishes that they had evidently been working on. To Skye's inexperienced eyes they looked passable, but not a patch on Emma's.

She went to pick one up, and was stopped at once by Desmond Lock's huge hand. Trying not to flinch, she heard him speak in a slow and ponderous voice.

123

"Don't touch 'un yet, Miss. 'Tain't dry, see? 'Twill come to slop in your hands if you try picking un up yet."

"I'm sorry," Skye said humbly. "So what happens next?"

But she half-knew. Hadn't she seen Emma's little oven and felt the fierce heat that emanated from it? For the first time she felt a kindling of interest to master a skill that Em, and two such unlikely folk as these could do so well, and when she had watched them for a while, she asked tentatively if she might have a try.

With a grin that did nothing to enhance his features, Desmond handed her a clay-encrusted overall from a hook on the wall, and she slid it over her head. And at Tom's suggestion, she tied back her hair to stop it falling into the wheel and the wet clay.

"Sit you here, Miss Tremayne," Tom said, "and feel how the foot-pedal works. And when you'm comfortable with the feel of the treadle, centre the dollop o' clay on the spindle, and if you'll permit me the liberty, I'll stand behind 'ee and guide 'ee in the process."

"Oh, please do," she said hastily, unsure exactly what he intended, but just as sure that if he didn't guide her every step of the way, her dollop of clay would end up as just another dollop of clay.

Ten minutes later she gazed in awe at the pot she and Tom Lock had made, though she admitted it was his skill and her clumsiness that had actually produced the lopsided pot. He had eased her fingers into the centre of the soft wet clay and helped her work the revolving mass into a cone-shape at first, then pressed down to change the shape of the mass.

He continually threw water over the clay to keep it moist, and together they had finally shaped the fluted rim, with Tom's thumbs pressing over hers to indent the soft clay at intervals. When he instructed her to stop the foot pedal, he ran a wire beneath the pot and lifted it on its square of greased metal to place it on the shelf beside the others.

"I never knew how quick a process it would be," she said, realising he was knowledgable about the craft but no expert after all. "But I know I couldn't do it myself, Mr Lock."

"Me name's Tom," he told her. "And o'course you could do it. You could come and work wi' we, if you'd a mind to it—"

His Pit Captain brother intervened quickly. "Tom, this is Miss Tremayne," Bert said sharply. "You can't ask her to come and work with you and Desmond."

"Why can't he?" Skye said, seeing his crestfallen face.

"'Twouldn't be right, Miss, and Mr Walter 'ouldn't like it," Bert said uneasily. "Besides, there's reasons . . ."

"Mr Walter needn't know. I'll come up here when I've got time to spare," she said recklessly. "Once we've got a number of pots to show him, he'll be amazed that we've been so enterprising. What do you say to that?"

The amateur potters said nothing, just gaped and nodded uneasily. And Skye swilled her hands in one of the buckets of water and removed her apron, thinking that it would be a diversion for her, no more.

For there were far more important things to be done now that war was a reality. As she had expected, Vera and Lily Pollard had gone off with the Red Cross, and were already somewhere in France, Charlotte had told her mother proudly. Skye needed to be useful as well, and not just an ornament.

She presented herself at *The Informer* offices in Truro a few days later.

"What can I do? I know you've lost some of your reporters," she told David Kingsley peremptorily. "Can I replace anyone?"

"I'm sorry, no," he said coolly. "If you want to send me any reports on local women's efforts from time to time, I'll print them if there's space, but I don't need you here, Skye."

She saw at once that he was paying her back for rebuffing him. She needed a job, and he wouldn't give her one, except to report on prissy women's doings, like Cathy's knitting circle.

No matter that women were already working in factories in large numbers now, and doing men's jobs. She had heard that those who could handle a vehicle were even driving tractors on farms. Some factories were already being turned into munition factories, and this nitwit couldn't see beyond the fact that she was a woman who hadn't responded to his flattery.

She left the offices in a huff, cycling aimlessly, and noting that Truro's Army Recruiting Office was awash with men of all sizes and ages, eager to go to war. Some were already marching about the town in makeshift lines. It was a mark of the male ego, she thought resentfully, and the days of the hunter stalking his prey were not yet over.

Without realising it, her cycle ride took her to the gates of Madron College. There were still people walking around the grounds and the grassy lawns, even though classes were over for the day. Some of the staff who had rooms would still be here, of course. Philip would be here.

She was lost in thought until she realised that the gate porter had come out of his lodge and was clearing his throat for a second time.

"I said, can I help you, Miss? Is there someone you wanted to see?"

"No. Yes. Well, if Mr Philip Norwood is available, I have a message for him. From my uncle," she invented wildly.

"Very well. Can I have your name, Miss?"

It was awful. As he looked her over, Skye could see he didn't believe her, and probably thought she was one of Philip's students, badgering him out of class-time.

For the first time in her life she wished she had cut her long hair, or pinned it up in a more sophisticated style, and didn't look such a hoyden after riding over the moors in the cool afternoon breeze. She lifted her chin, staring at the man, her candid blue eyes daring him to think any such thing.

126

He picked up a telephone and pressed a few buttons, while Skye waited, her thoughts milling in all kinds of directions. And the one uppermost in her mind now was that, if Philip's room had a telephone, she had only needed to know his number to have spoken with him at any time. She had never done so, nor thought she had the right, any more than she had the right to be here now. She turned to go.

The porter spoke. "Mr Norwood requests that you take tea with him, Miss. Room number forty-five, at the far end of the long corridor. You may leave your bicycle here, and it will be quite safe until your business is completed."

"Thankyou." And he would know exactly when she left, and how long she had been here. Not that she intended staying more than a few minutes, or even knew why she was doing this at all, unless it was to lay a ghost. They hadn't communicated at all since the night of her party. And, she told herself frantically, this was just to see him once more, to know that the mad passion that had flared between them was over.

The moment she entered his room and was drawn into his arms, she knew the foolishness of such a thought.

"Philip, I honestly didn't come here for this," she said faintly.

He ignored her words, his thumbs gently caressing her shoulders through the fabric of her jacket.

"Sweetheart, it was like a miracle to hear old Trethewy's telephone message just now. You don't know how many times I've wanted to call you at your home all these weeks, just to hear your voice for a moment. There was something I was desperate to tell you, but I could never find the right words."

"I think I know," she murmured, half ready for flight at the intensity of his voice.

"No, you don't know," he said, to her surprise. "You can't know how guilty I felt at wanting so badly to tell you that Ruth and her aunt left Truro for Wales more than a month ago, and

127

that they intend to stay there until the war is over, and then return to London."

"Why should it make you feel guilty to tell me?" she said, not daring to think any further for the moment.

"Because the engagement is off, my dearest girl. Ruth made it plain that she no longer wanted to marry a man who was so obviously in love with someone else. And the fact that she put into words what I was too cowardly to say, was what made me feel the guiltiest of all."

"Oh, God, no!" Skye whispered, shocked at how much she must have hurt the other girl. "You know I never meant for this to happen, Philip . . ." she tried to back away from him, but he held onto her too tightly.

"No more did I, my love. But if it comforts you at all, it was apparently no hardship for Ruth to tell me it was all over between us. We had been like brother and sister for too long, and there was no great passion between us, you see. We both knew it wasn't the right basis on which to build a marriage, but I would never have let her down."

But nor could Skye help feeling acutely embarrassed at being the unwitting cause of all this, even though she couldn't agree more with Ruth's sentiments. There could be nothing worse than a loveless marriage, or a humdrum one.

"I just don't know what to say," she said at last.

"Then I suggest that you don't say anything, and let me do what I've ached to do for so long."

He was still holding her close, and she felt the first sweet touch of his mouth on hers. And then the kiss became harder, more demanding. The flame in her heart became a fire, and she was responding with a passion that had been far too long denied.

"You know that I want to make love to you, don't you? To make you mine, for always?" he murmured against her mouth.

She took fright at once. She was modern, sophisticated . . .

128

and a virgin who had always strongly believed that a decent girl saved herself for marriage.

"I can't . . . we can't . . . I've never . . ."

She was babbling, because for all her high ideals she knew that she wanted this too, more than she had ever wanted anything. But she was so afraid of the consequences, of scandal, of bringing shame on herself and her family.

"I'd make it safe for you, Skye," Philip's voice was desperate with need. "I promise I would let nothing happen to you. I never would."

He was gently unbuttoning her jacket now, and she felt his hand slip inside it to cup her breast. Her so-willing breast that responded immediately to his touch . . . She seemed hardly able to catch her breath as desire swept through her as she felt her nipple surge into life beneath his fingers. And she gave a shuddering sigh, knowing that nothing on earth was going to make her resist . . .

They moved towards his bedroom, and sank down on the narrow bed together. For just a little while, she thought faintly, they could pretend that this was forever.

They could pretend that there was no war or devastation going on in another part of the world. No guns or bombs or men being slaughtered. It meant nothing to them, and they were not part of it. There was only this . . .

He made love to her sensuously and considerately, knowing it was her first time, and when it was over, Skye still held him tightly. For all her self-confidence in other ways, this had been a new and deeply emotional experience, and she needed to know that she hadn't failed him in any way.

"Did I disappoint you, Philip?" she whispered.

He gathered her in his arms more closely. Their flesh was still damp from exertion, and everywhere they touched they clung together. Such closeness made her feel wanted and loved, but she also needed him to tell her so.

"You could never disappoint me, my darling girl. I love

everything about you. Your quick voice, and your laugh, and the way you tilt your head when you're considering something. I love your mouth and your eyes, and your glorious hair. I love the way you smile and the way you walk. Now, if I've left anything out – oh yes, there is one thing," he added with mock solemnity. "I love the way you make love with me."

"Oh, stop it – you'll make me blush," she said, giggling nervously at his audacity.

"I love the way you blush," he said.

Chapter Nine

"There's something else I have to tell you," Philip said slowly against her cheek.

She was still wrapped in him, skin-close, glorying at the wonder of it all. Despite her so-called worldliness, she knew she was a babe in arms at making love, and he was such a willing, wonderful teacher . . .

"Do I want to hear it?" she said provocatively. She ran her hands slowly down the broad expanse of his chest, amazed at how quickly she had become so unembarrassed at her first naked encounter with a man, and knowing she could never bear to be apart from him now.

She couldn't think beyond the thought that they were obviously destined to be together. Ruth had seen it, and so had Morwen . . . and, in their hearts, so had they.

"No, you won't want to hear it," he said, making her heart stop for a moment. "And I don't want to say it. But I had made my decision before seeing you again, and I can't go back on it now."

"Philip, you're scaring me," she whispered. "What decision have you made?"

He moved slightly away from her body, so that a small chill separated them. It seemed ominously significant to Skye.

"You know I'm here for six months and that my time will be up at Christmas. I've been offered the option to stay on if I wish, but I decided I could be better occupied elsewhere."

"You're returning to London?" she said.

131

He shook his head. "No, I'm enlisting in the new year. I don't have any military experience, but I've a more than competent knowledge of the French terrain, and I'm a perfectly capable driver. I'm sure I'll be of some use."

His words took her breath away. Her first reaction was of shock, because it was the last thing she had expected to hear. Her second was anger, and without warning, she found herself pummelling his chest.

"How can you do this, just when we've found one another?" she almost wept. "How can you think of leaving me? You'll be killed at worst, or taken prisoner and tortured at best, and I'll never see you again—"

"Well, thank you for that tremendous vote of confidence," he said calmly. "Some people do come out of a war unscathed, you know."

"And some of them don't."

She could hear herself, shrill and bitter, unlike herself, behaving like a shrew, but she was knocked sideways by his words, and full of the direst dread.

For no reason at all she remembered the weird old woman she had seen on the moors, and she felt a great temptation to find her again and beg her for a potion to keep her lover safe, and she would sacrifice anything for such a charm . . . and even more shocked, she knew her thoughts were enveloping the old Cornish belief in witches and omens and premonitions.

But then, as the images that filled her mind became more wild and unreal, they seemed to steady her, and she clung to Philip wordlessly as he stroked her hair.

"If you're going to do this, then so am I," she said.

His hands were stilled and he tipped up her face to meet his. "Don't be foolish, Skye. I know your sabbatical is only for a year, and come the spring, you'll be thinking of returning home; if not before."

"No, I won't. My brother is already urging me to go home and implying that America won't be drawn into a war that has nothing to do with us. He may be right, but he makes me ashamed. Besides, my heart was here the moment I stepped ashore, and if you go to France, you'll take it with you, and I shan't be able to live without it."

He ignored her agitation, remaining as calm as possible, considering his own feelings at the thought of parting. "Your family will be upset. Your parents will think you've been influenced by your grandmother and your uncles."

"My parents know me well enough to know I've never allowed anyone else to influence my thinking – until now. Until you. So you see, it's no use. If you go, I go too."

"And what will you do, my brave darling?" he said.

"I'll be a hospital helper," she said recklessly. "Or a roving lady reporter – or I'll pack food parcels, or drive an ambulance."

"You can't drive – can you?"

"Not until you teach me."

The words tumbled out, nervously and urgently. She had never considered them before. At home, there had always been someone to drive her anywhere she wanted to go, and she had always preferred the freedom of the bicycle and the open air. But there were limits as to how far you could cycle, and the battlefields of France were hardly within pedalling range . . .

"Are you serious?" Philip asked.

"Why not? Don't you think I'm capable?"

He began to laugh at her indignant face.

"I think you're capable of doing anything your heart sets out to do. It's one of the things I love you for."

"One of the things?"

His hands slid down her body beneath the bedclothes, and she felt her skin shudder erotically beneath his touch.

"Let me show you the rest," he whispered seductively, and proceeded to make love to her all over again.

It was mid-evening by the time they left the college, and Skye was alarmed to discover how long she had been in Philip's room. She felt as if they had crossed a mountain in that time, and life would never be the same for them again.

But perhaps she was being selfish, she thought, more soberly. Her euphoria had begun to subside a little, for life would be irrevocably changed for so many people in the days to come. Already the appalling casualty figures had started to filter through, and the thought that it would all be over by Christmas was the most unlikely one of all.

They collected her bicycle from the porter's lodge, and Trethewy looked after them thoughtfully as they walked away.

Miss Tremayne, he ruminated . . . he knew of a family by that name. One of them was a well-known artist living in the town who'd once lived a bohemian life, by all accounts . . .

There was also a preacher of that name over Prazeby way, where his sister lived, and he remembered her saying in passing that a young American relation was coming to stay with the old grandmother. He wondered if there was any connection between them all. In any case, he had a juicy bit of gossip to tell Gracie, next time he saw her.

Philip had already decided it was too late for Skye to cycle back that evening. It would be dark long before she reached New World, and he suggested that she stayed with Albert and Rose for the night. She could telephone her grandmother from there to tell her what was happening.

She agreed. Their last hours had been so intense that she felt the need to talk about ordinary things, and on the way to the studio she told him about the proposed Killigrew pottery, and about the Lock father and son.

"It makes sense," he said. "But it will need more than two amateur potters to make it a going concern."

"I'm sure you're right, and Walter will need to bring in some experts in due course and set up proper premises. In any case,

I have a feeling that nothing's going to happen very quickly after all."

They reached the studio and were invited up to the living quarters. Skye made her request clumsily, hugely embarrassed at the strange way Albie was looking at them.

As if he could see all that there was to see, and knew that she had spent the last clandestine hours in this college man's arms. Rose looked at her oddly too, but it was Albie's expression that disturbed her most. She had seen it in a man's eyes before now.

It was jealousy, pure and simple – except that there was nothing pure about jealousy. It was ugly and destructive, and without examining the reason why, she shied away from the very thought of staying under the same roof as her uncle.

"Perhaps this wasn't such a good idea after all," she said, glancing at Philip. "I think I really should get home, or Gran will worry. Would you drive me back instead, Philip? I'll collect my bicycle some other time, if Uncle Albie doesn't mind me leaving it here."

"That's the best idea," Rose put in before either of the men could speak. "We'll telephone your grandmother to let her know you're on your way, Skye. I gather she's far from well."

She *wanted* her out of here, Skye thought at once. She could also see that Albie was jealous of Philip Norwood, and of course, neither of them knew about the engagement being broken with Ruth. They would think she and Philip had been cheating on the deaf girl.

Her cheeks burned at the very thought, but she could hardly bring Philip's personal details out into the open. All she could do was to get out of there as quickly as she could.

"I feel dreadful," she gasped to him, as they walked to the garage where Philip kept his hired car. "They didn't say anything, yet they made me feel so cheap!"

"You'll never be that, darling," he said quietly. "Don't concern yourself, although I think we must tell your grandmother

135

right away that I'm a free man, and not about to besmirch your honour in any way."

"Oh? I thought you'd already done that," she said with a shaky smile.

He squeezed her hand. "Any regrets?" he asked.

"Not a single one," she said honestly.

Skye hadn't expected Morwen to be still up by the time they reached New World, but the house seemed to be ablaze with lights. It looked welcoming as always, and yet Skye felt decidedly uneasy as they approached. And even more so as they saw Theo's car outside the front door, parked alongside his father's.

"Oh Lord, what's this? I hardly think it's going to be a welcoming committee," she murmured. "Please don't stay, Philip, but may I call you tomorrow?"

"I'll be mortified if you don't," he said, and scribbled his telephone number on a piece of paper before discreetly kissing her good-bye, well aware of the many windows that seemed to watch them like kaleidoscopic eyes.

The moment she entered the house, it was to hear the sounds of weeping, and the realisation that more important things were happening here than worrying about one wayward relative.

"What is it?" she said, grabbing Birdie's arm as she came hurrying towards her, her eyes red and swollen. "Is it Granny Morwen?"

For of course, it had to be. Why else would Walter and Cathy and Theo be here ... but whatever it was, Albie and Rose obviously hadn't heard of it before she left them.

"We didn't know where you were, see?" the woman gabbled. "So we couldn't let you know, and then 'tothers called to say you were on your way with your gentleman friend, so I daresay they'll be comin' here sometime—"

"For God's *sake*, Birdie, is my grandmother dead?" she screamed. And even as she said the words, the terrible thought ran through her mind that while her grandmother had been dying, she and Philip had been making love . . .

Birdie's teeth rattled in her head. " 'Tain't her that's dead, though she looks near to it with the upset of it all."

"Then who?" Skye whispered.

Cathy came hurrying out of the drawing-room, a handkerchief pressed to her eyes, and Skye's heart sank. As if seeking any kind of comfort, or maybe to give it, Cathy put her arms around Skye at once. Skye still had no idea what had happened, and she was embarrassed at this show of emotion from a woman she didn't altogether care for.

" 'Tis the other son," Birdie mouthed over Cathy's head. "The one up north, only he weren't up north no more. He'd gone and joined up."

Theo came to join them at that moment, his face grim.

"Please see to Grandmother, Birdie, and Mother, come back inside. We'll stay here tonight. It will be best for us all to be together. I've called your mother, and although she's distraught she intends coming down here to be with us as soon as possible."

"Will somebody please tell me what's happened?" Skye said in a strained voice. She could guess, but she had to know. She was a journalist, and she had to hear it in the words that were her business . . . the incongruous, useless thought flashed in and out of her mind.

"Jordan's been killed in France," Theo said curtly. "He was caught up in some shell-fire, and didn't stand a chance. At least we were told, it was mercifully quick."

Oh, Theo, Skye thought, *don't you know that's military and newspaper jargon to gloss over any ghastly truths*?

But she could see by the way he avoided her eyes that he knew it all too well. She could see how he was suffering. Jordan was his brother, and although Skye had never met him, he was her kin too, and she was caught up in the family grief. And the bigger the family, the more they clung together and prolonged the grief.

She felt a wild urge to remove this clinging woman from her embrace and run out of the house to go somewhere safe. Running back to Philip where she was loved, and where all that mattered was being together. Or running back home, where there was no urgent talk of war, except in distant Washington conference rooms that were so far removed from the reality that was here and now, and in their midst.

And in those moments of sheer terror she knew she had never really grown up at all. Her lips trembled, and she saw Theo give a short nod as he took his mother away, as if he could read every damn thing going around in her head.

"Will they – when will they bring him back?" she whispered, assuming this was the reason that Jane Askhew would think of travelling all the way from Yorkshire to Cornwall to be at her grandson's burial.

She heard Theo give a harsh laugh. It was a terrible sound in the midst of the weeping she could still hear from the drawing-room, and from the woman still clinging to her.

"No, they won't be bringing him back, Skye. When you're in the direct line of fire from an enemy shell there's nothing to bring back. Tom Askew might keep the truth from his readers, but he was never shy at giving out the truth to those that needed to hear it."

And she presumed that he thought he had needed to hear that too, thought Skye, hating the very thought of Tom Askhew, and unwittingly echoing all Morwen's old feelings about the man. *Morwen . . .*

"I must go to my grandmother," she said quickly, almost pushing Cathy towards Theo. "How has she taken this news?"

"As you would expect." Theo said brutally. "We thought there'd be few of the family going to France, and Jordan wasn't even a soldier in the regular sense. He was just doing his job, reporting the news."

"Every family is touched by war," Cathy murmured in a

shuddering voice. "Even Charlotte's silly girls were foolish enough to think they could be of use."

"They thought correctly," Skye said. "Everyone should do what they can to stop this horrible war."

She didn't look at Theo as she spoke. Nor was she going to tell them yet, that she had every intention of doing what her cousin Jordan had done and report the news. Nothing had changed. If anything, it had made her more determined than ever, and if the *Truro Informer* didn't want her reports, she would send them directly to this Tom Askhew and his *Northern Informer*. There would be a poignancy in her reports following on her cousin's death, that she was sure he wouldn't miss seeing and exploiting.

Her reasons were both patriotic and personal. But the one that was still uppermost in her mind was that if Philip was going to France in the new year, then so was she.

It was hard to forget that terrible night and the weeks that followed. The whole family seemed to congregate on New World as if it was truly the centre of the universe, until it felt as if there was no air left to breathe.

Cathy had recovered from her grief like the lady she was, but Walter had become alarmingly morose and introverted, unable to speak to anyone, and losing interest in everything. Jordan had left the family home years before, but losing a son seemed to affect him as deeply as losing an arm.

"It's not as if other families aren't losing their menfolk and having to deal with their emotions," Philip reminded her, during one of her erratic driving lessons. "But I must say I never thought your Uncle Walter would take it this hard. He's almost going into a decline."

"I know," Skye said, crashing the gears and making Philip wince. "He seems to have lost heart in everything lately. The two potters are still dabbling at Clay Two, but any real business plans have been abandoned for now. I

might take a look at it sometime, just to keep the interest alive."

And maybe wander over the moors to find that old witchwoman
. . . The thought was in her head before she could stop it. But
she had no intention of doing any such thing.

"Did Jordan's grandmother arrive safely?" Philip asked.

"She did, and she also called to visit Granny Morwen one
afternoon." She frowned, remembering the tense atmosphere
between them. "It was so odd, Philip. They once knew one
another pretty well, I gather, and yet you wouldn't credit how
distant they were. They were both suffering, and yet these
two eighty-year-old dames sat there facing one another like
old enemies!"

He tried to overlook what she was doing to his car as she
put it through its juddering paces on the moorland road.

"You're exaggerating, of course."

"I am not! Granny Morwen seemed quite frigid just talking
to Mrs Askhew, and I know she was glad when she left. I felt
rather sorry for her – for Mrs Askhew, I mean. She seemed
a soft sort of person, and well under her husband's thumb, I
should guess."

"Quite the little philosopher today, aren't you?"

"No. Just observant, and my guess is that those two had
quite a past between them," Skye said thoughtfully.

She suddenly felt Philip jerk the steering-wheel out of her
hand and pull it round to the right.

"Well, I'd prefer to think we have a future ahead of us,
providing you don't run us off the road," he snapped.

For once she didn't answer back. And anyway, what did it
matter what those two old dears had once fought over, if they
had fought at all? It may be just her imagination playing tricks,
of course, even though she was perfectly sure it was not. Her
instincts were very strong on that point.

But Philip was right. The casualty lists were becoming longer
than ever now, and every family who had sent their sons or

daughters to war had a tale to tell, either of bereavement or bravery, or hideous wounds and lingering mental disorders. War was evil, but Skye was just as determined to be in the thick of it. She knew exactly how those clayworkers, forming their own Killigrew Pals Battalian, had felt now. She had never known Jordan, but he was her kin, and she felt a violent need to go to France to avenge his senseless death.

She brought the car to a sudden stop, her heart pounding too fast for her to carry on with any safety, her knuckles white on the steering-wheel.

"If you're going to take offence every time I criticise you—" Philip began.

"I'm not. Truly," she said in a small voice. "I suddenly felt very aware of my mortality, and everyone else's in this damn awful world. Hold me, Philip. Just hold me. Please."

Christmas came and went without too much in the way of celebration in the family, even though they all gathered at New World as usual. But there didn't seem much to celebrate with Walter's long face, and Theo snapping at everyone in sight, and Cathy acting the brave martyr who had lost a son.

Charlotte and Vincent Pollard resisted telling the rest of them of the exploits of their two madcap Red Cross daughters, who had now been elevated to the status of heroines in their eyes, and Skye resisted telling Morwen her own plans until it simply became unavoidable. When she did, it was with Philip by her side.

The response was inevitable. Morwen's face went white, and she clutched at Birdie's hand.

"You can't do this, Skye. I forbid it. Your mother and father would never forgive me if I let you do it—"

"I've already written to tell them, Granny Morwen, and they can't stop me. And neither can you," she said quietly. "Philip's contract at the college is over, and he's going to enlist next

141

week. He's taught me to drive, after a fashion, and I want to be with him."

Morwen looked at them both sharply.

"And this is something else I shouldn't allow," she said.

"Mrs Wainwright, we hope that if we enlist together we may be sent to the same detachment in France."

"And why do you suppose they would agree to that, young man? You're not family, or a special group like the clayers."

"But as an engaged couple, we shall press to be allowed to stay together," Philip went on steadily, playing his trump card, the one that he and Skye had planned for just this moment. Unconsciously they moved closer together, as if to present a united front before this indomitable old woman. For all her frailty, Skye knew how badly she needed to win her over. She needed her blessing to be her talisman.

"You realise you would be entering into an engagement for all the wrong reasons, however noble they seem to you now," Morwen said at last.

Skye rushed to her, kneeling down beside her chair.

"Granny, you're wrong," she said passionately. "The only reason Philip and I want to be engaged, and to be together, is because we love each other so much that it would take far more than a war to keep us apart. Can't you understand that? You, of all people?"

She hardly knew why she said what she did, nor how she knew that Morwen Tremayne would have gone through fire and tempest to be with the man she loved, whether he was a Killigrew or a Wainwright. Just as she would.

And she saw the softening in her grandmother's eyes as she stroked the long black hair of the girl at her feet. The shimmering cascade of hair that was so much like Morwen's own had once been, and which somehow seemed to symbolise the empathy between them.

"I know that you must follow your heart, my lamb, and if it sends you to foreign shores, then I'm sure the Lord will go

142

with you. And now I'm in danger of sounding more like Luke than Luke himself, so away with you both and let me rest."

Skye kissed her creased old cheek, her eyes moist, and then she and Philip left her to her afternoon nap. They went outside the house, breathing in the crisp, wintry air.

"What a woman she is," Philip said softly, for no reason at all. "And what a beautiful grand-daughter she has. I hope our children will have the spirit of you both."

"Then you think we'll have children one day?" Skye said, catching her breath at the charm of the thought.

Not only the thought that she and Philip would produce a child out of their love, but that life would go on, beyond the holocaust where they were about to go so voluntarily. The hope of these shadowy children who would develop their own lives, was another talisman to keep safe within her heart.

"Of course we will," Philip said, his arm around her waist. "We have to continue your family dynasty."

"So we do. But we'll also be starting a new Norwood dynasty, won't we?"

They smiled in complete harmony, and then squinted their eyes against the winter sky, seeing a fine dust being thrown up by a horse's hooves approaching. Yet another visitor. They had intended leaving for Truro, to spend an idyllic couple of hours in the rooms Philip was now renting since leaving the college, but they could hardly drive off when someone was nearing the house in such an almighty hurry.

"Oh no," Skye groaned, seeing who it was. "We should have left earlier."

Luke Tremayne almost scorched his trap to a halt beside the pair lounging against the motor at the front of the house. His temper was sorely put out, and the sight of the flighty young miss standing so blatantly with the man's arm around her, offended him greatly. And he didn't care to have a relative's name bandied about in idle gossip by the lower members of his community.

Gracie Trethewy had reported with great glee what her brother had told her about the goings-on at the college during the final weeks of term. Shocking, disgusting things to relate to a God-fearing and celibate man, and he had berated the woman soundly for repeating them. He had been far too busy over Christmas to investigate immediately, but seeing the accused pair now, he was in no doubt of their guilt.

"Good afternoon, Uncle Luke," Skye said. "Granny Morwen was about to take a nap, but she'll be glad to see you."

She was quite sure that Granny Morwen wouldn't, but she spoke as dutifully as she could.

"It's you and your companion I've come to see, Miss, so it's fortuitous that I've caught you together. I suggest that we go into the house and discuss things in private."

Skye didn't miss his use of the words *caught you together*. She glanced at Philip, frowning, and knowing they were in for a roasting for some reason or other. Luke had been oddly absent over the Jordan affair, clearly finding it easier to deal with strangers' grief than his own family's.

But he went straight into the drawing-room, rousing Morwen without any apology, and obliging them to follow.

"Now then, Mother, you'd best hear what I've got to say in front of these two," he began.

"Good afternoon, Luke." Morwen said mildly.

"Yes, yes, I know all about the formalities, but this is far more serious. It's been brought to my attention that your grand-daughter has been spending hours at a time in this gentleman's college rooms in Truro, bringing shame on us all."

In the small silence following his words, Skye gasped, and Philip exclaimed angrily at the pomposity of the fellow. And Morwen . . . incredulously, Skye heard her grandmother give a loud chuckle at her son's scandalised expression.

"Oh Luke, my dear, I'm sorry to say so, but you do resemble a strangulated pig when you go on so."

144

"*Really*, Mother! Is that all you can say? Sometimes I think you're either going senile or you've simply taken leave of your senses. And as for condoning fornication—"

"How dare you speak to me like that, you pompous oaf," Morwen said, more sharply.

Philip spoke furiously. "I'll ask you, Sir, to apologise to Skye, for the inferences you've just made."

Skye stared at her uncle unblinkingly, knowing that what he spoke was the truth, all of it, and that it was even worse than his narrow, bigoted mind could possibly imagine. How could he know of the deliriously erotic times she had lain in her lover's arms, and how she ached to be there at all times? How could he know the feeling, that as soon as they were parted, she felt lost, bereft . . . ?

She caught sight of Morwen watching her, and thought immediately that *she* knew. She had once known those feelings exactly. Before anyone could say another word, Morwen had lifted her hand.

"You're a fool to heed such gossip, Luke, and as for fornication, since I presume that you have never experienced it, you cannot possibly know what goes on between a man and a woman behind closed doors. It may be perfectly innocent, and as the two people concerned in this instance are betrothed to be married, I hardly think it's any of your business, nor anyone else's."

She couldn't have knocked the wind out of his sails more effectively. Skye was filled with admiration for the way she had deflected Luke so well from his purpose in coming here.

"Betrothed? Since when? Why wasn't I told about this before now?"

"Because it's none of your business, Uncle Luke," Skye repeated, flaring at once. "And if you want some more news for your gossiping busy-bodies, you can tell them that we both intend enlisting next week. I presume it's acceptable for us to go to war together, is it?"

She was near to tears, but Luke was ready to back down now, knowing when he was beaten, and already concocting a more civilised story for Gracie Trethewy to pass on to her brother than the contemptible lies he had told her.

He finally muttered a miserable attempt at an apology and blundered out of the house. Morwen waved the others away as they attempted to thank her.

"Perhaps I can have my sleep now," she grumbled. "I'm fair weary with all this upset, but I think you can forget about Luke's interference. From now on he'll be keen to uphold you as shining examples to us all, if I know him."

They left her then, and far from feeling shame, there was no question of not spending the time together that they had planned, for who knew how little time any of them had left? Neither said as much, but it was in both their thoughts.

And they would have been more than surprised if they had known the thoughts and memories swirling around the head of the matriarch they left behind them at New World. For they were not the dreams of old age, but the dreams of a young and vivacious woman, revelling in the sensual passions of the two men who had loved her.

In her lovely water-colour dreams, the memories all merged so beautifully into one, so that she couldn't have said where the love of Ben Killigrew ended, and the love of Ran Wainwright began. But she understood and applauded the passionate heart of her grand-daughter so very well . . .

Chapter Ten

Their plans were postponed when Philip was persuaded to remain at the college for another term. In the circumstances he didn't have the heart to refuse.

"My replacement has lost his brother in France and gone into retirement," he told Skye. "We all have to adapt to changing circumstances these days. But young men still need education, and I can't leave the college under-staffed."

"Doesn't it make you wonder just what you're educating them *for*?" she said. "The moment they're old enough they go off and enlist, and become another statistic."

"Perhaps that's one advantage of not being young any more," he said.

"You're not *old*."

"No, but they prefer young men to go to war, my love, and now that I've agreed to remain at my post, I'll have to wait until April to volunteer. But I'll continue renting my rooms in Truro, rather than live at the college as before. It will be easier for us to meet discreetly in town."

There was no question of Skye volunteering before he did. The last thing they wanted was to be parted. And guiltily or not, it relieved Morwen's mind considerably to know that her ewe lamb was going to be safe at home in Cornwall, rather than in the reported mud of the battlefields.

But then, in the bitterly cold and wet weeks of January, something happened to throw the entire family into chaos.

Philip had been invited to dinner, and the three of them,

together with Birdie, were enjoying the meal, when Theo came roaring up to the house in his motor, flinging open the door and leaving it creaking on its hinges as he hurtled into the house. That fact alone would have alerted anyone that something was terribly wrong.

He pushed past Mrs Arden and rushed straight into the dining-room. His face was ashen, his eyes wild. Morwen half rose from her seat, and then sank back again. As if she already knew . . .

"What's happened?" Skye said sharply, as the atmosphere become as charged as if a bolt of lightning surged through it.

He ignored her, and went straight to his grandmother's side, holding her hands in a vice-like grip, and neither could have said whose hands were the icier.

"Gran, there's been a terrible accident. Oh God, now that I'm here I don't know how to say it – how to tell you – it's too Goddamn bloody awful to put into words—"

"It's Walter, isn't it?" Morwen whispered in a reedy voice. "It's my Walter."

Skye rushed around the dining-table to kneel at the other side of her grandmother. Her arms went around the old woman's thin shoulders, wishing she could protect her from whatever she was about to hear. As yet, no one but Theo knew what had happened, but Morwen's expression frightened her. It was almost as though she was seeing what had happened, before she even heard it.

"*Tell* me what it is you've come to say, Theo," Morwen almost gasped out the words, as if she was drowning.

He seemed unable to speak for a moment, which was totally unlike the frequently bombastic Pit Manager he could be.

"For God's sake, man, don't keep her in agony like this," Philip's angry voice broke into his stunned silence. "Whatever it is, let her know."

"I do know," Morwen said dully. "My Walter's dead, isn't he, Theo?"

His own voice was tortured as he answered. "Yes, Gran. You know how he's been all these weeks since hearing about Jordan. He took it far harder than Mother – well, you know Mother," he said, dismissing her as easily as if he swatted a fly. "We all thought Father was getting over it, but he just couldn't cope. The doctor's at the house now, and he says he must have gone into a serious decline to do this."

Skye felt her heart begin to thud sickeningly. The news was terrible enough, but there was clearly more to come. They hadn't learned the full horror yet.

"To do what?" she asked, looking at Theo above their grandmother's bowed head.

She saw him bring Morwen's hand to his lips and kiss it briefly. The action was so touching and so unexpected it sent the weak tears rushing to Skye's eyes. She dashed them back, knowing she needed to be strong for Morwen.

"They found Father's car parked on a headland above the cliffs. They can't be sure whether he fell or if he threw himself over. There was a storm raging, and the sea was evil, and it was a long while before they recovered his body from the rocks and brought him home—"

They all became aware of Morwen's keening then. It was loud and awful, like an animal in pain.

"I'll fetch her one of her sedatives," Birdie said at once. "She can't deal with this—"

"*No!*" Morwen screamed. "Do 'ee think I'm too frail to deal wi' my own darling's death? I'm not as soft as my own clay, woman! I have to feel the pain o' this, same I felt it when Celia, my sweet Celia . . ."

She slumped forward then, and needed all their attention to get her out of the dining room and upstairs to her bed. It was no more than a faint, but the shock had evidently been too much for her. Her last words had shocked Skye as well, until Theo muttered in her ear.

"I should have known 'twould bring it all back to her, but

149

you'd never think a young girl's drowning in a clay pool all those years ago would stay in her memory so vividly."

"Not unless it was a very particular kind of memory," Skye said. She glanced at him. He had lost his brother in a war, and now his father too. She put her hand on his arm.

"I'm so sorry, Theo, and for your mother too. How is she bearing all this?"

"As you would expect. She'll keep her dignity in public, and shed her tears in private. But once we've had the burying, she says she intends leaving for Yorkshire for a long visit. My grandmother Jane won't make the journey down here again, and Tom Askhew never had much time for my father."

Skye didn't know what to say. They seemed such a cold mother and son, and Cathy was preparing to abandon Theo, while her darling Granny Morwen was suffering over her beloved Walter. She heard Morwen moan as she half-regained consciousness, and the drink Birdie urged her to swallow contained the sedative Morwen didn't want, but badly needed.

"This'll settle her for a while, poor soul," Birdie told them all as Morwen drifted off again. "She's had a fair amount of tragedy in her life, but somehow she rides it all. A body wonders how long it can continue, all the same. I'll sit with her, while you folk have your own business to discuss."

Tactfully, Philip left the house soon afterwards, promising to call Skye the following day. It wouldn't be Morwen's place to host a funeral for a son who had a wife and son of his own, but they all knew it would end up here for the ritual bun-fight, as Theo was now calling it.

There were so many family members to inform. All the ones remaining in Cornwall, and those farther afield. Albert was Walter's brother, and Primmy was Walter's sister . . .

"I'll send a telegram to Mom first thing tomorrow," Skye said quickly. "She'll be devastated, I know."

Maybe not quite as devastated as if it was Albie, but that was an unworthy thought at such a time, and she pushed it

150

aside, thinking of what she could do instead. It was far better to be doing something than to sit and brood.

"I don't know everyone yet," she said diffidently. "I'll call Emma and Charlotte if you like, and Uncle Luke if I must. But the others in Ireland and Sussex . . ."

"No, I'll see to it all," Theo said briefly. "It will take ages, but I'll call Albert and the rest of them from here. My mother won't want to be alone for too long, but I daresay the doctor's sedated her as well by now. I'll call Luke first. He's sure to want to be in the thick of it."

Sometimes Skye wondered if she could really be related to this cold, aloof man who seemed to have shut himself off from the horror of his father's death, now that he'd gone through the ordeal of telling his grandmother. But everyone had their own ways of dealing with grief, and this was probably his.

She suddenly longed for Philip's warmth and love. It wasn't the time or the place, but she knew it was far better to be alive to all your emotions than to cut them off completely. Morwen knew that, and so did she.

She was glad when Theo was finally ready to leave. It had taken an interminably long time to make all the telephone calls, but he had arranged the funeral date for a week ahead. Luke intended to conduct it himself. The Irish folk, as she thought of them, wouldn't be attending, but sent their condolences.

Jack and his wife promised to travel from Sussex if the weather improved, but as Annie was habitually unwell, he hoped the family would excuse their absence if they didn't arrive. Emma and Will would come the previous day and freely offered to stay overnight on the day to give Morwen support.

Skye presumed they all asked after Cathy, Walter's wife, and yet it was Morwen they were all concerned about. Walter was her adopted son, along with Albert and Primmy, but by now Skye was well aware that Walter had always been the one closest to her heart.

They were all the children of Morwen's oldest brother Sam,

151

who had died when Ben Killigrew's rail tracks had collapsed all those years ago. And she and Ben had taken in the three orphaned children and loved them like their own.

"What the hell does it matter who comes and who doesn't?" Theo snorted when he put the phone down at last. "My father won't be there to see 'em, and there'll be plenty of clayers to turn up to see him properly planted."

Skye felt shocked at his words, but by now, having listened to him on the telephone to the various family members, she knew it was the only way he could get through these first raw hours.

On the day, it was just as Theo had said. The long stream of clayers from other pits as well as theirs, walked in silence behind the cars taking the family to the church where Luke Wainwright presided over the service for his step-brother.

Cathy was as pale and composed as if she was made of ice, while Morwen's suffering showed all too well in her face, and she had to be assisted by the men of the family. Only Albert was one of her own boys, thought Skye. But Charlotte's husband Vincent, and Em's husband Will, were stalwart seconds.

Jack and Annie had thought better of their reticence, and travelled from Sussex in this dismal January weather to stay a couple of days with Morwen. Matt had sent a telegram from California expressing his sorrow, and a distraught one had arrived from Primmy, begging a detailed letter from Skye.

Skye was thankful for Philip's presence at New World that day. Inevitably, much of the talk was of the past and those no longer with them, and she felt very much the outsider.

"So you're Primmy's daughter," Jack stated unnecessarily for what seemed like the tenth time. "I can see the likeness to her, and to our Morwen as she was, o' course. She were always a corker of a girl."

Skye wasn't sure which of the two he was referring to. She didn't like him much. He was noisy and stout, a prosperous businessman who had made good out of his boatbuilding skills,

152

and nothing like the adoring sibling of his brother Sam that she had imagined from Morwen's description.

But for heaven's sake, she chided herself, how could he be! He was an old man now, and those childhood days were far away. She shivered as they ate their funeral fare and drank their wine and fruit cup, listening to the talk between the older ones, and the younger generation, and feeling that she didn't fit in here. Not at all. Despite all she had once felt and dreamed about this place, she didn't fit in. She was an intruder.

"It will be over soon, and then we can get on with our own lives," she heard Philip say quietly beside her.

She was glad of his understanding, and yet unwittingly as contrary as Morwen Tremayne had ever been, she resented it too. "You mean we'll mark time until April, and then we'll both go to war and be killed, and join the rest of the family in the churchyard."

Appalled, she heard her voice rise passionately, and some of the others paused in their conversation and stared at her. Jack cleared his throat and spoke again.

"By God, she's a true Tremayne, ain't she, Morwen? And she's Primmy's girl all right with all that fire in her belly. Wouldn't you say so, Albie?"

To her horror, Skye saw Albert's face go red, and as if it was written all over him, she knew instantly what his feelings had been for her mother – and for her. Without thinking, she linked her arm through Philip's, as though to affirm their relationship for everyone to see.

"I think we're rather forgetting why we're here." They all heard a genteel voice break into the embarrassed silence.

Cathy stood in the middle of the drawing room, holding her audience with quiet dignity, her face pale above her black dress, a glass in her hand.

"Mother, perhaps you should sit down—" Theo began, but she shook him off.

"I'm perfectly calm, thankyou, Theo. But I would like us all to drink to Walter's memory before we part company."

She was as good as saying the wake was over, thought Skye, as they dutifully did as she asked. She remembered how Morwen had once told her in an unguarded moment that the adolescent Walter and Cathy had run away together, hiding in the turret room of this very house, because they couldn't bear to be parted.

And here was this calm, controlled woman, dealing with a social gathering so efficiently, as if she hadn't just buried her husband and so recently lost a son.

She seemed unnatural . . . but watching them all as they began to make their goodbyes, and knowing what she already did about her family, Skye could see how life changed people. Her thoughts ran on frighteningly, turning inwards. Life changed them all. It would change her and Philip.

As well as Jack and Annie, Emma and Will were staying overnight, leaving the farm in the charge of their stockman. And at the last minute, Skye clung to Philip.

"Don't go," she whispered. "There's plenty of room here. I feel so isolated, and I need someone of my own."

She knew it was the oddest way to feel, surrounded by her family, but it was true. Apart from Morwen, they were still strangers to her, and Philip was her dearest, her darling, her lover . . . her eyes held a mixture of pain and passion, and despite the solemnity of this day, she knew what she was offering. She needed his arms around her so desperately, to feel that life was still warm and vibrant, and didn't merely consist of ghosts of the past.

"Of course I'll stay if your grandmother agrees," he said quietly, and they knew they wouldn't be parted that night.

Whether the others knew, or guessed, that he had come to her room that night, she hardly cared. She was safe in his arms, where she most wanted to be. He made love to her gently at first, until she made it clear that she wanted more, and finally she cried out as she felt the moment of climax approach. She clung to him fiercely, but, as always, he withdrew from her, leaving her momentarily lonely, but knowing this was the way it had to be. They couldn't risk the shame of creating a child out of wedlock.

He left after breakfast the following morning, along with the rest of the family. And only then, when they were alone, did Morwen make any comment.

"Philip is a good man, Skye, but be careful, my lamb. I know how feelings can run away with you, and you're not planning a wedding just yet, I take it?"

"We haven't discussed it, Gran," she murmured. "There's time enough for that, and there's a war to get through first."

"You still intend to go with him, then?"

"Wouldn't you, if it were Ben? Or Ran?"

Morwen gave a small smile. "Oh ah. I'd have followed either one of 'em to the ends of the earth."

"Well then," Skye said.

There were no surprises in Walter Tremayne's will. He left his shares in the clayworks to his son, and Killigrew House was also left to him, with provision for Cathy to live in it for as long as she wished. Theo came to New World a week or so later to discuss it with Morwen.

"There was no need for a formal reading, Gran, as everything was straightforward. It was a recent will, with no mention of Jordan."

To him, it was a sure sign that Walter had known exactly what he was doing when he went over the cliff. But he knew better than to say so. Morwen had taken to her bed more and more now, and the doctor had put her on permanent sedatory medication, though she constantly railed against it, saying caustically that she was no cabbage-head yet.

"So what have you come to say, Theo?"

"I think we should make a decision to close down Clay Two for now. There's work enough for those remaining at Clay One, but we'd be wasting machinery to keep both pits open at present. Stokes and Keighley are willing to extend their contract with us for the next five years. The war will be over long before that, of course, and we'll be on our feet again with the overseas markets," he added optimistically.

But he knew the war reports didn't look good. After the initial burst of patriotic fever, more men were dying than enlisting now. He had toyed with the idea of going himself, but somebody had to run the clayworks, and he was the only Tremayne left here to do it. It shook him to realise it.

"And what about the pottery notion?" Morwen asked. She was too tired to be overly interested, and other folk could deal with the hustle and bustle of business.

"We leave it for the time being," Theo said. "We can lease the linhay at Clay Two to the two dabblers there now, but this is no time to go into production on our own account, when we'd probably lose half the workforce to the army."

She nodded in agreement, knowing that Walter had been the keener of the two. Theo kissed Morwen's crumpled cheek, unconsciously echoing his cousin Skye's thoughts that it was sad that life changed things, and people.

He could remember Morwen when her hair was as black as Skye's and her eyes as startlingly blue, and it saddened him to see her now. But he was too much in control of himself to stay sad for long. He had all the Tremayne passion when it came to the clay, but he had more than a smidgin of his mother's icy control. And that made a more successful business brain than all the passion in the world.

"Where's Skye today?" he asked now.

"She and Philip are choosing an engagement ring," Morwen told him, brightening. "It's Philip's birthday at the end of February, but they don't want any fuss or parties."

Theo grunted. Philip Norwood seemed a decent fellow, so

good luck to them. Anyway, he might have plans of his own in the marriage direction, though with his father just cold in his grave, he wouldn't introduce the subject yet.

But with his mother gone to Yorkshire, and, he suspected, planning to stay there, Killigrew House was large and empty. It needed a wife, and children. And nobody was immortal. That was swiftly coming home to him.

"I'll leave you to sleep now, Gran," he said, planning to drive to his lady-friend's house in Grampound. He passed it on the way back to St Austell, anyway, and it was too tempting to resist calling in for a cup of something and a warm at her fireside. Far too tempting.

Skye admired the ring on her finger, its small sapphire surounded by the cluster of diamonds in its Victorian setting. She had refused to have anything ostentatious. It seemed wrong to be celebrating birthdays and engagements when men were dying, even though she knew how foolish that was.

Life went on, though the reports from the Front were becoming ever more serious. At the beginning of February the total British casualties had amounted to more than 100,000. And one thousand suffragettes were shortly going to France to do war work. Skye found herself wishing she were there too.

But when April came, Philip enlisted alone. Morwen was ill and begged Skye not to leave her, often calling her Primmy in her confusion. Skye wouldn't ask Philip to stay, no matter how she feared for him, nor how desperately she would miss him. So she stayed behind while Philip went to war.

The spring and summer dragged on, and she was still getting letters from home, entreating her to return, but she was adamant that her place was now here. Her brother, Sinclair, washed his hands of her, thinking she was completely stupid, but despite her fears, Primmy understood, as Skye had known she would.

Hadn't she once sacrificed everything to be with Cresswell, whom she loved, despite all the threats of family and public scandal? But Skye admitted she felt useless. Charlotte's girls were practically heroines in their parents' eyes now, both seasoned nursing auxilliaries in France. Philip was driving an ambulance through the territory he knew well from the past. Morwen was improving and Skye resolved to stay at New World only until she recovered her health fully, and then she would join him.

"You need to get out of the house, my dear," Birdie told her one morning. Skye's face was clouded from reading the latest letter from Philip, in which he made no secret of the numbers of casualties, and the futile way in which a piece of ground could be gained, only to be lost almost immediately.

"Get on up to the moors and get some colour in your cheeks," Birdie went on, "or you'll be as pasty as t'other un. She'll be sleeping like a babby for a coupla hours."

"I think I will, Birdie," Skye said gratefully.

She rode her bicycle, revelling in the clean summer air, and realising that the house had been full of a sickbed smell lately. She had better get used to it, she thought grimly, if she intended working in one of the field hospitals in France, but for today she was going to forget it, and pretend that a war wasn't raging across the Channel, and that her lover was not in the middle of it.

After a laborious ride and bicycle-push up the steep moors, she reached the old cottages on the ridge. She gazed down on the glistening sky tips, always beautiful in sunlight, and the gouged out hillside with the little trickling streams emptying into the milky green clay pool of Clay One.

She could see the clayers, busy as bees, but she didn't want company, and she turned away, pedalling over the firm moorland turf towards the abandoned Clay Two. The only activity here now was in the old linhay, where the unskilled potters muddled about, according to Theo. He was scathing of their efforts, and Skye agreed he had reason to be. When they started up the pottery properly they needed to employ skilled people, to support the proud name of Killigrew Clay.

She had reached the linhay before she realised it, and as

Desmond Lock caught sight of her and waved his beefy hand, she felt obliged to throw down her bicycle and wander across to say hello. She resisted taking his proferred hand, seeing it caked in oozing clay.

"All alone?" she asked.

"Me Pa's off doing a job for one of the farmers, Miss. Do 'ee want to have another try wi' the clay?"

"Oh, I don't think so. I just thought I'd see how you were getting on."

She became aware that the grin on his face was becoming salacious, and she edged back a little, registering that he didn't smell any sweeter than the dank, earthy clay.

"I been waitin' for 'ee, I have. I knew you'd come, sooner or later."

"What do you mean?" She tried to laugh, but the laugh stuck in her throat as he came swiftly around the workbench, his club foot being no hindrance to the lustful intent she could see in his eyes now.

"I seen it first time you came 'ere wi' my Uncle Bert. I told meself that fine pretty wench is just right for the pluckin'."

Skye smelled liquor on his breath, and knew she had better assert her position fast. She tried to sound as imperious as her Aunt Cathy.

"I'll try to overlook what you've just said, Desmond. Now, if you'll just get out of my way—"

How he had come between her and the means of escape, she didn't know. But the next minute she screamed as he lunged for her, his clay-soggy hands pushing inside her coat and fumbling for her breasts. He was large and rough, and his words had become leering and slobbering.

"Knew you was asking for it soon as I saw 'ee, wi' them big blue eyes and that maid's-hair. If I be the first, 'twill be an even bigger bonus than any yon pit bosses ever pay out."

"Keep away from me, you bastard," Skye screamed, fighting him off. He had bullish strength, and she was very frightened.

159

And the last thing she wanted to do was to be practically mud-wrestling with this drunken oaf. Then the heavily-booted club foot shot out and hooked itself behind her ankle, giving it a vicious wrench.

She lost her balance at once, and went flying to the ground, hitting the back of her head with a sickening crack. Desmond Lock fell on top of her, winding her, his hands fumbling for her skirts now, and pushing upwards with those slimy, sausage fingers, hurting her.

Dazed and sobbing, Skye's head twisted this way and that in her terror, her lovely hair unkempt and dirtied on the dusty ground. She tried desperately to clamp her legs together, knowing this awful thing was about to happen, and there was nothing she could do to stop it.

Then, out of nowhere came an unholy screech, as if all the demons in hell were being unleashed. Desmond's head jerked up, and as he paused in his fumbling, Skye scrambled away from him, staggering to her feet and clutching at the edge of the workbench. Her head swam, and her eyes were blurred with tears as she made out the outline of what looked like a horrendous gargoyle standing against the light.

The bedraggled figure, with its tangled, wispy grey hair, pointed an accusing finger at Desmond.

"Keep away from me, you evil witch bitch!" he screamed, backing away with his eyes rolling in terror.

The old woman moved menacingly forward. "You'm doomed for defiling this pretty miss, Desmo Lock, and tain't the first time you've dabbled with young maids, from all I hear tell. Such wickedness allus comes back to roost, sure as night follows day."

"You bloody old crone!" Desmo screamed again. "You don't scare me wi' your spells and potions!"

Without warning she flung a handful of something hot and peppery towards him, and he howled with pain as it reached his eyes. He blundered out of the linhay and away from the

160

makeshift pottery, hollering that he'd have her pool-dunked and strung up yet for the she-devil that she was.

Still shivering with shock, Skye recognised her unlikely saviour now as the old woman she had seen when she first came here. The woman from the hovel on the moors.

"Thankyou," she croaked.

"No need for thanks. I've fair taken to 'ee, my pretty, and that one's due for the fiery furnace, never fear."

Skye didn't heed her words. She smoothed down her clothes and her hair with shaking hands, wincing at the lump on the back of her head. The old crone took charge.

"You'd best come back wi' old Helza, and I'll give 'ee summat to make 'ee feel better."

"Oh, no, it's not necessary. I should get home—"

"What, and stir up bad thoughts and memories for old Morwen Tremayne by your appearance? You come along wi' me, my pretty, and take a warmin' cup, and I'll tell 'ee a tale o' the past that I'll wager none of your kin have told 'ee," she went on slyly.

Skye was starting to feel that she had no will of her own any more, and she was unable to resist the enticing words. The shambling old crone led her to where a disreputable hovel stood alone on the moors. She went inside, and was enveloped in a choking, cloying mixure of smells that made her heave.

"You'll soon get used to it," Helza cackled, kicking a yelping cat out of the way. "Now then, you drink this, and if you cross my palm with silver I'll tell 'ee the ancient tale my sister witch passed on. Old Zillah were a good teller o' tales, and this one were a beauty, concerning Morwen Tremayne an' her flighty young friend Celia Penry."

Skye stared, her heart thumping. She had heard the name Celia before, and she knew there was some long-buried secret concerning her and Granny Morwen. And this strange being knew it all . . .

"Tell me what you know," she croaked. "I'll pay."

161

Helza cackled again. "I know it all, my pretty. All about how Zillah gave the two young 'uns a potion so they could see the faces of their lovers through the Larnie Stone. And how Ben Killligrew and his cousin Jude got to know of it, and made sure they was the ones on the moors at midnight that night."

Skye gasped. She was still in shock after Desmond Lock's rape attempt, but her eyes were glazing with the effects of the narcotic herbal brew Helza had given her.

"Oh ah, yon Morwen were a comely young piece in them days, by all accounts, but 'twere t'other un who enticed a bad 'un like Jude Pascoe and got more'n she bargained for. Like you nearly got today, if 'ee gets my meaning, girlie."

"You mean he raped her?" Skye whispered, her tongue thick and furry now.

"An' left her wi' a child in her belly. So the wenches came back to Zillah for another potion to rid Celia o' the waste, and they buried it on the moors."

"Dear God, how terrible—"

"An' then the Penry maid got struck by her conscience and drowned herself in a clay pool. 'Twas one o' Morwen's brothers that found 'er."

"And what of this – this Jude person?" Skye forced herself to say, willing away the awful images of a young girl drowning in a clay pool.

No *wonder* Morwen had got so distraught, hearing about Walter's drowning.

"Went to America wi' Matt Tremayne—"

"*What*? But Matt Tremayne is my grandfather."

"Oh aye, they're a tangled bunch o' folk all right."

Skye couldn't bear to hear any more. She couldn't breathe, and she had to get out of there. Of course she knew her parents were cousins, and Grandfather Matt and Granny Morwen were brother and sister, but this . . . all this terrible information Helza had given her, information that she knew instinctively was all true . . .

162

She was so befuddled by now that she hardly remembered thrusting some coins into Helza's hands, nor how she got back to the linhay to collect her bicycle and rode like the wind back to New World, praying that no one would see the state she was in until she collapsed on her bed and slept off the effects of the drug and the day.

On the way she passed the Larnie Stone, the gaunt standing stone with the hole in the middle, through which could be seen the sea at St. Austell. The stone that two young girls had once circled at midnight, chanting a witch's spell to produce the faces of their lovers.

It took Skye days to put the incident with Desmond Lock properly behind her, vowing never to go to the linhay alone again. But then Theo brought the news that there had been a raging fire on the moors one night, and the old linhay had been burnt to the ground, with Desmond Lock in it. All they found of him was some charred clothing and the heavy boot from his clubbed foot.

It was a mystery how it had happened – except to Skye Tremayne. She couldn't even be sorry for the man, but she was perfectly sure who had set the linhay on fire, and hadn't Helza said he would go to the fiery furnace for his sins? As if she had all the second sight in the world at her disposal at that moment, Skye knew. But it would remain a dark secret between her and the witchwoman.

Chapter Eleven

In September Philip came home on leave, staying at New World for eight days' respite from the Front. After their first rapturous embrace, he held Skye away from him, shocked.

"Your lovely hair," he said. "What have you done to it?"

She gave a shaky laugh. "I thought it was time I acted my age and had it cut. Don't you like it?"

Her eyes were brimming, and she prayed he would think it was due to the emotion of their reunion. But it was more than that. The memory of Desmond Lock's attack had affected her more deeply than she imagined. She felt shamed by her own femininity, and one way in which she could alter herself was to hack off her hair – or rather, to let some sympathetic salon person do it for her. It hadn't helped but to Philip now, she looked gamine and appealing, her eyes huge and anxious that he should approve.

"I love it," he said, gathering her close once more.

"Anyway," she went on in a bright, brittle voice. "They collect hair now, for stuffing mattresses or something, so I'm told, so I'm doing my bit for the war effort as well."

"What's wrong?" he said quietly.

As an engaged couple, they had been left discreetly alone, and Skye had thought she could ride out the horror of Desmo Lock's attack without ever telling Philip. But he knew her too well. She blurted it all out, finding more relief in the telling than she could ever have imagined.

"The bastard," Philip said savagely. "He should be hung,

drawn and quartered. What did Theo have to say about it? I trust he hounded the bastard out of the place."

Skye looked at him mutely. She hadn't told him everything yet, and nor could she. Not *everything*. But the sinister thought of history repeating itself didn't escape her. Morwen and a witchwoman had once shared a dark secret. So did she.

"I told no one," she choked out. "I couldn't. But it's all over, anyway. The linhay burnt down one night, and they discovered that he was in it."

"Good God! That was poetic justice, if you like. And you're *really* all right, darling? He really didn't hurt you?"

He sounded so blessedly normal, so concerned for her, that she clung to him wordlessly for a moment. She had been so afraid that the encounter with Desmo Lock would have turned her against any contact with another man, even her beloved Philip . . . but it hadn't and she needed him more than ever.

"I'm more than all right now you're here," she said huskily. "And when you leave for France, I'm going with you. Granny Morwen's well enough now, and I've already been to the recruiting office and got the necessary papers."

He folded her to him, glad to his soul that no harm had come to her, but knowing that if he had any savvy at all, he would tell her to stay in Cornwall where she was safe. He had witnessed too many horrors of war to want her exposed to them, but he knew it would be useless to try to dissuade her.

They stayed close for a long while after that, needing to talk, needing to touch and hold, and to renew the sweetness of their feelings for one another.

"Philip, there's something else I want to say," she said eventually. "I've been thinking about it for weeks now, and I know it's right. I want us to be married before we leave. I don't know if married women are acceptable at the Front, and I know Granny Morwen would make a fuss, so we must keep it secret. But I need to know that we really belong together—"

He put his finger on her mouth as she babbled on. She was

166

desperate for him to agree to this. To know that they were truly married would be her talisman.

"We've always belonged. And you're a crazy woman," he told her. "What man in his right senses would marry the woman he loves and then take her into danger?"

"What man in his right senses would desert the woman he loves and go to war without her?"

"I'm not deserting you—"

"Then agree to it. I'm begging you, Philip – and that's a first!" she said, reverting to her more peppery self with a shaky grin. "*Please?*"

"You wouldn't even want your grandmother to know?" he asked at last, and she knew she had won. She hugged him close.

"When we go, we'll leave an envelope containing our marriage certificate for safe-keeping for her to open later. I'll also write to my parents to tell them. I'm not being heartless, truly, but I don't want anyone to stop me."

"You've thought this all out, haven't you, my clever little witch?" Philip said dryly. "So I take it you don't intend asking dear Uncle Luke to perform the ceremony?"

"I do not!" But she was laughing now, despite his odd endearment that had made her heart stop for a moment. But now that they had established their future she was starting to feel more reckless and carefree than she had done in weeks.

Philip was nothing if not resourceful, and she wasn't the only one to put plans into action.

"Then I suggest we drive to some other town for a few days and get a special licence. You look peaky, and a change will do you good. A tactful word to your grandmother should get her to agree to it."

Skye put her arms around him. "One of the things I love about you is your willingness to change direction when the need arises. You're a very satisfactory lover, Philip."

167

"Oh, really? Just because I change direction when the need arises?" he said provocatively.

"Not just because of that," she said. Her eyes were full of dreams as she looked into his. "Oh, and did I mention that Granny Morwen is asleep, and everyone else is out?"

"You didn't, but I think we should take advantage of the situation," he said. They walked towards the stairs, arms entwined. "And have I told you lately that I love you?"

"I think so. But you can always tell me again."

It was simpler than Skye had imagined to carry out her longed-for plan. It didn't disturb her that she had taken the initiative and proposed. It was going to happen eventually, anyway, and after a couple of respectable days in Bodmin, they became husband and wife, and spent one night of bliss in a country hotel, registered as Mr and Mrs Philip Norwood.

But they both knew it was an idyll that was soon to end, and they clung to one another almost ferociously in the dawn light of their last morning, knowing they must return to New World and act out their expected roles.

"Promise me we'll never lose this feeling of oneness, Philip," she whispered to him, stroking the strong, muscled back of her husband.

"I promise," he said, bending his head to kiss her breasts. "Whatever happens to the rest of the world, you and I will always be constant, my darling."

His words made her feel cherished and loved, even if they also sent an unwanted little chill running through her veins. For these few brief, blissful hours, they were cocooned and safe. But they knew they were part of a wider world, and that they couldn't ignore it for much longer.

Their plans were followed with precision-like efficiency. Birdie was instructed to give the envelope to Morwen the morning after they sailed to France, and by then Skye had penned the letter to her parents, telling them that she and Philip were married, and asking for their blessing.

She had begged and cajoled the recruiting officer to allow her to be sent to the same hospital where Philip was driving ambulances to and from the Front and on to the hospital ships.

She had stated her credentials, which amounted to very little, until the man snapped that they always needed intelligent people who could spell correctly for clerical duties, and to record the names of the incoming wounded and the outgoing dead.

"He was so callous," she raged to Philip. "Eyeing me up and down as if I was some do-gooder who was going to fall by the wayside at the mere mention of dead and wounded."

But all the same, the reality of what she was doing was only just coming home to her. Philip was sympathetic, but he pointed out the sense of the man's words.

"If you'd fainted right off, he'd have seen through you in a minute. They have to be sure you're made of the right stuff to deal with whatever comes."

"And they obviously think I'm only made of the right stuff to be pushing a pen," she said indignantly. "How does that make me sound, for pity's sake?"

"Like a journalist," he said.

Her eyes gleamed at a sudden thought. "Can we call at the *The Informer* office in Truro before we leave?" she asked.

And miraculously, maybe because of the bereavements in the Tremayne family, allied to the death of Jordan Askhew, the revered journalist in their northern sister paper, David Kingsley had softened towards her and agreed to her request.

She didn't care what the reason behind it was. All that mattered was that she was going to send back reports to *The Informer*, albeit under a male pen-name. She was going to tell the truth about the conditions and the casualties, and David Kingsley had promised to publish them, however gruesome.

If she was reduced to filing reports for the hospital in a clerical capacity, at least she could hold her head up high,

knowing she was also doing a worthwhile job, even if she
didn't get the credit for it she deserved.

They knew they couldn't spend their nights together. They
were officially an engaged couple, and that was all. But there
were nights when Philip managed to come to her room when
her fellow nurses were on duty, or she could sneak into his.

It was far from ideal, but they were not the only couple to
need time to be together. And Skye was never sure how much
of a blind eye the authorities took to such clandestine meetings.
The progress of the war was always uppermost in everyone's
minds, but they also aknowledged that there had to be time
for personal feelings, or they would all go mad.

At the end of September there was a huge autumn offensive on
the Western Front. The French attacked the German lines at
Champagne, and the British attack was near Loos in Flanders.
Casualty numbers were immense, and the influx of them to the
field hospital where Philip and Skye were stationed shocked
the most hardened medical staff. No one was immune.

"Leave that book work for now, Tremayne," Sister Bell
snapped at Skye. "We've been sent reinforcements from
another hospital, but everyone's wanted on the wards. Tie
a surgical mask around your mouth and nose if you feel
like gagging at the smells, and be prepared to help the
surgeons."

Skye felt her heart beat sickeningly fast. Help the surgeons?
She couldn't do this. It wasn't what she had volunteered
for . . .

"Come *on*, girl. There's one of your own out here, leastways,
she says she is. She'll show you what to do."

Philip . . . even as she thought it, she knew it couldn't be
him. He was busy transporting the poor devils from one hell
to another, and besides, Sister Bell had said *she*.

"I guessed it was you, Skye!" she heard a bright voice say
a few minutes later. "This is a lark, isn't it? I bet you never

thought you'd be doing this sort of work when you came to see dear Grandmama!"

"Vera, it's you!" Skye stuttered, seeing the cheeky face of one of Charlotte's girls.

"Right enough, so let's get on with it, shall we?" she said cheerfully. "Some bloke's got to have his leg off, and another one's lost an eye and is losing blood by the bucketful, and they're screaming for helpers."

And she had sneered at this girl and her sister, for their keenness to roll bandages! Skye had never felt so ashamed in her life, sensing the grit that was behind Vera's words now. But all the same . . .

"I can't go out there," she whispered. "There's so much blood, and the smell of it makes me want to vomit."

Vera gave her a withering look. "I don't suppose the poor Tommies care for it much, either, but they've got no choice, have they? Some of 'em aren't going to make it anyway, but we can hold their hands and give them a smile while the surgeon does his best to patch them up. A pretty girl's smile is worth a lot when you don't have much else to live for, so stop being a daffodil and come *on*."

Vera pulled her to her feet, and she knew she had no option. At the last minute, her cousin gave her a piece of extra advice.

"If you've got some strong perfume or linament with you, stuff it up your nose to deaden the less savoury smells."

"Sister said I could use a surgical mask."

Vera laughed. "None left, sweetie. You've got a handkerchief, haven't you? Or do like I do and ignore it, and just let the fellows see you smile. It cheers them up – providing you don't puke all over them."

God, she was so *hard*, thought Skye. She was so changed from the rather simpering girl she had thought her to be.

But after an hour, then a day, and then weeks on the wards, in between doing her clerical duties and falling exhausted into bed at night, and snatching an occasional meeting with Philip,

Skye knew she was changing too. Everyone did. Everyone had to, if they were going to survive.

The year dragged on, and in October they received the shocking news that a British nurse named Edith Cavell had been shot by a German firing squad for treason.

"Her only crime was in running a nursing school in Brussels all these years, and then choosing to nurse the wounded of both sides," Vera stormed. "Where's the humanity in a system that can condemn such a woman?"

It was one of the few times Skye saw her lose her composure. But the sights on the wards made everyone lose all sense of decency and privacy, and they also lost much respect for men who could so humiliate and maim their own kind.

On the rare occasions she seemed to see Philip alone now, Skye wept in his arms, berating the whole human race.

"Hush, darling," he said. "You have to accept that war makes animals out of all of us."

"Not *you*," she said stubbornly. "And certainly not *me*."

"So if you were to come face to face with a Hun, and it was a case of kill or be killed, you think you would be too full of humanity to pull the trigger, do you? I think not, my love. The need for survival is as strong in us today as it was in the Stone Age."

"Oh, I hate it when you're so logical and make me feel such a ninny," she stormed.

"Then let me make you feel human again," he said softly, but she couldn't and in the end, neither could he.

"This war has got a lot to answer for," he said grimly, knowing that this wasn't the time or place, after all, to be making love. "There was never a more apt saying about the spirit being willing, but the flesh weak."

"We're all exhausted," Skye told him, knowing his male pride was suffering right now. "But one day it will end, and we'll be home in Cornwall again, doing all the ordinary things we always took for granted."

172

It had never sounded so poignant nor so sweet.

"Is Cornwall truly home to you now, Skye? Don't you have hankerings to go back to America? If it was what you really wanted, we should think about it—"

"It's not," she said flatly. "Of course I'll want to see Mom and Daddy sometimes, but I can live without my brother's pomposity, and Cornwall feels more like my spiritual home than anywhere else on earth now. And if you don't start talking about something else, I'm going to cry."

They had occasional leaves, but the timing didn't always coincide, and they only went back to England a few times during the following year. Most times they preferred to stay where they could be in touch with each other, and Skye's fellow nurses had long since begun calling them the love-birds. But it was said with affection, and not a little envy.

In the September of 1916, tanks arrived on the scene to give them new hope for an early end to it all. And there was fresh excitement as the news was relayed about the Zeppelin that had exploded over Essex, with the crew being almost bizarrely arrested by a lone Special Constable. And then something far more heartbreaking occurred to bring home and war more closely together for Skye than anything else so far.

"There's a large batch of casualties for you to detail, Tremayne," her immediate superior said. "You came from Cornwall, didn't you? I'd better warn you that some of the names might be familiar to you."

She didn't get much sympathy from that one, thought Skye, and she took the bundle of papers into the small office that had been allocated to her, steeling herself for seeing Cornish names among all the others. But there was only one section of casualties that turned her blood to water. They were all dead. The whole unit had been wiped out, and they were collectively known as the *Killigrew Pals Battalion*.

173

For the first time in a long while, she couldn't think. Couldn't write. Could hardly breathe. She simply sat there with tears streaming down her face, her chest so tight it felt as though it would burst as so many names that were familiar to her leapt out of the columns at her.

David and Harry Penry . . . Drago Trewithin . . . John Penhale . . . Lenny Pollard . . . Tommy Dark . . . Lance Jerram . . . Jemmy Praed . . . Ronnie Wells . . . Denzil Trethorne . . .

"For God's sake, Skye, what's happened?"

She heard her cousin Vera's voice as if through a mist. Vera was about to be posted, and Skye knew she would miss her badly. They had become good friends in the last traumatic months they had shared.

"I have to detail the lists of casualties, and I'll have to send a special list back to *The Informer*. It's our boys, Vera. Our lovely Killigrew Clay boys . . ."

She couldn't say any more as the sobs were wrenched out of her. She didn't know many of them, or their families, but they were part of her heritage, and she wept for them. Vera hugged her, sharing her sorrow because of who they were, but more hardened to war than Skye, and finally speaking to her like a Dutch Uncle.

"When you do your reports, remember that this is the last thing you can do for them, Skye. Write about them as if they were the heroes they were, and this time write with your own name, and insist that David Kingsley acknowledges it. Let the folk back home know that you're here and that you care. It will give them comfort."

"You're so wise, Vera," Skye said through her sobs. "And you're so right. All the articles I send back in future will be from a woman's viewpoint, and not some anonymous male observer. If David won't publish them, I'm sure there will be other editors who will."

"That's my girl," Vera said softly.

*   *   *

All the same, it was the hardest job in the world to send in the lists and the article about the *Killigrew Pals Battalion*, insisting that her name should be beneath it. And then she took it on herself to write personal letters to every family, knowing it was what her family would have wanted. It was what Morwen would expect, and it was certainly what Walter would have wanted.

She didn't know about Theo, but she wrote to him separately, telling him what she had done, and hoping that he would follow up her initiative by visiting the families concerned. To her surprise she received a package from Theo a few weeks later, a surprisingly humble Theo from the one she remembered.

'Well done, Skye,' he wrote. 'And well done for telling that oaf Kingsley where to credit the reports in his paper. Your name is now there for all to see, and I'm enclosing the latest issue for you. I've done as you suggested, and visited the families, and a pretty harrowing task it was. But nothing like the harrowing scenes I'm sure you and Philip and young Vera have to face.

'Anyway, in the midst of all this misery, there is some happier news to tell you, though I'm sure Gran will be relaying it all as well. As you know, I was married in the summer, and my wife Betsy is preparing for a happy event in the spring. We're naturally hoping for a son, since the child will be the heir to Killigrew Clay, such as it is.

'But life goes on, and since my mother has decided to live permanently in Yorkshire now, it's time that Killigrew House had some young blood in it. Be pleased for us, Skye, and God willing, you'll all be safely back with us before the new sprog makes his appearance.'

Skye folded the letter slowly. He was kind, but there was still an underlying selfishness in Theo that she couldn't deny, and she would never really warm to him. She wished his wife Betsy well of him, and according to Granny Morwen the lady had brought money to the marriage, so Theo was undoubtedly well satisfied.

Which was more than could be said when news of her own marriage had broken, Skye thought with a shiver. When she had sailed to France, leaving the wedding certificate in Morwen's safe-keeping, she had begged her grandmother to say nothing to anyone else, lest their relationship should scupper their chances of being here together. But she had received a less than complimentary letter back from Morwen, condemning her for her deceit. And only at the end did the words soften.

'. . . but because I know only too well the strong Tremayne passions that are in your heart, my dearest Skye, I wish you and Philip all the happiness in the world, and a safe return to normality in this mad world.'

"What do you think?" Skye said to Philip, when they snatched a few moments together a few evenings later. "Theo's wife is expecting a baby, and knowing him, he'll be bragging that it's the most perfect child ever born on this earth."

"So it will be, to him and Betsy," Philip told her. "Just as ours will be to us."

"Oh, so we are planning to have children, then?" she said, glad to be jocular after a very painful week.

"Of course. Didn't I tell you?" he said, matching her mood, and caressing her bare arm. "Once this war is over, we'll plan on a dozen or more, if that's what you'd like. We'll have lots of little cousins for the princely Theo's offspring to fight with."

"Fight? Don't you mean to play with?"

"Not if I know the fiery Tremayne brood," Philip teased.

"But ours will be Norwoods, and anyway, who said I wanted a dozen? One will do for a start – but not yet, thankyou!"

She crossed her fingers as she said it, for apart from the times when the horrors of war seemed to make them both mentally and physically impotent, they were such passionate lovers, and everyone knew that for people like them, this was no time to be making babies . . .

Morwen wrote to Skye in her usual blunt fashion.

'You did a good and wonderful thing in writing separately to the families of the boys who were killed, dar. All of them were touched, and there was a grand service for them all that Luke managed to conduct less pompously than usual. Even his stuffy heart was stirred by the magnitude of such a loss.

'It was held on the moors at Clay Two, since the workings have stopped there now. In fact, Theo has suggested that we close it permanently, as the workers are so depleted, and with none of the young 'uns coming back to carry on, it seems the most sensible course to follow. But when the war is over, and things are a bit more regular, we'll think again what we intend to do.

As for your writings in *The Informer*, I hear nothing but good things about the way you describe it all. I'm sending copies to your Mammie every week, and she's letting the folk where you used to work see them, so I daresay some of it will appear in your American magazine as well.

'Apart from that, we're all tolerably well here, though you can't expect miracles of an old biddy like myself. But Theo's Betsy is sprouting nicely, and it's good to have something to look forward to. So you and Philip take care of yourselves, and be sure that you're in our prayers.

'Your loving grandmother, Morwen.'

Her words brought tears to Skye's eyes. Morwen wrote as she talked, and she could almost hear that soft Cornish accent, and the quaint way she referred to Betsy's 'sprouting'.

And she could just visualise the service on the moors at Clay Two, which was the right and proper place for a dedication to

177

all those young boys who had served Killigrew Clay so well, along with their fathers and grandfathers.

The sweet continuity of it all wouldn't have escaped any of them, and it didn't escape Skye now.

The searing sadness of that time was three months behind them when they learned that she and Philip had been granted a few days' Christmas leave together, but it was far too short a time to travel home. And the weather was less than clement.

Instead, they managed to hire a service car, begging and scrounging just enough petrol to get them away from the hospital and into the countryside, where blessedly, there were still little hotels ready to accept folk who had money to spend on a couple of nights' lodging and to sit and talk in front of a roaring wood fire before bedtime.

And they were happy to linger in front of the fire, talking of old times and future plans, knowing that they had all night to be together. And letting themselves pretend, however selfishly, that this was the first of so many nights when war was a distant memory.

The first night of the rest of their lives, Skye thought with a catch in her throat . . . and that was how it felt to her, as Philip undressed her slowly, kissing every inch of her exposed flesh as her clothes fell to the ground, and he gathered her into him.

"God, I love you so much," he said, almost savagely, "If I thought this was all we had—"

She put her fingers on his lips, realising almost with a little shock that his thoughts hadn't been on the same plane as hers after all. She spoke with a passion.

"It won't be. Our marriage is our talisman, remember? One day we'll go home and set up house, and live a mundane life with our children."

"It will never be mundane with you, sweetheart. Not with my mad, fiery, beautiful Skye who I love with all my heart."

"Do you? Then why don't you show me how much?" she said, provocative now, and utterly comfortable in her lack of inhibitions.

178

He lifted her in his arms and lay her gently on the creaking bed, while he undressed swiftly. She gazed at him through shuttered eyelids, marvelling at the strength in his body, and the taut, powerful maleness of him.

And then the desperate urgency to be lovers, to shut out everything ugly and evil in the world, transcended everything else. And as he covered her with himself, the vibrant heat of him filled her, and exalted her, making her gasp out loud at the surging joy of their oneness.

The brief leave was too soon over, and they drove back to the hospital through dank and misty roads in almost complete silence. Another Christmas had come and gone, however sweetly memorable it had been for them, and another year was just around the corner. Already this war had stretched into unbelievable lengths. Weeks, and months, and now years . . .

And no matter how she tried, Skye couldn't rid her thoughts of the dread that this unreal half-life they all led, seemed destined to go on for ever. That there would never be an end to this bitterly-fought war, and more and more people would be killed and maimed so senselessly.

"Do I offer a penny for your thoughts, or are they too dismal for sharing?" Philip asked her eventually.

"I'm sorry," she said contritely, realising she had been staring gloomily out of the steamy car window at the dripping branches of the trees for the last ten minutes. "After our lovely time together, I shouldn't seem such a grouch."

"You don't have to apologise to me, darling. I can guess at the thoughts in your mind. Wondering when it will ever end, and when we'll get back to normality. Right?"

"Right," she said, thinking it odd that he could be so in tune with these dire thoughts, and yet his thoughts had completely missed connecting with hers when she had been able to imagine they were in some kind of never-ending seventh heaven at the small hotel.

179

She had been able to believe themselves suspended in time for those blissful hours, while he apparently had not. But that was the prosaic in him, of course, while she was the romantic . . . and *somebody* had to be the practical one, she reminded herself. It didn't mean he loved her any the less. She *knew* how much he loved her, with all his heart and soul, the way she loved him.

"I do love you, Philip," she said. "I thought I'd just mention it, in case there was any doubt."

He laughed, putting his hand on hers for a moment before returning it to the steering wheel on the muddy, bumpy road.

"Oh, I think I know it by now, my lovely, uninhibited angel! I think the whole hotel must have been aware of it!"

She blushed and laughed with him, remembering how the bedsprings in the lumpy bed had creaked appallingly with their vigorous love-making – and she herself had been less than silent in the magic of it all. But this was the middle of a war, when such rare moments were too precious to lose, and she didn't regret a single thing.

Chapter Twelve

"You should have a nurse permanently at the house, Gran," Theo told Morwen in annoyance. "These constant bouts of pneumonia are weakening you, and it's hardly fair on Birdie, is it? She's not a trained nurse, and the doctor agrees with me."

Morwen glared at him as best she could while her eyes streamed with the attack of coughing she had just managed to suppress. It hurt her chest abominably, but she had no intention of letting him see it, especially with the anxious eyes of his whey-faced wife hovering beside him.

Betsy was a nice enough soul, Morwen conceded, completely under Theo's thumb, of course, as one would expect, and looking like the side of a house in the last months of her difficult pregnancy. She shouldn't have come here with him on such a miserable February day.

"Have you been discussing my affairs with the doctor?" Morwen wheezed at Theo now.

"Who else is there to do it, if not me? Luke's too busy saving souls, and the girls have their own families to care for. Albert and Rose rarely venture out of Truro now that Rose has got the consumption, and besides," he wound up without pausing for breath, "your affairs *are* my affairs, or have we grown too far apart for that as well?"

"I'm sure Grandmother Morwen didn't mean any such thing, Theo dear," Betsy put in anxiously.

Morwen glanced at her. She was always anxious to please, the daughter of monied parents who had left everything to her, and yet she had the self-confidence of a flea. It had to be said that she irritated Morwen with her constant need to appease Theo's caustic words, and she longed for the robustness of Skye to fill this house with laughter again. Primmy's daughter had become so very dear to her.

"So what did you and the doctor discuss for me?" she said to Theo now, ignoring Betsy.

"Just what I've said. We think we should engage a permanent nurse to live in the house, Gran. God knows we can afford it, and it would ease us all to know you were being taken care of properly."

"Ease your consciences, you mean," Morwen said dryly.

For a moment she had a vision of her own Mammie, the stoical Bess Tremayne, living out her early married life with the five children in the cramped little cottage on the moors, through whose slates you could sometimes see the stars, and wondered how Bess would have scoffed at such a namby-pamby suggestion of a living-in nurse. It was odd that Theo's wife had almost the name as her Mammie, yet never were there two women so totally different in spirit.

But all the same, however reluctantly, she could see the sense of what Theo said, and times had changed for them all since those scratch-penny days. The owners of Killigrew Clay were Somebodies in this community, and she probably owed it to her relatives to show that she was being properly cared for.

It was almost laughable. Morwen Tremayne, who had once run barefoot across the moors as free as the wind, with her black hair streaming behind her, her cheeks glowing with health, and her blue eyes blazing . . . where had she gone?

She felt a burning, innate sadness for the loss of that young, vivacious girl, and then she mentally chided herself, for allowing herself to forget, even for a moment, the happiness that two husbands had brought into her life. Her cherished Ben, and her darling Ran. She had had it all . . .

"I daresay you're right in all you say, Theo," she said at last with a heavy sigh. "You can see to it then, but it will have to be somebody that Birdie approves of as well as me, mind. I'll not have some starched body in the house who thinks she can rule the roost."

"There's no danger of that while you're still in control, Gran," Theo said with a relieved grin.

It was like entering another era, thought Morwen a few weeks later. Here she was, relegated to matriarch of the family, as she had been for many years now, but never feeling it quite as much as when Nurse Mabel Jenkins from Bristol, armed with a fistful of recommendations, attended to her every whim, whether she wanted it or not.

She meant well, but it put Morwen severely in her place, and the only way she could rid herself of uneasy thoughts of the impending end to her life, was to write long letters to Emma, and to Primmy in New Jersey, and to Skye in France, and to write as humorously as possible.

Skye laughingly related one of these letters to Philip, imagining the indignity in Morwen's musical voice as she read out her words.

'She even wants to sit me on the blessed commode, if you please, but I told her I'm having none of that. When I can no longer manage to do my personals for myself, it'll be time for me to bid farewell to New World, and not before.

'Besides, I've still got to see this wonder-babe of Theo's and Betsy's. To listen to the pair of them, by all accounts he's going to be nothing short of a genius of the first order. We'll all have to mind our country manners when he arrives.'

Philip laughed at her turn of phrase. "Are you sure this isn't where you get your writing talent from, sweetheart?"

"Maybe so, but I doubt that Granny Morwen ever saw it like that. She simply writes down the way she feels – which is the best way of all, of course."

It charmed her all the same, to think that she and Morwen had something else in common. And in between her duties, she wrote many letters of her own, to Morwen, and to Primmy.

Letters were a vital and important link with home and family, as they were for so many of the wounded soldiers. And eventually Skye took on the voluntary task of writing for those who could no longer see to hold a pencil, or had no hands left to do so. It was heartbreaking, writing to wives and sweethearts in the words the men whispered to her, but she did it, knowing it would mean so much to them.

"You're killing yourself with kindness, Tremayne," her superior told her sharply. "You'll be no use to us on the wards when the next wave of casualties comes in if you stay up half the night writing letters."

"I shan't fail in my duties, Sister, but while the men want me to do this for them, I shall do it," she said, lifting her chin. "If anything ever happened to my–my fiancé," she remembered to say at the last instant, "I'd like to think there was someone who would write to me on his behalf."

She immediately felt chilled, wishing she hadn't said it, as if it was inviting disaster.

"Well, we'll soon be having reinforcements, and not before time," Sister Bell said, clearing her throat at the defiant young woman who stared her out with those enormous blue eyes.

"What do you mean?"

"You've heard the news, haven't you? Your President Woodrow Wilson has decided your people are going to enter the war at last, though God knows how long it will be before any of them get here. Still, better late than never, I daresay."

Skye felt her cheeks burn with patriotic pride. "You seem to forget that it wasn't *our* war in the first place," she snapped. "But I'm glad we're in it now, if it stops your snide remarks."

184

"I'll stop yours, Miss, and send you packing, if I get any more insubordination like that!"

"Oh, go stuff yourself," said the elegant Skye Tremayne Norwood, in as bawdy a comment as she dared to make.

And of course she wouldn't be sent packing! They needed all the female help they could get in the hospital, and she couldn't have cared less about Sister Bell's tightly-pursed lips and even tighter backside as she swished away, Skye thought irreverently.

She hadn't seen Philip in days, since he was out on manoeuvres, but the moment he returned and sought her out, he was full of news. By then it was the beginning of April.

"Have you heard that America's entered the war?" he asked, once he had hugged her tightly for a few minutes.

"Of course I've heard it. And have you heard the family news? Well, no, you haven't, since I only got the letter a day or so ago. But it seems that the sainted Betsy has had her son, so all is right with cousin Theo's world."

He held her away from him, seeing the darkened shadows beneath her lovely eyes, and hearing her cynicism.

"That's good news, isn't it? A son and heir for Killigrew Clay, I mean?" he said cautiously, not quite sure of her mood yet. They had hugged and kissed, and been joyful at their reunion, but he sensed that Skye's feeling of well-being had quickly passed.

"Of course it is. I just pray that I'll be back in Cornwall soon to share the good news with Granny Morwen. She sounds really sick, Philip, and I fear for her. I had a letter from Birdie as well, and she confided her fears as well. Now, when *Birdie* takes it on herself to write a letter, it's got to be serious, wouldn't you say?"

She tried to make light of it, but her voice broke. It was bad enough to think that Morwen might be seriously ill, but not to be there to care for her was one more thing to blame on this bloody, bloody war, Skye thought savagely.

Apart from Theo, who did his dutiful best, there was no one

of her own who visited Morwen regularly. Out of all that large family, Morwen must be lonely in that big house that held so many memories of times past, Skye thought.

Primmy, her own mother, was three thousand miles away; Emma was too busy with her farming life to be able to spend time at New World; Charlotte had her Good Works to contend with; Albie . . . why didn't Albie visit her more?

But of course, Rose was ill. Bradley and Freddie were away in Ireland; Jack and his family were in Sussex or somewhere, and Luke had his wider flock to care for.

Besides, Morwen wouldn't give a thankyou for Luke to be piously pandering over her, and as for the others . . . even as she thought it, Skye knew there was only one person Morwen would really want with her at this time. The one with whom she had had such an extraordinary empathy, from the moment they had met. Herself.

"You should go home," Philip said quietly, reading her mind. "You've had enough, my love."

Angrily, she turned on him, perverse as ever.

"Oh, really? Well, why don't you go and say the same thing to those poor bloody boys who come in to the hospital more dead than alive, to get themselves patched up and sent back to the Front to get slaughtered all over again? Tell them when they've had enough, and then tell *me*."

"Good God, don't take it out on me! I'm only thinking of your health. You'll be no good to anyone if you collapse on the wards, will you?"

She was contrite at once, seeing the hurt in his eyes. "I'm sorry, love. But I'm all right, truly I am. I've just had a bad day, worrying about Granny Morwen, but I know she has this nurse at the house, and Birdie is full of praise for her, so we must just hope she doesn't decline any more."

Not until Skye Tremayne was there to see her safely on her last journey . . . the insidious thought ran through her head,

186

sending cold shivers down her spine, and she dismissed it as best she could.

"So what's the perfect infant to be called?" Philip asked her, ignoring the sight of her shaking hands as she made tea for them in her room. For a moment she couldn't follow his thoughts, and then she gave a small smile.

"Would you believe he's to be called Sebastian Walter Jordan? Poor babe. Chances are he'll be landed with a nickname anyway. But as long as he's healthy, that's all that really matters."

"That's all any of us wants," Philip said, and she couldn't find an answer to that.

Events at the Front kept them apart for a while after that, until Skye began to wonder if they were even in the same war. There was no news of Philip, except that he was doing extra ambulance duties transporting the wounded back and forth across the Channel. The lack of communication did nothing to help Skye's fragile temper, and more than once she snapped back at Sister Bell in a white rage after being reprimanded for some petty misdemeanour.

Two months later, Sister Bell sent for Skye to come to her office, and she thought immediately that she was due for a real wigging. She stood stiffly, her hands clenched by her sides, wondering if there was any humanity in the woman at all. But, shamefacedly, she knew that there was. She had seen it in the many patient hours that Sister Bell had held a wounded soldier's hands as his life slipped away.

"Sit down, Tremayne," the woman said without expression. "I'm afraid I have bad news to tell you."

Skye immediately thought of her grandmother. But just as immediately she dismissed the thought, for why and how would any dire news from home have come to Sister Bell and not directly to her?

"I'm sorry to tell you that your fiancé has been wounded," the woman went on. "I have no information of how serious his

187

wounds are, except that they are head and chest injuries and therefore must be seen to be grave. The report has come to us, being his base hospital, and because it is known that you are his fiancée."

Skye registered vaguely that Sister Bell was talking rapidly as if to ward off any undignified emotion from the straight-backed young woman sitting on the edge of the hard seat in front of her. She needn't have worried, thought Skye briefly. She had been too well indoctrinated in the behaviour of hospital personnel in all this time, not to fall apart now. Even when she felt so very much like it.

"Where is he?" she asked in a stifled voice.

"He's in the Sanctuary of Our Lady Hospital, fifteen miles north of here, Tremayne—"

"I must go to him. You must see that. You *will* let me go, won't you?" she said jerkily. She had never really got on with this woman, and she couldn't expect any favours from her now. She was needed here, but she knew that Philip would be needing her too.

"It has already been arranged, after some consultation with the surgeons. You'll be slacking in your duties if you're constantly fretting over the young man."

"Wouldn't you, if you had a fiancé?" Skye snapped.

She saw the woman flinch, and for the first time, her eyes flickered with something like pain.

"I did, once," she said. "Feelings weren't invented for your generation, Tremayne. And it's agreed that you should take no more than five days' leave. That's stretching the bounds, so I hope you won't abuse the arguments in your favour. There are others here who need you."

And that was all Skye heard her say on the matter before she stalked stiffly away. But the implications were there, and she guessed who had persuaded the surgeons to let her have five days' leave, and why. It cooled her anger and shamed her anew, to think she may have misjudged the woman all this time.

You just never knew with people. Some opened up their hearts, and others kept everything bottled up inside like a time-bomb waiting to go off.

She hitched a lift with another ambulance driver taking wounded to and from the Front, and managed to reach the hospital where Philip was detained. It was all alien to her, and the sound of distant gunfire they could hear from her own hospital was suddenly, frighteningly nearer to this one.

And Philip looked so white and ill. She wept and prayed over him as he raved in delirium for several days, without ever knowing she was there, until at last he opened his eyes and spoke her name weakly.

"Thank God you've come back to me," she whispered. She clutched his hand so tightly he winced, and she released him slightly. But only a little. She felt as if she never wanted to let him go, and she had already learned from the surgeons here that he was to be sent back to England as soon as he was well enough to travel.

His injuries were too severe for him to continue at the Front, but as yet he hadn't been told. She didn't know how he would take it, knowing that she would be remaining here without him. It was her duty to do so . . .

When he learned the truth, he was furious with her for not agreeing to take the easy option that was open to them. Telling them they were married, that he needed her to look after him, that she was exhausted, but somehow she couldn't do it. Unless she was sent home forcibly, she had to stay.

"Do I mean so little to you?" he asked her, when he was finally allowed to sit out in a chair for no more than five minutes.

"You shame me by even asking it," she said passionately. "You know you mean everything to me, but how would it be if every nurse who ever loved a man turned turtle and went home when he was wounded?"

And, having seen it so many times before, she knew he was

189

allowing himself to slide into the selfishness of the sick, when all the world needed to revolve around them. But this was war, and he wasn't the only one who needed her.

"And what if I was to let your Sister Bell know that we're married?" he said, confirming her thoughts.

She stared at him. "I know you won't do that. You couldn't be so self-centred, Philip. You've spent your working life guiding students and helping them. Can't you see that this is my one chance to be as useful? Sister Bell saw me as some flighty thing when I first arrived, and it's taken me a long while to prove myself, so don't tempt me into being a coward and throwing it all away."

It took a lot of persuasion and coercion to make him see how determined she was, but finally he gave in. The arguments exhausted her still further, and almost guiltily, she was thankful to leave him in good hands after her five days' leave, promising to come back if she could. Providing he continued to improve, he was due to leave the field hospital in two weeks' time, as his bed would be needed, but, for Philip, the war was over.

And in the end, Skye believed he understood. With a wry smile, he told her he would have done exactly the same thing.

After Philip had left for England on the hospital ship, Skye felt desperately alone, terrified in a foreign country, with a war raging all around her, and her husband sent back to an English hospital to recover and recuperate. She had never felt so bereft. While he had been here, she had had his strength to draw on. Now she had nothing.

Despite her resolution, she felt spineless and lonely. To try and combat it, she threw herself into doing the things she had been doing for so long, caring for the sick and wounded, clearing up after the surgeons, and trying to ignore the appalling sights and sounds and smells that made her retch constantly.

She wrote her articles for *The Informer*, knowing they would reach her family's eyes, and playing down the loneliness of one

scared American girl with Cornish roots, and a longing for
England that was almost painful. She longed for Philip, and
the love they shared. And she wrote to him every day.

Sister Bell sought her out one evening when she had fallen
asleep over some letters she was writing for the soldiers on
the ward.

"You know, this just won't do, Tremayne," the woman said.
"The other girls take their time off and go into the town to the
cafés. You should do the same. Your fiancé wouldn't begrudge
you a little time chatting and laughing. In wartime we all have
to keep up our morale as best we can."

"He's not my fiancé. He's my husband," Skye mumbled, still
half-asleep, and hardly knowing what she was saying.

"*What* did you say?"

For the first time since coming to France, Skye's demeanour
crumbled. The tears rolled down her cheeks unchecked, and she
simply gazed mutely at the older woman. Sister Bell reached
into the pocket of her starched apron, and handed her a clean
handkerchief.

"Are you telling me you're married to this man? When did it
happen?" she said sharply. "You're not pregnant, are you?"

Skye felt a wild desire to laugh. To say that yes, yes, yes,
she was pregnant, so now could she please go home and lead
an ordinary life, bringing up her children in the clean, green
English countryside, away from the horrors of war . . .?

But just as she had refused one easy way out, she was too
honest to take this one.

"I'm not pregnant," she said tonelessly. "And we were married
before we enlisted."

"Then you're a fool, Tremayne."

"Oh, really?" Skye shot at her. "Perhaps it wouldn't have
seemed so foolish if Philip had been killed in action. At least
we would have something to remember."

She bit her lip, knowing instinctively that Sister Bell had no
such memories.

"What are you going to do about it?" she muttered now. "Am I going to be reported and dismissed?"

"I shall do nothing," the other woman said after a moment. "It's up to you whether you go or stay. But if you stay, then you'll get enough sleep and you'll take your time off and not be a danger to my soldiers. Believe me, my dear, I know what I'm talking about."

The small endearment was enough to start Skye off again, but by then, Sister Bell was turning away and leaving her to mop up her own tears. And of course she would stay. She owed it to all the poor devils in the wards. Philip had been one of them, and now he was safe. Not all of these would be so lucky.

But Skye knew the sense of Sister Bell's words, and she made proper use of her leisure time with the other nurses, and went to bed as early as she could, knowing she would be all the stronger for it.

And then came two letters that changed everything.

'Your grandmother is seriously ill, Skye,' Theo wrote. 'There's no way I can dress it up in fancy phrases, but it seems very doubtful that she'll last another winter. Personally I doubt that she'll last the summer, but that's between you and me. I tell you this, because she asks for you constantly. She's dependent on Nurse Jenkins for her physical needs now, and Birdie dotes on her.

But it's you she needs and wants more than she wants the rest of us, and I say that without rancour. She's grown closer to you than anyone else in the family, partly because you're so much like her beloved Primmy, but because of who you are. I'm not given to flowery speeches, Skye, as my wife well knows, and I don't intend to start now.

It seems to us that you're the only one who can make your grandmother's last weeks or months less harrowing, and for that I suggest that you apply for an extended leave

192

at the very least. If she can only see you for a week or two it will mean so much to her.

Talk to the harridans at the hospital, and see what you can do. And, since we know that your fiancé has now been transferred to a serviceman's hospital in Truro, you would be able to visit him as well.'

He signed it, formal as ever – 'Your cousin, Theo.'

To mention Philip was moral blackmail, of course, but Skye couldn't deny the thought of being close to him was tempting as she read the gist of the letter. The other one was from Morwen's doctor.

'Your cousin has asked me to add my thoughts to his, Miss Tremayne, and there's no doubt that Mrs Wainwright has gone into a decline in these last few months. She is asking for you constantly, which is very wearing on the rest of the household at New World, as you can imagine. Her mind wanders, and sometimes she seems to think you are in the room, and her reaction is pitiful when she discovers you are not.'

There was more of the same, and by the end of it, Skye was alarmed and upset. And enraged at the way these two seemed to be ganging up on her. It was her moral duty to stay here where she was useful to so many . . . and it was just as much her moral duty to go home and care for her grandmother. Her mother would expect it.

In the end she sought out the advice of the hospital chaplain. She showed him both letters, and explained the situation. Since she assumed he was bound by his own moral code, she also told him that she and Philip were married, even though it was obvious that Morwen had respected her wishes, and not told the rest of the family.

"Go home, my dear," the chaplain said at once. "You've done more than your duty here, and there will always be others to take your place. In your grandmother's eyes, and in your husband's, no one else can ever do that."

"Is that truly what you think?" she said, her eyes larger than ever in the face that had grown considerably thinner.

"It's what every sane person would think. And if it will help, why don't we say a prayer together?"

"I'm not a religious person," Skye mumbled.

"But you came to me, and I turn no one away, any more than God does," he said simply.

She allowed him to say a short prayer, thinking that he and Uncle Luke were poles apart in the way they expressed their faith. This man had seen the very worst degradations of humanity, had heard men screaming and blaspheming against the very God he served, and yet he still had faith. It was the most humbling moment of her life to realise it.

There was no doubt that Sister Bell and the higher authorities at the hospital agreed with the chaplain's advice. It took relatively little time and effort to get the papers signed that released Skye from all duties at the hospital, and by the end of that summer in 1917, she was on her way back to England in a hospital ship, feeling as if all the stuffing had been knocked out of her.

But, undoubtedly, as the white cliffs of Dover came into view in the misty morning, there was a soaring feeling of jubilation in her heart as well. She had failed no one, and even though she was going home because of Morwen's frailty, she was gong home to Philip too.

No matter how long this interminable war stretched on, there would be time for them to get to know one another all over again. They could reveal their relationship proudly, instead of having clandestine meetings in a foreign country.

To Skye, the future suddenly looked full of hope.

*   *   *

The hospital ship spent several hours at Dover discharging the men going to south-east hospitals and on to the north. They would all wear the honourable blue uniforms of the wounded in action, the uniform which Skye assumed that Philip now wore. From recent letters, she gathered that his recuperation was taking longer than they had expected, and he was angry and frustrated because of it, so she was anxious to see for herself that he was improving.

The ship continued along the south coast until it finally reached Falmouth, and Skye had such a feeling of *déjà vu* as it sailed into the great natural estuary, with the twin castles of Pendennis and St Mawes on either side of that great stretch of water, that she was filled with raw emotion. This is *home*, she thought, this is where I belong.

"Cornwall's never looked so beautiful, has it, Miss?" she heard one stretcher-bound soldier say beside her.

She turned to smile at him and agree with him, and then saw that his eyes were tightly bandaged. He could see nothing, but he still registered that Cornwall was beautiful. That the sun was sparkling on the water, and the sky was a cerulean blue, and the green of summer was burgeoning all around them as they neared land.

By now the open moors would be richly scented with wild flowers and bracken and golden gorse, and the Killigrew sky tips would be gleaming with diamond-bright minerals in the sunlight.

"I know I ain't seeing none of it right now, till they fix me eyes," the soldier went on confidently. "But 'tis all there in me mind, Miss, and no Hun can take that away from me, can he?"

"That's right, soldier," she said softly, swallowing the lump in her throat as the orderly attending him shook his head at the man's words, affirming that he had seen all he was ever going to of England's green and pleasant land.

195

They were so *brave*, all of them, Skye thought with a passion. Heroes, every damn one of them. And they wouldn't give you a red cent for telling them so.

Chapter Thirteen

Even in the middle of a war, life went on. Businesses continued to thrive or went under; people got married and babies were born; and old folk died . . . but thankfully, as far as Skye was concerned, her arrival home from France seemed to have given Morwen a new lease of life. So much so, that she even began to suspect it had all been a ruse on her grandmother's part to get her back. Birdie assured her it wasn't so.

"Though if you'd seen her a coupla months back, you wouldn't have thought she'd live to see the next morning," Birdie confided. "She was near to expiring many times, and the doctor and Nurse Jenkins will bear me out on that."

"Oh, I'm not doubting what you say, Birdie," Skye said hastily, before the companion began to get ruffled. 'I'm just thankful that the worst seems to be over."

"Aye well, let's keep our fingers crossed on that until the winter's over, and spring's here again. 'Tis a good job the Cornish winters are so mild, and the doctor says that providing she stays in out of the damp, all will be well. And she'll not want you constantly fussing over her, mind, 'specially with the young 'un's party coming up. She'll not miss that, nor thank you for saying she should."

"I wouldn't dare," said Skye with a grin.

It had been arranged that Sebastian Walter Jordan should be christened on Christmas afternoon. His great-uncle Luke would perform the ceremony and there would be a family celebration at Killigrew House, combining the Christmas festivities with naming the heir to Killigrew Clay.

Skye and Philip walked slowly around the grounds of the Truro hospital in which he was still slowly recuperating. It had taken far longer than anyone had anticipated, months instead of weeks, and only now was he starting to come out of the mental trauma his head and chest injuries had produced. And as yet, none of the family in Cornwall, save Granny Morwen, knew that they were married.

However foolish and poignant it seemed to Skye at times, they had reluctantly decided it was for the best. Philip needed time to face a normal life again. The mental scars he had suffered went deeper than the physical ones, and Skye was anxious to put no undue pressure on him, even while she longed to be with her husband and to feel properly married, and to proudly wear the wedding ring she kept on a chain around her neck inside her everyday clothes.

Sometimes, she admitted uneasily to herself that the marriage ceremony seemed more like a dream than reality. The times they spent together in one anothers' arms, so few, and so precious now, still seemed like the clandestine reunions of lovers . . . and in some ways she was superstitious enough to keep it that way.

The marriage had been her talisman, her secret, and once a secret was told . . . she couldn't explain herself properly, but she knew that Philip couldn't cope with any fuss, or questions, or scandalised family discussions. Besides, if it was a case of keeping their heads in the sand until they both felt able to cope with the barrage of gossip it would produce, it was their choice.

"How grand Theo's formal christening card looks!" Skye said to Philip now, after showing the gilt-edged card to him.

"It has every reason to. The boy is the natural heir to the clayworks after all, and Theo is justifiably proud of that fact, so it should look grand," Philip replied to her comment now, leaning heavily on a walking-stick with one hand, and with her hand through his other arm, supporting him. "Your family has a fine tradition behind it, and the children who come after should never forget it."

"And what of our children, Philip? Will they go into the family business, do you suppose? Will they be clayers, or will they be celebrated potters – if the new venture ever comes to fruition, of course?"

She spoke lightly, hardly daring to mention children at all, for it was so long since they had touched on so personal a subject. She was almost frightened to recall now how long it was since they had made love, or had the opportunity, or the inclination, at least, on Philip's part, and for all her fiery spirit, she was not yet brave enough to question it.

There would be time enough for loving when he was well and strong, she thought fervently, and if more than a fleeting shadow of unease crossed her mind as she thought it, she dismissed it quickly. Of course that time would come . . .

"They must be whatever they choose, because I've always thought children should find their own way in the world, and not be dictated to by their parents," he told her, in what she privately thought of as his pompous lecturer's voice. She was sure it worked fine with his students, but sometimes it irritated her so much. She kept her voice even as she answered.

"Doesn't that rather undermine the heredity angle? As I understand it, my family fought tooth and nail to keep Killigrew Clay alive, so don't you think their descendants have a duty to continue that fine tradition you spoke of?"

She knew she was trying to provoke him into as passionate a discussion as they used to have, when they could thrash out any topic, no matter how controversial and come out laughing at the end of it. But once he had put his own views across, Philip seemed less inclined to have a healthy argument these days, and it alarmed her.

199

"I daresay everything will sort itself out, and those days are a long way off yet, Skye. I doubt that Theo will be thinking of sending his child out to work just yet."

She supposed he intended it as a humorous remark, and if so, it was the first glimmer of it she had seen in him for a while. It depressed her that it was so laboured. They had always laughed together, and had fun together, and suddenly Philip seemed so much older, so serious and remote from the lover she yearned for.

Still feeling the frustration of it, she confided some of her feelings to her grandmother that evening as she made her habitual visit to Morwen's bedroom to bid her goodnight.

"I feel as if I hardly know him any more. He's changed, and everything's different now."

"You've changed too, lamb. So has everyone who was ever involved in a war. None of us stay the same, however much we'd like to. You must give him time to recover mentally as well as physically, and you've said as much often enough—"

"But how much time does it take?" Skye burst out. "It's been months now, and I want him back. I want my—"

She felt her face burn, knowing what was in her heart and trembling on her lips at that moment. *I want my husband and my lover back.* She turned her face away, but she felt Morwen's hand cover hers for a moment.

"I know what you want, dar, and I know what you're missing. But I promise you, it will all come right if you're patient a little longer."

Skye spoke restlessly, hardly heeding the words as her thoughts raced on. "I keep wondering just how stupid we've been in not telling the family we're married. The longer it goes on, the more bizarre it will seem when the truth comes out, and what's the sense in putting it off for some mythical proper time? How can there *be* a proper time? Everything feels such a muddle in my head. You know, sometimes it feels as if it will burst!"

"I can only tell you that you'll know when the time

is right, my love," Morwen said. "Perhaps at the boy's christening . . ."

Skye shook her head vigorously. "You know very well Theo wouldn't thank me for spoiling his son's special day, Gran. No, it will have to wait until later, and until Philip is ready. If he ever is, that is."

She looked down at her hands, held loosely in her lap now, feeling sheer misery wash over her.

"Now you listen to me, Skye," her grandmother said, suddenly sharper. "If you think this little trip-up in your married life is going to mean the end of it, then you don't have as much Tremayne spirit in you as I think you have. And you've been doubly blessed with that, on your Mammie's and your Daddy's side, so don't let me see that drooping face one minute longer, or I'll start to wonder if you came into my room to cheer me up or depress me."

The effort of such a long speech started her wheezing and coughing, and Skye was instantly contrite. Here she was, moaning and groaning over her own problems, when the fiery Morwen Tremayne had overcome far more desperate ones than these in her long life, and suffered more heartaches too.

Once the paroxysm was over, Skye kissed her grandmother's creased cheek.

"Thankyou for putting me in my place," she said humbly. "You always do me good, and Mom told me more than once how you always found the right words to say. I bet you didn't know that Philip reckons I got my writing talent from you too."

"Did he now? Then he's not as green as he's cabbage-looking, is he?" Morwen said, chuckling at Skye's blank look. "It's a tease, my love, a Cornish bit of nonsense. And for what it's worth, I always thought he was the only man to hold a candle to you."

"It's worth a lot for me to know it," Skye murmured, and went to bed, a mite less disturbed than before.

*　　*　　*

The Christmas celebrations turned out to be more joyful for Skye than she could have imagined. The family gathered at the church for Sebastian's christening as planned, and then they all decamped to Killigrew House for the evening dinner and present-giving. Some of them would be staying overnight, including Morwen and Skye, and Philip too. And he had the best present ever to give to his wife.

"They're discharging me from hospital next week, and the hospital folk have found me some rooms in Truro. The college bursar has been to see me, and if I feel up to it, I'm starting back to work on a part-time basis in a couple of weeks' time."

"That's absolutely wonderful," she said, hugging him, her eyes shining. And doing her best to hide her miffed feeling too, that all this had been happening without her knowing any of it. If they had known she was his wife, it would presumably have been so different.

But to all intents and purposes, she was only a fiancée, and the engagement had been so long-lasting, the family must be speculating among themselves if that was all it was ever going to be.

"Philip, shouldn't we tell them about us soon?" she urged him under cover of the general merriment at the house. "Not now, of course, with Sebastian holding court like a disgusting little princeling, but *soon*?"

He kissed her cheek. "Let me get used to these new arrangements first, darling," he said. "After all this time away from teaching I feel as if I'm being thrown to the wolves, but of course I'll want you to see my rooms, and help me choose some curtains and womanly things like that."

She suddenly realised how nervous he was. It certainly wasn't Philip's style to be referring to her choices as *womanly things*, nor to think that domestic doings were going to be of paramount importance to her. He *was* being thrown to the wolves, and she had to let him do things at his own pace, however frustrated it

202

left her. But since he intended renting rooms outside the college, she could visit him frequently.

In that alone, it would be like old times, the way it used to be . . . and she was full of optimism as she raised her glass to the appallingly spoiled infant who was now puking all over the silk-covered sofa to his parents' indulgent smiles.

And much later, to her incredible joy and surprise, she sensed that her door handle was being turned during the silent hours of the night. She held her breath for a moment, and then she felt her beloved slide into bed beside her, and Philip's arms were holding her as close as she had ever dreamed of him holding her all these long, lonely months.

And if their love-making was slower and less frenetic that it used to be, it was none the less beautiful and emotional and so very dear to her.

"Welcome home, my darling," she whispered silently into his shoulder, knowing that because of their self-enforced denial of their marriage, he must leave her before morning, but content enough to have the memories of this special Christmas night to hold on to.

Primmy had other ideas about the sense of her daughter keeping such a secret. Her Christmas letter didn't arrive until the middle of January, and her words were crisp and to the point.

'You're completely mad, my girl. Your father and I can see no reason why there shouldn't be a proper celebration of your marriage to Philip. Are you ashamed of it? With Mammie's failing health, don't you think she'll be itching to acknowledge Philip as her grandson-in-law? Unless he's not the paragon you've always led us to believe, of course – and knowing you, I can't think that's the case. So do the proper thing and bring it out in the open, Skye, while Mammie can still enjoy seeing the shock and disbelief on the rest of their faces at having known the truth of it all the time!'

Reading her mother's words, Skye laughed a little and wept

a little, knowing she was right. But she wasn't the only one to be considered. It had to be a decision that both of them made, and she questioned Philip seriously about it when she showed him Primmy's letter.

By then they had spent many hours in Philip's rooms. The secret meetings produced their own excitement and eroticism, and his physical energy had returned to their mutual satisfaction, but Skye longed to be with him all the time. So far, their marriage had been a completely unnatural one, and they were still leading separate lives.

It wasn't right, and she still didn't know how she had been patient enough to let it go on so long. By now Philip was of the same opinion. But once on a treadmill of deceit, it was hard to break away from it. And the timing had to be right.

"Philip, what do you think about our putting an announcement in *The Informer* giving the date of our marriage? We'd have to tell the family first, but perhaps we could send them all a formal announcement card like Sebastian's christening card, since there's bound to be an uproar. What do you think? I know I'm being a chicken in not wanting to face them all . . ."

She stopped, for wasn't she making it sound more of a hole and corner affair than it was? As if she was ashamed? To her relief Philip folded her in his arms.

"It sounds fine, and afterwards we'll do the thing properly and hold a party at New World, with your grandmother's permission. *The Informer* announcement sounds like a good idea to me, and you'll know how to word it."

"That's another thing I wanted to talk to you about," Skye said carefully, pushing her luck. "I'm tired of doing nothing, and I'm wondering if David Kingsley will give me a regular column in the newspaper. What do you think?"

She held her breath. She had been independent all her life, and never had to answer to anyone, but she needed Philip's approval on this. Women were already doing all kinds of things they never used to do; driving army vehicles; working in munition factories; working on the land, not only digging potatoes and planting cabbages, but doing the heftier jobs that were once the men's prerogative.

Women were proving themselves, and the war had been the catalyst for that, the way war always made changes in people's lives, she thought.

"If it's what you want, then it's fine by me," Philip said now. "I'll be taking up permanent duties at the college at the end of this term, and we can start looking round for a house after the April term finishes. Can you bear to wait until then to make it public?"

Skye thought she could wait for ever, if it hadn't been a contradiction to all her dreams. But at last they had a goal ahead of them, and she could wait a couple more months. She was sure David Kingsley would let her continue with the work she loved, if only on a freelance basis, and she and Philip would soon be together permanently. After April . . .

Morwen approved of their decision, and the party was planned, with no special explanation as to why, though most of the family assumed that Skye and Philip were going to announce the date of their wedding. And not before time, some of them thought, seeing the passionate looks the couple could barely disguise even when they were in company.

In early March there was a unexpected visitor at New World. Morwen and Skye were waiting for Theo's regular Monday morning visit, with the inevitable report of the minutiae of Sebastian's progress, and a report on the clayworks. The spring despatches, so depleted now from the heyday of Killigrew Clay, had been safely sent north. They were holding water, just.

Before Theo arrived, Skye and her grandmother were almost gleefully discussing how the rest of the family were going to take the shock news that Skye and Philip had been married before they went to France.

It was a relief to be able to share the secret with her

grandmother, Skye thought, and there was no one she would rather share secrets with – except Philip.

"There's a young person come to see you, Mrs Wainwright," the housekeeper announced. "He's one of those American servicemen and he says he has some connection with your family. If you don't feel up to seeing un, I'll send him away wi' a flea in his ear. I'm told there's a lot of these so-called Doughboys in Truro now, and probably with nothin' much to do, so they come bothering folk on the flimsiest excuse, if you ask me – and wi' Mr Theo due at any minute, you've got a good enough reason to be rid of un—"

"Thankyou, Mrs Arden," Morwen said, when she could get a word in edgeways. "If he's one of Skye's compatriots and far from home, then of course we'll see him for a few minutes. Show him in, and bring us all some tea, and don't be so cantankerous, woman."

Mrs Arden snorted. "I'm only thinkin' of your best interests," she grumbled, leaving with a swish of her skirts.

Skye laughed at her grandmother. "You do love to stir her up, don't you, Gran? And she may be right. The soldier may be no more than a fly-by-night, trying to get a decent meal with a family instead of eating boring army food all the time."

"And he may not. If he's meant to have some connection with us, I suppose he could be one of your brother's acquaintances, so we should be on our best behaviour."

Skye groaned. "Lord, I hope not. Sinclair mixes with the stuffiest of Washington folk."

She stopped talking as Mrs Arden showed in the tall, rugged-faced young man wearing what she recognised as the American army uniform of a lieutenant. Skye certainly didn't recall ever having seen him before, but he gave her an admiring glance as Morwen bade him sit down.

"I apologise for intruding, Ma'am," he said. "But all my life I've heard about the Tremaynes and the Killigrews in this area, and it took quite a while for me to realise that a lady called Mrs

Wainwright had any connection with them. It was your first name that did it for me, and when I discovered it, I plucked up my courage to come see you."

"Well, I assure you I'm not at all formidable," Morwen told him, waiting for more.

"Oh, but you are, Ma'am," the soldier said. "At least, your reputation is, and if you'll pardon my saying so, the young lady here is just how I imagined you to be when my grandaddy spoke of you and your family."

"Your grandfather?" Morwen said, diverting his attention, when it seemed as if he couldn't take his eyes of the vision of her granddaughter.

She couldn't blame him for admiring Skye. Now that her glossy black hair had grown long again, she was more beautiful than ever, which undoubtedly came from the fulfillment of her relationship with Philip.

But there was something about this newcomer that Morwen couldn't define, something that bothered her . . . some fey sixth sense that she had always been blessed, or cursed, with. And no matter how she tried she couldn't dismiss the feeling.

She didn't know him, but she supposed it could have been some acquaintance of her brother Matt who had gone to America all those years ago, who had mentioned the Tremaynes and the Killigrews and set him on this track of discovery when a chance billeting in a war had sent him to Cornwall.

For a few disorientated seconds Morwen felt the room swim. It was almost as if she knew exactly what the stranger's next words were going to be. He stood up, so that she was forced to look up at him, seeing his smiling face, the rather fleshy lips, and the dark gleam in his handsome eyes and she knew . . .

"Forgive me, Ma'am, but I was so struck with the pleasure of finding you that I was forgetting my manners. My name is Lieutenant Lewis Pascoe."

Past and present came rushing together for Morwen in a single instant. It felt to her as if all the waters of the Atlantic were crushing her at that moment. As if she was one of those tragic victims in the Titanic disaster as the weight of pain threatened to crush her chest and take away her breath and her life.

"Gran, for pity's sake, what's wrong? Please say something. Please don't die!"

She seemed to hear Skye's panicky voice from a great distance. It sounded thin and shrill . . . it sounded like her friend Celia's terrified voice, coming at her from another age. But pretty, foolish Celia had drowned long ago, in the milky waters of a Killigrew Clay pool . . .

The thoughts in her head struggled to make some kind of sense, but it was difficult to think at all when she didn't even know where she was. She thought she had been sitting upright on a chair, but now she was lying crumpled on the Chinese carpet, and four faces were staring down at her.

Her tortured Skye, the anxious Birdie and the resident nurse who was feeling her pulse and thumping her chest, and a stranger she didn't know . . . yet knew only too well.

"What the devil's going on here?" came her grandson Theo's roaring voice. "Get away from her, all of you, and let her breathe. She's trying to say something."

He leaned over Morwen as the others backed away, hearing the authority in his voice. Even the nurse, resentful at him taking charge, stood silently now, after muttering that if her patient had had a stroke, then she was the best one to deal with it, and not some amateur quack.

"A stroke? Is that what you think this is?" Skye whispered to her in agitation.

"Could be. The doctor would have more knowledge about that. Birdie, go and send for him – and fetch a blanket to cover her so she doesn't get chilled," she ordered.

"Right away," Birdie said, clearly distressed, but glad to get away from the reprimand in Theo Tremayne's eyes. Nasty piece of work he was, and always had been, she thought savagely, as she pushed past the American soldier and rushed out to the telephone.

"She's coming round," Theo said. "Can you hear me, Gran?"

"Of course I can hear you. I'm not deaf," Morwen's voice said feebly. She tried to get up, but the nurse insisted that she stay exactly where she was until the doctor came.

In the small silence that followed, accompanied only by Morwen's ragged breathing, the soldier spoke directly to Theo.

"Say, I'm real sorry if it was my visit that upset the lady in any way, Sir. It was certainly not my intention, and I only wanted to make contact because of family connections."

"Who the devil are you anyway?" Theo said, never one to waste time on graciousness.

The soldier drew himself up to his full height, towering over Theo, which Skye could see annoyed her cousin even more.

"Lieutenant Lewis Pascoe, Sir—"

"*What*! Pascoe, you say?" Theo bellowed. "Don't you know that's a bastard name that's never mentioned in my grandmother's presence?"

"Theo, how could he possibly know?" Skye said nervously, appalled at the swiftness of his rage, and wondering from the way the ropy veins stood out on Theo's forehead now, if he was going to be the next one to collapse. She knew she should recognise the name as well, but somehow she couldn't.

She had been told something about a man with that name that was too terrible to remember . . . it had to do with a visit she had made to the witchwoman on the moors, Skye thought desperately. But because of the narcotic drug old Helza had given her, and her own desire to forget, most of the horrific memories of what she had been told that day were as totally wiped from her mind.

"Look, I'd better go," the soldier said, backing away. "The lady's ill, and my presence is obviously not helping."

"Hindering, more like. And if you take my advice, you'll stay well away from any member of the Tremayne and Killigrew family. You're not wanted here," Theo said savagely, as Birdie returned with a blanket to cover Morwen who had regained a considerable amount of colour by now, to everyone's relief.

But Theo's last words had obviously riled the soldier.

"Why the hell not – beg pardon, ladies," he said angrily. "The Killigrews were my kin, and Mrs Wainwright's first husband, Ben Killigrew, was my grandaddy's cousin. Is this the way the Cornish folk treat strangers? I'd heard they were an insular race, but I hadn't expected such a welcome."

"No one who bears that name will get a welcome here."

Morwen's voice took them all by surprise. It was slightly stronger now, and almost venomous. She pushed aside Nurse Jenkins' restraining hand, and propped herself up against the sofa where she had been sitting previously.

Lewis Pascoe's face took on a dark red hue, and Skye felt sorry for him. She didn't know the full reason for her grandmother's violent reaction to the soldier, but there was surely only one person who could produce this amount of hatred. She was slowly remembering the witchwoman's tale of the girl who had drowned herself after being raped and left with a child. The witchwoman had told her more than she had gleaned from Morwen, or the old newspaper reports at *The Informer*, and it was all coming back to her now.

The name too, was one she had seen before in the family's tangled history. So this soldier had to be related to the man who had raped Morwen's dearest friend. But to harbour such violent hatred all these years was frightening. Skye had never considered how such hatred could fester in a person's soul for so long without forgiveness.

But she had never known the closeness and friendship of two simple bal maidens who had lived in a very different world from the one she knew, and she conceded that too.

"I'll show you out," she said to Lewis Pascoe now, as he

210

seemed unable to know what to do. It wasn't his fault, and she felt a brief pity for him. He had apparently come here in all good faith, presumably knowing nothing about his namesake's part in the turbulent family history she was still discovering here. To be met with such rage must be devastating to him.

"I never meant to upset her so, and you surely must believe that." He told Skye in great agitation once they were outside the house. "You don't sound Cornish any more than I do, Miss, but you must be one of the family, so do you have any ideas on it?"

"A few," Skye said reluctantly. "But I never gossip about my family business."

"I've been trying to explain that it's *my* business too. My grandaddy was Ben Killigrew's cousin. His name was Jude Pascoe, and he went to America years ago with one of the lady's brothers, Matthew Tremayne—"

"So it *was* him," Skye said unthinkingly. She was completely shaken now, trying to unravel the truth of it all in an instant. "Matt Tremayne is *my* grandfather, so we're – we're sort of related, I guess."

She wasn't keen to acknowledge it, after seeing the effect that his name had had on Morwen. Then she saw the doctor's car approaching, and brought the awkward discussion to an end.

"I'm sorry, but I have to go inside now."

"But we must meet again. I feel that you and I have much to discuss, if only to untangle the mess that I don't understand at all. Look, I haven't seen these clayworks yet. Couldn't we meet later – please? I have a boneshaker of a car, so maybe we could go see them together?"

All Skye's instincts told her to refuse. The guy's hand was on her arm, and she didn't want it there. He had a roguish look in his eyes that she didn't like. He certainly wasn't oafish like Desmo Lock, but she'd met his sort before. Charming, dangerous, sexually attractive . . . yet he was right. They both had a stake in this family, and there were still things neither of them understood.

211

"I'll meet you at Killigrew Clay around three o'clock this afternoon," she said swiftly. "Clay Two is deserted, and you'll find it easily enough. Then we'll talk to someone who may clarify things for us both."

She went into the house with the doctor, her heart beating sickly, still wondering why she had agreed to it. Philip wouldn't like it, but then Philip wasn't going to know. Morwen wouldn't like it either, but there was no way she could question her on her reaction at present. And Skye had been born curious and questioning.

But there was one person who knew everything. Her so-called witch-sisters had passed down the knowledge to her, and she would know why the name of Pascoe was so evil to Morwen. Helza would know, and she must be made to tell, without dulling the senses of her listeners as she had done so effectively the last time Skye had spoken with her. This time, Skye intended her brain to be clear.

"How is the lady now?" Lewis Pascoe greeted her when she reached Clay Two that afternoon to find him already waiting.

"The lady is my grandmother, and she is recovering," Skye said crisply. "But she suffered a slight stroke, and her speech has since become impaired."

"Say, I'm sorry to hear that—"

"Are you?"

"Well, of course! Do you think I intended this to happen? What kind of a guy do you think I am?"

"I don't know," Skye said slowly. "What's more to the point, what kind of a guy was your grandfather?"

"The best, as far as I'm concerned, which makes it even more bewildering to meet with all this hatred. And by the way, what *is* your name?"

"Skye. Skye Tremayne."

"That's the prettiest name for a very beautiful young lady, if I may say so."

"I'd rather you didn't. I'm not in the mood for compliments. Now, shall we take a walk over the moors, Lieutenant? There's someone I want you to meet."

He snorted, his dark eyes flashing at the rebuff. "Hell, I'm not going to move one step until you cut all this British formality and call me Lewis. We're *cousins*, aren't we?"

"I guess so," she said slowly. "Lewis it is then."

The waft of herbs and indefinable cooking smells came towards them long before they reached the hovel Skye pointed out.

"Good God, what kind of a person lives in such a dump?" Lewis exclaimed.

"Some say she's a witch. Others say she's just a harmless old woman who mixes potions and herbal cures for any gullible person who asks for them."

She watched him closely as she spoke, but his face gave nothing away. If he had any idea what she was talking about, he was being as close as a clam, she thought. And she wished she could remember the details properly. As it was, they merely swam about in her brain like water-colour memories, indistinct and unclear.

Helza must be persuaded to repeat it all while her senses were fully alert, Skye thought determinedly. There must be no herbal concoctions, no drugs. Then they would both learn of the tragedy of the past and the part their forebears had taken in it, and try to relate it to the present.

Chapter Fourteen

Skye sat down gingerly on the edge of a stool. She just managed to resist the urge to gather her skirts around her and make herself as small as possible in the stifling atmosphere of the cottage, added to by the vile-smelling stuff Helza smoked in her clay pipe. Lewis Pascoe seemed to have got over his initial distaste, and stared around with interest now.

"Jeez, I never knew such places existed," he exclaimed.

Skye saw Helza cock her head on one side and study him.

"You bain't from these parts, are you? Mebbe you've come from the same place as the pretty maid here."

"I'm American," Lewis said. "Lieutenant Lewis Pascoe of the United States Army, to be precise."

"Oh-ho, so now I see why you've come. You want to know if 'tis true what I told missie here, do 'ee?"

Skye leaned forward, anxious not to offend the old biddy.

"I've told him nothing, Helza, because I can't remember any of it clearly. You gave me a drink, remember?"

"You needed it, as I recall, to steady your nerves."

But not to wipe out all memory of certain things that once occurred in my family, thought Skye in annoyance.

"Can I offer 'ee both a drink now?" she wheezed.

"No thankyou!" Skye said quickly. "But will you tell us again, Helza – the things you told me then? About ..." she dragged the memories to the front of her mind as best she could, "about the old Larnie Stone, wasn't it?"

When the old witch said nothing, she became more agitated, her words rushing out.

"It was to do with two young girls and a potion, and seeing the faces of their lovers at midnight."

"Go on," Helza cackled. "The memories are still in your head, my pretty, and you don't need me to bring 'em out."

"But I do," Skye snapped. "I want you to tell my cousin exactly what you told me. He has a right to know as much as I do, and my telling would be biased."

"So it would," Helza agreed, glancing at the now silent Lewis. "Well then, how do it feel, my fine young feller, to know that one o' yourn despoiled a young girl and caused her to drown herself?"

"One of *mine*?"

"Oh ah. 'Twere one o' yourn all right that forced hisself on her. Name of Jude Pascoe, the felon were, and this here pretty maid's granny witnessed every gory bit o' the agony t'other 'un suffered because of the raping and the shame of it, afore she drowned herself."

"You lying old witch!" Lewis burst out furiously. "You should be hounded out of here for weaving such evil tales."

"It's the truth, Lewis," Skye cut in. "All of it. Every word of it is true."

And with every word old Helza bit out in her hoarse, lascivious croak, the memory of the first time Skye had heard it came surging back, every bit as horrific as it was then, and just as convincing.

Without warning, Lewis knocked over the stool he had been sitting on and stormed out of the hovel. Skye stared at the old woman dumbly, realising she had no coins to give her, but it seemed that Helza wanted nothing.

"He'll take time to adjust to it," she said complacently, just as if she'd told him no more than a fairy tale. "You should never have brought him here if you didn't want him to know. Just beware of one thing, pretty maid. Don't let history repeat itself."

216

"What do you mean?" Skye said, starting to back away as the stink of the old crone's clay pipe became even more excruciatingly rank. She heard Helza cackle again.

"If 'ee don't know by now what 'tis like to lie beneath a man, missie, then mind you don't find out by lying beneath a wrong 'un, that's all."

Skye turned abruptly, needing to get out of the cottage and breathe clean air before the overpowering stink of the place overcame her. She ran outside, to see Lewis stalking away from her, back in the direction of the sky tips, more menacing than usual without the sunlight glinting on them, like great grey-white sentinels crouching over the clayworks and the gouged-out earth and murky clay pools.

"Lewis, *wait!*"

He stood still, not turning around, until she caught up with him. Then he whirled on her.

"You should have warned me. Christ, that filthy old crone got as much excitement out of the telling as if she was being groped. And you believe it, do you?"

His crudity didn't shock her. She had heard and seen enough in the hospitals in France to know how men hit out verbally when they were hurt and shocked, and impotent to do anything else.

"Of course I believe it," she said quietly. "And so must you. Can't you see that it explains why Granny Morwen was so shocked at hearing your name? Her friend Celia was more than a sister to her. What Jude Pascoe did to her was unforgiveable."

She carefully avoided calling Jude his grandfather, distancing him from the act that was still so despicable and unforgettable to Morwen, even after all these years.

They walked on rapidly without speaking, until the gaunt, holed standing stone reared up in front of them.

"Is this the place then?" Lewis almost snarled. "Is this where I'm meant to believe that that harmless old man I loved until he died, raped a young girl?"

217

"This is the Larnie Stone," Skye said woodenly. "They drank a witchwoman's potion and circled the stone at midnight like they were told, and Ben Killigrew and Jude Pascoe were waiting for them."

"How convenient. And you don't think these flighty young dames encouraged them?"

He oozed sarcasm and scorn, and Skye flinched. If Morwen had been vindictive over what had happened, then so was he in defence of his grandfather. And she was here alone with him, with Helza's warning suddenly ringing in her ears.

"I don't know. I wasn't there, any more than you were. I only know what I've been told."

"And maybe they weren't the only dames ready for a bit of fun, eh? There's nobody to see, honey."

He suddenly grabbed her to him, almost winding her. The stink of Helza's cottage was still on him, and to Skye it was as if he was the evil one, he was Jude, and she was Celia, reincarnated, and it was all about to happen again . . .

She wrenched herself away from him, her eyes full of terror, forcing the images away.

"How *dare* you!" she screamed. "My grandmother was right to mistrust you. You're tarred with the same brush as the other one, and if my husband gets wind of what's happened here, he'll kill you."

She stopped abruptly as he grabbed her left hand.

"There's no wedding ring, sweetheart, only a token—"

"It's here." She pulled the chain from her neck and thrust the gold wedding ring under his nose.

"What's this? Another secret in the family? Does the old lady know about it, I wonder?" he taunted.

"She knows. And I advise you to forget this conversation ever happened. Otherwise, well, you don't know these clayers like I do. They're a violent bunch with a tradition of protecting their own, and if it was known that Skye Tremayne had had trouble with a soldier, I wouldn't give a red cent for your chances.

Things have happened on these moors that have no logical explanation, like old buildings being burned to the ground and nothing found of the occupant but his boots."

She didn't know why she was saying these things, nor why her voice had dropped to a husky, sing-song quality, as if someone other than herself was saying the words. She stood there defiantly, old Morwen Tremayne to the life, some might say, her black hair streaming in the wind, her blue eyes flashing with anger, her voice accusing and threatening.

To her amazement, Lewis Pascoe began to back away.

"You're bloody mad!" he shouted. "You're in cahoots with that black-hearted bitch back there, and if you're married at all, it must be to the devil. This family will hear no more from me, and the sooner I'm shipped out of here, the better."

Skye sank to her knees as he ran over the moors the way they had come, presumably to drive like a crazy man in his boneshaker car and back to his billets. For one awful, terrible moment, she felt a fleeting hope that he might lose control of the car and go hurtling into oblivion, to pay for all the pain his ancestor had caused Morwen, and Celia.

Even though the thought was gone almost before it was formed, she shook uncontrollably. Because for that black-hearted instant, she knew it was in her power, as it was in everyone's, to think evil thoughts, and to wish someone dead. And she had never done so in her life before.

She gathered her senses together and ran back over the moors to the deserted Clay One, and her own car. There was no sign of Lewis Pascoe's. There was no sign of anyone, and she wandered restlessly around the silent clayworks, unwilling to go home yet, and trying to piece together what it must have been like when it hummed with activity and workers.

She closed her eyes, imagining Morwen and Celia, and her great-grandmother Bess, and a host of other bal maidens in their white aprons and bonnets, made even whiter by the constant clay dust. Whole families had spent their lives working for Killigrew

Clay – lived and died for it, she thought, remembering the *Killigrew Pals Battalion.*

It was too big to be destroyed by the lust of one evil man, or those who had sought to take control of it by other means. No strikes, disasters or losses had completely ruined it, and none would. There was something fundamental and enduring about a livelihood that had existed for generations. Theo and his little son, whose precocious antics she so scorned, would see to that. It was humbling . . .

"Skye, what the devil are you doing? I've been looking everywhere for you."

Her muddled thoughts were shattered as she heard a voice calling to her. She scrambled to her feet, brushing down the dirt and dust from her skirts, and saw Philip hurrying over the uneven ground towards her. He caught her in his arms.

"Are you hurt?"

"Is Granny Morwen all right? Has anything happened?" she said through trembling lips, ignoring his question.

"Your grandmother is tolerably well, though I had a shock when I went to the house to discover what had happened. But what are you doing up here? I've searched everywhere."

She leaned against him. He was so blessedly normal, so quickly regaining strength and vitality now, at a time when she felt as if her bones had turned to water and there was nothing substantial inside her at all.

"Philip, I'm perfectly well," she said shakily. "I was just so upset after Granny Morwen's attack that I had to get away and be alone. It was cowardly of me, I know—"

"No, it wasn't. You've had a hell of a few years, as we all have. You've seen worse sights than any young lady should ever see, and eventually, something had to crack. But now it's time to go, Skye. Your car will be safe here until tomorrow. You're coming home with me."

Home to New World, of course, because that was where she needed to be. She felt safe there. She had gone through a war, and she had never felt quite as disorientated and afraid then, as she did now. Lewis Pascoe had done that.

"What happened? I know about the visitor," Philip asked as he drove them slowly home. "Mrs Arden told me some of it, and how he upset your grandmother."

"I'll tell you everything, Philip," she murmured. "But not now. I'm only just coming to terms with it all myself."

He glanced at her, seeing the pinched look around her mouth. He already knew more than she suspected. Theo Tremayne hadn't been reticent in explaining who the visitor was, and his connection with the family. And the more he learned about them, the more intrigued he was by the bonds that had kept this huge family together, and dragged them apart.

"Stop the car, Philip!" she said suddenly. "Quickly!"

Almost before he did so, she had wrenched open the door and stumbled out, retching violently and spewing bile over the ground. He was beside her, holding her, while she sobbed helplessly.

"I'm sorry, and I know I'm being a soft-ball," she gasped. "I've just always hated being sick. Mom used to say I'd better get over it if I'm ever going to have a baby, since she was sick every inch of the way with Sinclair and me."

She was gabbling, because the truth of it was only just beginning to dawn on her. It wasn't the first time she had felt so nauseous, but because of her all-time aversion to the indignity of it, she had always managed to fight it down until now. It had been happening for a couple of weeks, and other things that should have happened, *hadn't*. And she had never even considered why . . .

"Are you saying what I think you're saying?" Philip asked her slowly, still holding her close to his chest as the nausea subsided and her colour returned.

"I think what I'm saying," she said shakily, when she could speak, "is that we'd better get those belated marriage announcements out pretty damn quickly, before the whole

221

family is scandalised when I produce a little cousin for Sebastian."

She tried to make a small joke of it, because it was suddenly scary to think she might be carrying another human being inside her. And she didn't even know for certain if it was true. Except in her heart, and in the feelings of new life that were suddenly surging inside her, blotting out the past, giving them a future that was theirs alone.

She looked up at Philip, searching his face.

"Is it . . . Philip, it *is* all right, isn't it?" she said, suddenly hesitant. "We always said we wanted children, but we never said when."

He gave a joyous laugh. "It still amazes me that it's never happened before now, my passionate little darling! And if there was anything to give your grandmother an incentive to get well again, I'm damn sure this is it. You know how she dotes on you."

"But I don't think we should tell her just yet," Skye said, guilty that she had totally forgotten Morwen in the intimacy of these last few minutes. "She's had enough to cope with just recently."

Even though Skye knew that Morwen would have understood completely. But even good news could be a shock, and they had to choose the right moment for this secret to be shared, the best secret of all, because the dynasty would continue.

In any case, the April party would have to be abandoned, with Morwen's health so uncertain. She would need time to recover from her stroke, and Skye refused to think that it could end in any other way. To her, Morwen was still invincible, even though she knew how mortal all of them were.

What was more urgent now, was for Skye and Philip to carefully work out the wording for the marriage announcements and then post the cards to all members of the family. Once it was done, Skye went to *The Informer* offices in Truro and asked to see David Kingsley. He greeted her more warmly than of old.

"This is an unexpected pleasure, Skye. I'm delighted with the articles you've been sending in recently, and happy for you to continue with a regular women's column, as you've hinted more than once." He paused. "I presume that *is* what you came to see me about?"

"Not entirely," she said, feeling her face flush. "I've come to ask if you would place this announcement in the paper, David. I've worded it very carefully as you will see, and if it could be included in one of my normal pieces of copy, it would reach the people most interested."

He took the envelope from her and took out the paper inside, scanning it quickly in his editorial way.

"Good God!" he exclaimed. "Skye – is this true?"

"Well, of course it is. It's hardly something I would invent, is it?"

"And you and your – well, I can hardly call him your fiancé now – have actually been married all this time?"

"That's right. But now that Philip's recovered from his injuries, we see no reason to keep it a secret any longer."

"So why did you?" he said, with the newspaperman's nose for a story.

She lifted her shoulders helplessly. "It seemed the right thing to do at the time. There was a great to-do about married women not going to war, and being together for part of the time was better than not being together at all."

He looked at her thoughtfully and then at the brief announcement she had handed him.

"Then I suggest that you write this in an entirely different way. It's far too formal a statement, and you should capitalise on the romance of it, Skye. Make it appeal to the readers as being the love story of the war, including your husband's slow return to health. Readers will love it."

"You think so? I'm not a romantic writer."

"But you're an emotional one, and your sympathetic reports meant a lot to the folk at home while you were in France. They'll love you for confiding how your own story unfolded now that you've become one of their own. Talk it over with your husband, if you must, and then come back to me, and I'll be delighted to run it."

"I don't need to talk it over with anyone. I'll do it," she said decisively, knowing Philip would approve. The idea of it charmed her as much as his casual remark that she had become one of their own. And it wasn't as if she intended giving away any intimate secrets of their lives. Some things were *too* private.

She had one more errand to run in Truro before meeting Philip once his college duties were over. It was a while since she had seen Albert and Rose, and she felt guiltily that she should have made more of an effort, as Rose was ailing now. They had been informed of Morwen's steady progress, and Albie had visited her when he could, though Skye had no idea whether or not Theo had revealed to any other family member the true cause of her stroke. She supposed so, though it was never spoken about now. But this was one announcement card she wanted to deliver herself.

"Skye, what brings you here? Is all well with Mother? I telephoned yesterday, and the nurse's report sounded reassuring," Albie greeted her, momentarily anxious as he drew her inside the studio and kissed her briefly on both cheeks.

Very continental-arty-farty, she thought irreverently, but at least he seemed genuinely pleased to see her.

"There's nothing wrong. And how about Rose?" she asked, as they climbed the stairs to the rooms above. He shrugged.

"She copes as best she can, but Rose and illness make poor bedfellows," he said eloquently. "She doesn't get out much, and she bemoans the fact that she's putting on weight."

That much was obvious as soon as Skye saw her. Once a pretty woman, Rose's petulance showed up all too well in her fleshy face now, but she brightened as soon as she saw the visitor. Presumably she had forgotten Albie's penchant

for the Tremayne girls, Skye thought cynically, now that he
was obliged to give her all his attention.

"So what brings you here, my dear?" Rose said, echoing
Albie's words, once the obligatory details of her condition had
been exhausted.

"I've got news. At least, it will be news to you, but not to
us, to Philip and me, that is."

As she floundered, Albie laughed. "You don't mean that you
two have actually set the date at last?"

"Yes, we have. September the first, actually – 1915."

She handed them their announcement card and waited until
they had read it. Nobody spoke for a moment, and then Albert's
face went its occasional dull hue.

"My dear girl . . . all this time . . . for almost three years you
and that man have been married?"

"Me and Philip, yes. Or is it Philip and I? I never can remember
the correct way."

"Does your grandmother know about this? And your mother?
Does *Primmy* know?"

Skye caught her breath, hearing the small softening in his
voice as he spoke her name. After all this time he still loves
her with a special kind of love, thought Skye. A very special
kind of love that could never be fulfilled . . . she was suddenly
sorry for him, understanding and forgiving him.

"Mom and Daddy knew right away," she said gently. "And
we left Granny Morwen our marriage certificate when we
enlisted and went to France. We wanted to be together, you
see, even though we couldn't be *properly* together, since we
told no one else. And the longer it went on, the more difficult
it became to let people know. But now we think the time
is right. We intended to put a formal announcement in the
newspaper, but David Kingsley wants me to write it up as
a romantic story for *The Informer* readers. What do you
think?"

If it was incongruous to be asking him, she no longer cared.

225

He had loved her mother, and he knew the pangs and torments of a frustrated love. He kissed her forehead.

"I think it's a lovely idea, and I'm sure Rose does too," he said, drawing her into their circle. "And what of the rest of the family?"

Skye shivered. "They'll all be receiving cards like this one in a day or so. I wanted you to know first, since you were always closest to Mom, and I daresay there will be varying reactions. But I know Mom and Daddy will be relieved it's out in the open at last."

"Primmy couldn't abide secrets," Albie nodded. "Not unless they were her own, of course."

And however enigmatic that statement was, they all chose to ignore it as Rose set about busily making them all tea.

The most predictable reaction came from Luke. A few days later he came roaring into New World like a raging bull, slamming the card on the hall table and bellowing for Skye.

"For the Lord's sake, man, don't you know there's a sick woman in the house?" Nurse Jenkins snapped, having no fears of a ranting preacher like this one.

"Don't speak to me about the Lord, woman. What was this chit doing, getting wed without the sanctity of a proper church service and the Lord's blessing?"

Skye came out of the sitting room quickly on hearing the rumpus, glowering at her uncle.

"I did have the Lord's blessing, Uncle Luke, and if I didn't have yours, then I'm sorry, but Philip and I are just as surely married as any other couple you ever droned over."

She held her breath, wondering if anyone had ever dared speak to him like that before. But she didn't care. She was a married woman, and she wore her wedding ring with pride now. The people who mattered didn't censure her.

Emma had telephoned, twittering with delight at the news, and so had Charlotte's girls, back from France now, and thrilled

226

to think it had all been *going on*, as they put it, right under their noses. Theo simply told her it was a good thing, and Betsy added her congratulations, and everyone else was too far away to have given their reactions yet.

Morwen was improving daily, and her speech had almost returned to normal again. It was easy to be lulled into believing that this strong woman was going to make a perfect, miraculous recovery, even though the doctor had warned them that a relapse and a second stroke was always possible. So the sooner Skye got shot of this one, the better, she thought, as Luke glowered back at her, then his pompous face broke into a reluctant grimace of acceptance.

"Well, since it was going to happen sooner or later, I daresay there's no harm done. Just so long as it didn't upset your grandmother."

He'd left it long enough to think of her, thought Skye indignantly. She smiled back sweetly.

"Actually, Granny Morwen has known all the time, and her blessing was the most important one to us. Oh, and didn't you come to see her, Uncle Luke? She'll be happy to know you pray for her as well as the rest of your flock."

Luke eyed her silently for a minute.

"You're your mother's daughter all right," he said finally. "Primmy were always a sparky maid, with a tongue like quicksilver when it suited her. You, and Primmy, and your grandmother – like three peas in a pod in more ways than one."

"You couldn't have given me a nicer compliment, Uncle Luke," she said, knowing he hadn't meant it that way at all, and completely flummoxing him again.

Philip had been invited to dinner that evening, as he was most days now, and Morwen said she had something of importance to suggest to them both. She was well enough to come downstairs for varying periods of time now, and with her returning speech she hardly stopped talking, but to Skye and all of them, she would never be quite the same again.

There was pain around her still-vivid blue eyes, and she seemed to have shrunk in stature, as well as in spirit. Lewis Pascoe had done that. He had come calling so innocently, and he had torn an old lady's heart apart so disastrously. But for all that she lived so much in memories now, Morwen was still in control of her faculties.

"You'll be looking for a proper home soon, I take it," she said to Skye and Philip now. "I won't want my granddaughter to be living in miserable cramped rooms in Truro."

"We shall be looking for a house soon, Mrs Wainwright," Philip agreed.

"And you can stop using that ridiculous name now that we're properly related, young man. Call me Morwen if you can't manage the Granny half of it. And you need look no further, if you've no objection to my proposal."

They waited, as she subdued a cough with difficulty.

"Can I get you something, Gran?" Skye asked anxiously, but she waved her aside at once.

"A bit of a cough won't kill me, girl. Now then, since it's high time this house rang to the sound of children's laughter again, and since you two are the best prospects of filling it, I want you both to come and live here. There's plenty of room, and you can have your own part of the house and do with it what you like until I'm gone. In any case, it'll belong to Skye then."

Skye gasped as the implications of the words sank in.

"Oh no, Gran! There'll be such a fuss in the family if you leave me this lovely house – and anyway, I don't want to talk about such things, it's bad luck—"

"Why? Do you think I'm going to live forever?" Morwen said dryly. "Now you listen to me, girl, and don't go all soft and sentimental on me. None of 'em want to live here, and they're all settled nicely elsewhere. 'Tis the right order of things, love – and you'll be wanting to fix up a nursery well before time too."

Philip's hand reached out for Skye's, but she shook her head. Seeing it, Morwen gave a small smile.

"Did you think I didn't guess? You may have kept it from the others, but there's a bloom on you, Skye, that only comes from one cause."

"But we hardly know for certain ourselves yet," she murmured, feeling her face go hot. "And the sickness I had only troubles me occasionally now, so maybe it was just a stomach upset."

"What's wrong with you, girl? Don't you want this babby?" Morwen said, her voice sharp.

"Of course I do," Skye said softly. 'I'm just superstitious enough not to hope too much until I'm sure."

"Then be sure. I've seen enough in my time to know when a woman's flowering, so what do you say to my proposal? Do you come and live here?"

Skye glanced at Philip, knowing it had to be his decision as much as hers. Hers was already made, she realised. She adored this house, and she had done so from the moment she stepped inside. But if Philip objected to these Tremayne womenfolk dictating the terms . . .

Neither of them were Tremaynes any more, Skye reminded herself swiftly. Morwen was a Wainwright and she was a Norwood. But she knew that none of that counted in the real order of things, as Morwen put it. They were still Tremayne women, strong and fiery, and ready to fight to the death for what was theirs.

She saw Philip move around the table to her grandmother. He knelt at her side, took her hand in his and raised it to his lips. The gesture sent the tears stinging to Skye's eyes.

"We accept your gift with gratitude and love, Morwen, and may you live to see *all* our children."

Morwen smiled gently. "Mebbe I'll just settle for this one,

229

dar. So start making whatever changes you want in the house, for I'm eager to have my family under my roof again and for things to be settled."

"She's a marvel, isn't she?" Skye murmured as she lay in her husband's arms.

The room they shared at New World that night was Skye's own, but now that the idea was taking hold, they were already making plans to convert the whole of the west wing for their own use. The room they would use for the nursery had a wonderful view of the distant sea, and Skye was already picturing the fittings and furniture, and the child who would nestle inside the crib.

And thanking God that her husband was not stuffy enough to worry his head over the fact that when her grandmother died, New World would belong to her.

Chapter Fifteen

Family members responded to the belated news of the marriage with gifts and letters, but Skye was even more touched to discover how many congratulatory notes and small gifts began arriving at *The Informer* offices. Once her revised article had appeared in her new *Women's Column*, the romance of what many saw as an elopement obviously appealed to local folk, finding this news a welcome diversion from the reports from the Front.

David Kingsley had been right, thought Skye, and perhaps it was time to write about more leisurely and normal activities to cheer up her readers, as this miserable war dragged on. With America still sending vast numbers of troops to add to their own, it must surely end soon.

There were other dramatic events to take people's attention and distract them, of course. In April, Germany's famous 'Red Baron', Baron Richthofen was killed in the second battle of the Somme, shortly after the Royal Fying Corps and the Royal Naval Air Service merged to become the Royal Air Force.

"Whether such a move means greater efficiency, only time will tell," Kingsley remarked sagely. "But anything to bolster up the public's faith in government strategy is worthwhile. And it gives us something positive to report."

But as soon as something positive happened, something seemed to happen to counter-balance it. The shock news in July that the entire Russian royal family had been murdered hardly made a ripple in some country newspapers, but Kingsley insisted

231

again that anything to stir the public's apathy was newsworthy, and it was reported with due solemnity.

Skye's condition was starting to be evident by then, and the closest members of the family had all been told. To her relief, the early nausea had passed, and she blossomed visibly. And as if determined to defy the doctor's private predictions and outlive the lot of them, Morwen rallied and took an active delight in helping the couple plan the west wing of New World, which quickly became home to them both.

"What does your mother have to say in her letter?" Philip asked her, when he found her smiling over Primmy's latest epistle on his return from college one afternoon.

"Oh, you know Mom," she said without thinking, and then looked at him in dismay. "No, of course you don't, and that's something I regret so much, Philip. Mom would love you."

"Well, maybe we'll go and visit them once things become settled, and then we can show off their new grandson to them."

"Grandson? What makes you so sure it will be a boy?" Skye said, laughing.

"Hell," he said fiercely. "We need *somebody* to offset the beastly Sebastian. He grows more obnoxious every day."

"Just be glad you don't *see* him every day."

Since Betsy had taken to bringing him to New World quite frequently of late, Skye spoke with feeling. Betsy was of the impression that everyone adored her son, and that Morwen must see as much of him as possible. And she was far too dense, in Skye's opinion, to notice how often Morwen retired to her room for a well-deserved rest while the two of them were here.

By the end of August the nursery was almost finished, and the old crib that had once seen service for all Morwen's children had been repainted and made respectable again.

"The babe should have something newer," Morwen told her. "This old thing is falling to bits."

"Your daddy made it, didn't he? I remember you once told me so, and therefore it's special. It has a history, Granny Morwen, and I want my baby to be a part of that history."

Morwen smiled at her. "You're a very satisfactory grand-daughter, Skye. Just in case I forget to tell you."

She laughed, pink-faced at the unexpected compliment.

"Why? Just because I say all the things you want to hear?"

"No. Because you mean them, dar."

But despite her determination to see Skye's baby born at the end of the year, Morwen knew that time was running out for her. She had had a good life, she told Birdie, and she wouldn't be sorry to see the back of it.

"Don't talk that way. 'Tis tempting fate."

Morwen smiled ruefully. "I'd say fate has already given me a good run, Birdie, and if you believe in such things, then my departing time has already been decided. And get that look of panic off your face. I'm not about to send for the grim reaper just yet, but when he comes I'll be ready."

"You upset folk by talking so," Birdie scowled. "'Tis as if you're seeing things other folk don't see, and you know how I hate that kind of talk."

Morwen put a hand on her companion's arm. "Dear Birdie, there's nothing to fear in anticipating your own death. It's the poor boys who died a violent death in the trenches before their time, whose souls will be wandering the earth."

"For pity's sake, stop these spooky tales, or you'll have me awake all night!" the woman said, white-faced now.

Morwen looked at her in surprise. Anticipating her removal from this life to the next had become one of her interests these days, and it held no fears for her. Not when she was convinced of an afterlife where she would see her Mammie and Daddy again, and her beloved brother Sam, and the two husbands she had adored, and sweet, sweet Celia . . . but of course, not everyone saw things the way she did.

"I'm sorry, Birdie," she said, contrite now. "You know I don't mean to upset you. But you should make plans for the future too. I'll not live for ever, and you must have a family of your own, or friends. What will you do when I'm gone?"

Birdie looked at her speechlessly. "You're *heartless*, that's what you are, and I don't know why I've stayed here as long as I have. Yes, I've got a family. I've got a brother who'll always take me in, but do you think I want to think of that now, when *you're* all the family I've cared about all these years?"

She rushed out of the room, passing Nurse Jenkins on the way and nearly knocking her over. The nurse pursed her lips as she cocked her head at Morwen.

"I see you've been upsetting her again with your cussedness. What gory tales have you been telling her now to send her rushing for her smelling-bottle?"

"Nothing for you to worry your head about."

Just putting the idea into Birdie's stubborn old head that she would have a future long after Morwen was gone, and that she should think ahead and not be left in the void that Morwen knew must come. Provoking her to remember the existence of the brother who would take her in . . . even though Morwen had every intention of leaving her independently provided for. It had had to be said, but tomorrow she would make up for it by being as sweet as she knew how.

She took the medicine Nurse Jenkins had brought her with a grimace, and waved the woman away, well satisfied with the way she had manoeuvred Birdie into thinking for herself, and knowing that she was gradually getting her own thoughts in order. You had to plan for all the big things in life, and that included your death, and she wasn't shirking that, any more than she had ever shirked anything in her life.

But that wasn't quite true, she admitted, as the sedative medicine began to take effect and allowed her mind to wander on its usual trail into the past. Long ago, when she had come up in the world and married Ben Killigrew, she had shirked telling

234

her adopted daughter Primmy of her own background. She had grandly pretended that they had always been clay bosses, instead of revealing that Morwen and her own mother had been humble bal maidens, working for the Killigrews.

For years she had omitted to tell Primmy and Albie and Walter that they were not her own children, but the children of her dead brother Sam, who had been killed in a dreadful accident when Ben Killigrew's rail tracks had collapsed. She had never been totally honest, and Primmy had hated her for it. Especially when the ghastly young Cresswell Tremayne had been the one to shatter all her vulnerable illusions.

The tangled threads of love and hate ran very closely together, Morwen mused. For of all people in the world, it had been Cresswell who had finally stolen Primmy's heart. Her cousin Cress, whom she adored with such a passion that she couldn't live without him.

And between them they had produced this golden child Skye, who was now the darling of Morwen's heart.

But she had upset Birdie more than she realised, and the companion did something she had always vowed not to do. There was a limit as to how much you should interfere in other folks' lives, but this was something that had to be done.

She wasn't even sure if Skye was aware of just how morbid Morwen's ramblings had become of late, but that was exactly how they appeared to her. And it was time her own daughter knew of it, and of how Birdie fretted and feared for the senses of her old lady. She wasn't a great letter-writer, but the more information she penned to Primmy, the more fluent she became, until she was opening up her heart.

"Your people are leaving it pretty late in the day, aren't they?" Theo asked Skye sarcastically, on hearing the news that a huge number of Americans had registered for conscription by the middle of September. "By the time they get over here the bloody war may well be over and they'll all have to be sent back again."

Skye bridled at once, ignoring the oath for which he didn't bother to apologise. "My Lord, that sounds as if you're actually complaining about the fact that things are looking more hopeful on the Western Front," she snapped.

They didn't like one another and never would, but they had to tolerate one another, for Morwen's sake. And with her journalist background, Skye's own knowledge of the war progress was every bit, if not more up to date than his.

"Of course I'm not complaining."

"Good. Then wouldn't you say that it must do every mother's heart good to learn about our forces' successes in Flanders and that the Germans are in an almighty hurry to retreat out of Belgium now?"

"I read the newspapers too, and if the bastards are rounding up every man between sixteen and sixty to help build up their defences as they retreat, as is reported, then that *ain't* exactly good news, is it, my clever little know-all?"

Skye stared at him unblinkingly.

"Why do you hate me so?" she said at last.

"I don't," he retorted. "I just think folk should stay where they belong, and women should attend to their knitting."

"Tell that to the American servicemen who have already died alongside the British and French – men *and* women," she whipped out, infuriated by the arrogant pomposity of the man. He and Uncle Luke together . . .

As they heard Morwen coming heavily down the stairs to join them, still adamantly refusing to stay in her room all day, she spoke more urgently to Theo.

"Look, can we please put our differences aside for now? Gran hasn't been so well these past few days. It's probably no more than a heavy cold, but with all this talk of an influenza epidemic everywhere, the less upset she has, the better."

"Agreed," Theo said coldly. "I've got some news to cheer her up, anyway. And since you seem to be her chief confidante lately, she'll naturally want you to hear it. Anyway,

I seem to remember you started the whole thing in the first place—"

"What in heaven's name are you talking about, Theo?" Skye said, exasperated as he burbled on.

"You'll find out," he said, annoying her even more.

When Morwen joined them, it was obvious that if this was no more than a heavy cold, it was taking a serious toll on an old lady who had recently suffered a stroke.

"Good God, Gran," Theo said at once, forgetting all else. "You should be in your bed, and I could easily have come to see you there. Has the doctor been to see you?"

She waved him aside irritably. "He's coming later today," she wheezed, her voice thickened and hoarse. "Now let's get down to business and then I'll think about going to bed for an hour to keep Nurse Jenkins and the rest of 'ee happy."

"Well, if you're sure it's not going to tire you."

As she glared as him, he shuffled some papers out of the leather briefcase he always carried so importantly. His next words startled Skye and made Morwen look at him more keenly.

"I've been thinking seriously about turning the abandoned site at Clay Two over to making pottery goods, as we've discussed on more than one occasion. I've taken the liberty of having an architect draw up some plans, as I feel now that we'd do more good for ourselves if we expanded in this way. Clay One can still take care of our present commitments as well as providing the raw material for our needs.

"If and when the European markets open up to us again and the orders get back to normal, the two smaller pits can be brought back into production again. Though I've got my doubts as to just how quick that's going to be. I fancy there's going to be a lot of resentment about consorting with the enemy, even when we're no longer at odds with 'em."

He paused, as neither woman commented. They all knew the old matriarch still had the final say-so on what they did with Killigrew Clay and its environs, and in Theo's opinion the American upstart had far too much influence over her. But she had started this whole idea, he reminded himself, and he continued with his spiel.

"So I'd like you to take a look at these plans, Gran, and tell me what you think. I'm not forgetting the roll-call of dead and wounded and our concern for them, but I doubt that Cornwall's in any danger of being invaded, so I think we should look to the future and put the Clay Two site into better use. I know my father would have approved."

It was his trump card and he knew it. Bringing Walter's presence into the discussion, however obscurely, was a sure way of softening any objections Morwen might have.

Before she could say anything at all, Morwen was racked by a sudden paroxysm of sneezing and coughing, and finally managed to gasp her reply at him.

"You've taken a lot on yourself, Theo, but then, that was always your way. So you'd best show me these plans, if you think I'm capable of understanding 'em."

"Look, Gran, if this is a bad time, perhaps we'd best let it wait," he said, eyeing her in some alarm as she seemed to shrink back in her chair, as if he thought she was going to expire there and then.

"Just get on with it, Theo. Skye can cast her eyes over 'em and give me her thoughts on it as well."

He spread out the plans for the proposed pottery without any more comment, biting his tongue at the blatant inclusion of his cousin in any decisions that had to be made. It was family business, and even though he couldn't deny that she was as much a part of this family as he was, he still wasn't ready to accept her wholeheartedly.

She hadn't been born here, nor born into the clay like himself, and his daddy and grandaddy before him. And ever since Walter had drowned himself, Theo's unreasoning resentment of any

238

family outsider, and this one in particular, had eaten like a cancer into his soul.

The fact that she looked so blooming and beautiful now, with the expected infant giving her a special radiance, did nothing to soften his feelings towards her. Especially when he knew bloody well that his own little Sebastian was turning into a monster, and at six months old he was already starting to rule the roost at Killigrew House, with his ineffectual Betsy doing nothing to curb it.

With an effort, he pushed such savage thoughts out of his mind and got on with the business in hand, explaining the various stages of the construction to the womenfolk. He was rewarded by hearing his cousin confirm his own opinion that the architect had done an excellent job in drawing up these plans to his own specifications.

"So what are you waiting for?" Morwen said, noting that the two of them seemed more in harmony over this little discussion than she normally suspected they were.

She wasn't daft, but she had no intention of playing up to their vanities by censuring them. They would have to get on with it long after she was gone, and she only hoped she'd be able to look down from heaven and see how the pair of them behaved. It was a thought to give her some amusement, but she pushed it aside now at their silent reactions.

"If you think 'tis a viable concern, Theo, then get it started before some other clayworks gets the same notion. Bult and Vine's have never been slow in following up our ideas."

"There's a little more to it than that, Gran," he said, despite his relief at this virtual go-ahead. "It's going to be a huge operation. We have to ensure there's no danger of subsidence from both old tin and clay workings, so surveyors will need to be consulted, according to Harrison Dean. He's the St Austell architect, so he knows the lie of the land, and he's perfectly trustworthy."

"So I should hope," Morwen said dryly. "So – how much?"

The figures he mentioned sounded astronomical, and Skye drew in her breath. Surely it couldn't possibly cost as much – and all this before the new buildings were even constructed?

She presumed Killigrew Clay was a rich enough concern, and it was well-respected for its continuing success over the decades. Other clayworks had come and gone, or been swallowed up in bigger concerns, but there must be a limit on how far the coffers would stretch.

"From the look of these figures, you'd best call in the accountants before you make any move," Morwen said at last.

"But if all is well, you think we can go ahead, then?" He admitted to himself that he could hardly believe his luck at this lack of objection.

"You can go that far," she said, more sharply. "I've already said 'twould seem like a good venture, and I'm too weary to be going over and over it. Providing it don't bankrupt us, then you have my say-so on it. 'Twill be summat for your young 'uns to work toward for when I'm gone."

"Gran, please don't talk like that," Skye said quickly, knowing that Morwen was tiring far more quickly than she cared to show. Nurse Jenkins would be hovering soon, insisting that she go back to bed, and she hoped fervently that the doctor would arrive soon as well.

"Now then, my girl, I've already told Birdie there's nothing wrong in planning your own demise, so don't you be the one to go and spoil my enjoyment of it," she chided Skye with a wicked smile.

She suddenly started to shiver, and Skye moved towards her quickly, wrapping her shawl more closely around her thin shoulders. She was alternately chilled and sweating, and she had admitted that all her bones ached, but insisting that it was all to do with advancing age, and nothing to fret about.

When she regained her breath, she spoke feebly, but pointedly. "Theo, go and leave me to the womenfolk, and sort out your business dealings with my blessing. And don't kiss me, unless you want what ails me, and drive yon Betsy to distraction with worrying that the babby will catch it."

He glanced at Skye, and the look they shared was mutually troubled. For all his bombastic ways, he truly cared for Morwen, she thought, and that went a long way towards tempering her own feelings towards him.

He was long gone before the doctor arrived, and after he had done his examination, and taken some swabs for further tests, he warned them gravely that it could be serious.

"Not the Spanish 'flu'!" Skye burst out, her eyes wide with horror. "I know that millions of people in other parts of the world have died from it, Doctor, but my grandmother never goes anywhere, nor does she meet foreigners!"

"My dear young lady, I would have thought your own intelligence and your knowledge of recent events would have alerted you to the possibility," he said testily. "We have become a global community, Mrs Norwood, and soldiers returning from other parts of the world bring the virus with them. Those who are weakened by age or war privations are easily susceptible, and if it *is* the particularly virulent kind of influenza, your grandmother is not the first case in Cornwall. And at the moment, I'm not prepared to say categorically that it is the so-called Spanish strain."

As he prevaricated, annoyed at her questioning, and obviously unsure of his own diagnosis, Skye already had her grandmother dead and buried in her mind. And all she could think about was that this strong old lady, who had gone through so much in her lifetime, including a stroke, was likely to be struck down by a miniscule virus that no one could see.

"But you can do something for her, can't you? You *must!*"

He sighed, clearly seeing he would be unable to get away until he had satisfied this imperious young woman's demands.

"She's in Nurse Jenkins' capable hands, and apart from giving her sedatives to calm her, influenza must always run its course. Time will tell if she has the strength to combat this disease. But you can do your part—"

"*Anything,*" Skye said passionately. "I'll sit with her day and night, if need be!"

"And much good that will do for you in your condition. You have another life to consider now, Mrs Norwood. You must think of your baby, and Mrs Wainwright wouldn't want you to do otherwise. But since I know it's useless to suggest that you stay away from the sickroom, I suggest that you take turns in relieving the nurse and companion's vigil. At all times you must see that the sickroom is well-ventilated, and that you constantly burn coal tar in a container to ward off any germs for yourselves. She's sleeping peacefully now, but I'll call back later this evening to check on her progress."

And that in itself was an ominous sign, thought Skye.

"There's only thing I'm glad about in this whole worrying business," she told Philip later, once the doctor had been and gone again, and Morwen was uneasily settled for the night.

"And what's that?"

She spoke slowly, hoping he would understand. "The fact that Granny Morwen knows I had decided to stay permanently in Cornwall, without any thought of this house being my legacy – which I still can't believe she truly meant. Cornwall is my home now, and I know she would go more peacefully to her grave, knowing I was always going to be here."

She clapped her hand to her mouth, immediately wishing she hadn't said such a thing. Like Birdie, she was afraid that putting it into words was tempting fate, an omen, a touch of fey presentiment that she didn't want.

Philip hugged her close, feeling her body shake. "Whatever is destined to happen, will happen, darling, and there's nothing you or I can do to stop it."

"That sounds more like me than you! Since when did you become so *Cornish*?" she said, trying to be smart.

"Since sharing your life, I suspect. Don't you know the old adage that people in love begin to share the same thoughts and feelings, and even start to look alike?"

"I thought that only applied to people and their dogs," Skye said, starting to laugh, despite herself.

"Oh well, maybe that's what I'm thinking about," he said airily, "but at least it made you smile. And Morwen won't thank you for walking around on tip-toe with a gloomy face all day. Even Birdie knows that. If you've got any crying to do, then do it in private, darling, the way I suspect she does. But Morwen would be the first to tell you not to waste your tears until it becomes necessary."

"And there speaks the college lecturer," she murmured.

"I'm not trying to lecture you. I'm trying to say, in my clumsy way, that if this illness is going to end Morwen's life-span, then you must let her go, Skye."

The silly comment that she could hardly stop the inevitability of death faded on her lips, because she knew exactly what he meant.

But she had known her grandmother for such a little while, for far too short a time, and in her heart she was already mourning her. She swallowed the lump that had suddenly gathered in her throat.

"You're saying that I must be strong for her," she said slowly, wishing she had the strength of a man. His strength. At that moment, she seemed to have nothing inside her at all.

"I'm saying you should be yourself, sweetheart, because that's all your grandmother ever wanted. You're so like her in every way, and she'll always be proud of you."

She had to be comforted by that, and by the gradual evidence of Morwen's own will to live. Even though there was huge relief when the doctor confirmed that Morwen was not suffering with the Spanish 'flu' that was ravaging countries around the world, she seemed to get no better, nor thankfully, any worse. It seemed as though something stronger than herself

243

was telling her to hold on to the thread of life, however tenuous it became.

Most of the family members who visited at intervals, kept well away from the old lady's bed, to which she was totally confined now, except for short periods of sitting out each day to avoid painful bed-sores.

At the beginning of October, autumn descended on them in crisp, misty mornings that turned the countryside into a ghostly fairyland, and the leaves on the trees changed to a fiery flame and gold. And Freddie and Bradley arrived on a brief visit from Ireland. Their appearance in her room brought a flash of the old spirit to Morwen's eyes.

"What's this?" she wheezed. "I suppose the pair of you have some horse-dealing business to settle, and thought you'd call on the old biddy before it was too late. Is that it?"

"Mother, of course it's not," Bradley blustered, but her brother Freddie chuckled, squeezing his sister's frail hand, his blue eyes as twinkling as ever.

"You know me too well, dar, and you'm right, o' course. Not that we ain't concerned about you, and Primmy's girl's been very obliging in keeping us up to date wi' what's been happening here."

"Including this idea of Theo's for branching out with a pottery," Bradley put in, unable to resist putting in his own objections as usual. "It sounds daft to me, Mother."

"Shut up, Bradley," Freddie said mildly. "Morwen can't be bothered with all that business talk now."

"Since when was I ready to ignore anything to do wi' Killigrew Clay?" she said, perverse as ever. "And 'tis not a daft idea at all, Bradley, so you can just keep your nose out of what don't concern you." She paused. "Unless you're wondering just how much it will concern you when I snuff it."

She had the satisfaction of seeing his face burn with annoyance, and Freddie put a hand on his arm to stop him blustering still more.

"Morwen, the boy meant no such thing, so keep your dander down, there's a love, and tell us a bit more about this pottery idea, if you've the breath for it."

The middle-aged 'boy' scowled, but decided to leave them to it. If any of them thought he was sizing up New World or the clayworks with any idea of cashing in on it after his mother died, they were on the wrong track. He had no more desire to come back here to live than fly to the moon, and he had no interest in clay in any shape or form. He and Freddie had built their own lives, and done well with it.

But it didn't hurt to stir things up a bit and watch the sparks fly. He wasn't a Tremayne for nothing.

And this girl of Primmy's . . . now there was the spit of her Mammie if he ever saw one, in every way. Primmy had always been a dazzler of a girl. And this Skye was more a Tremayne than his sister Em, and certainly more than the insufferable Luke . . . how the hell the three of them could be so closely related, Bradley couldn't think.

He sought out Skye in the conservatory, watching her for a few moments before she realised he was there.

"Lord, you startled me," she said with a forced smile.

He looked and sounded what he was, a rough-talking horse-dealer, but he was family, and deserved politeness.

"So how do you think Gran looks?" She asked him.

"At death's door," he said dryly. "She should have been kicking up the daisies long ago, but knowing her, she won't go until she's good and ready."

But there was a limit to politeness . . .

"That's a pretty callous thing to say about your own mother, isn't it?" she snapped.

Bradley shrugged. "When you deal in horseflesh as I do, you realise that life's cheap, girlie. I thought you'd have learned that much from the time you spent in France. Mother's had a bloody good innings, and she's just hanging on by the skin of her teeth, if you ask me."

"I'm sorry I ever did. Now, if you'll excuse me, I'm expecting my husband home at any minute."

She brushed past him, but he caught her arm.

"I ain't meaning to upset you, cuz, and I'm no threat to you, if that's what you'm thinking. Me and Freddie are moving on tonight, and all this," he waved his arms about, as if to embrace the entire county, "well, it's like another world to us now, and we don't want none of it."

"Is that meant to reassure me in some way?"

"You can take it any way you want."

Chapter Sixteen

Morwen's shadowy daydreams took her anywhere she wanted to go. That was the best thing about daydreams. Not a second was wasted before she was breathing in the aromatic scents of yarrow and bracken and gorse on the glorious moors above St Austell, as surely as if she was there.

Pictures of the past flitted delightfully through her mind, filling her with memories and images . . . seeing herself and Celia, teasing and scolding young Freddie for not bringing their tea quickly enough, and slopping half of it in his haste to be with his big brothers, working the clay.

And proudly watching her brother Sam in his pit captain's hat like her Daddy's, striding across the wet earth in his long boots, while Jack followed his every move, copying him and envying him.

And Matt, there was her darling brother Matt, so dreamy-eyed, and always wishing himself somewhere else . . . across the Atlantic ocean, perhaps, or hatching up impossible plans with Jude Pascoe at one of the kiddleywinks, more like.

Her dreaming thoughts abruptly changed direction, bringing them more sharply to the present, and an imaginary picture of what was happening at Clay One now. The autumn dispatches would have been sent safely off to their various destinations, and the depleted army of clayworkers would be resting briefly before they continued on their endless treadmill, gouging out the riches of the earth, and building the mountains of waste until they almost reached the sky.

Sky tips, Morwen thought, with the same satisfaction she always had. Was there ever a more apt name for the glittering white mountains that reached towards heaven? The thought of it had charmed her as a girl, and it charmed her now. Especially since she would be climbing one of 'em herself very soon.

She was thankful for the family's sake that the doctor had finally decided she hadn't had this terrible case of 'flu' that was killing so many folk now, or they'd all be scurrying away from New World to their own bolt-holes like frightened rabbits. But, with a strong sense of fatality, she knew that life was ebbing away from her. It didn't scare her. The time was almost here.

She was still in control of her senses, thank God, and aware of what was going on in the world. And since all the signs were that the war in Europe was almost at an end too, it was a good time for Theo to be planning ahead.

The final plans for the pottery would have to unfold without her, but that was right too. Young uns should take on the responsibility for the future, and there was a great joy in her heart that Skye was so ready to take her place in the doings of Killigrew Clay and whatever this new venture was to be called.

Skye had already voiced a few ideas to her, just to keep her amused, Morwen suspected, but so far, nothing had seemed right. It could just be called the Killigrew Pottery, of course, but since there were no Killigrews left, they all felt that it should be named something completely different. A new name for a new way of life, alongside the old.

But there was time enough for that, and why should she worry her head about it, anyway? It wouldn't be her concern, and she didn't have to worry about anything any more.

"What *is* she hanging on for?" Charlotte whispered to Birdie from the foot of Morwen's bed a few weeks later. October was drawing to a close, and Charlotte decided she may as well end her weekly tearful visit to her mother, since Morwen had fallen into a raggedy-snuffling sleep.

"She was always stubborn and determined to do things her own way," Charlotte went on, as if resentful of the fact, "but you'd think that when it came to dying, she wouldn't have any say in the matter. She'd just *go*."

Birdie was outraged at such heartlessness.

"Only the Lord will decide on the time a body takes to arrive in the world, and the nature of their journey out of it, Mrs Pollard," she said, as they crept out of the room.

"Oh, of course! And not for one minute am I wishing to hurry it up, but I do hate to see her in such distress with her breathing," she said quickly, in case the woman thought she was hinting at anything else. "Perhaps she's hanging on to see Skye's baby born. Do you think that could be it?"

"Mebbe," Birdie said. "And mebbe not. I'm not in possession of any second sight, and nor do I care to speculate on such a notion."

Charlotte put a hand on the woman's arm. "I know you'll be feeling this as badly as the rest of us, won't you, Birdie? What will you do . . . afterwards?"

Birdie blinked rapidly, half wishing the insensitive woman to Kingdom Come, and fearfully thankful that she didn't have the wherewithal to make such wishes come true.

"Get on with things, same as we all have to. I'll be staying with my brother, I daresay, until I decide what to do. But I'd rather not talk about it if you don't mind, not while she's still with us. It ain't decent."

"Of course," said Charlotte. But she left the house feeling uneasy, knowing they all had to think about it.

Everything would change after Morwen died, though she guessed that Skye and Philip and their coming baby would remain in the house. Morwen had made it plain to anyone who would listen that it was her wish. Charlotte didn't begrudge them that, though some might. But they all had their own homes and

249

were comfortably off, and they certainly didn't need the cold monstrosity of New World to live in.

She drove her smart little motor back to town with a feeling of relief at getting away from the sickroom. But all the time, her own words were swirling around in her head. What *was* Morwen hanging on for?

The sitting room door opened abruptly after the briefest tap while Skye and Philip were talking quietly that evening. Dinner was long over, and they had said goodnight to Morwen and sat with her until she had drifted into sleep. It was late, but this quiet hour alone before they retired for the night had become precious to them both, when they could talk over their respective days, and pretend for a little while that there were no battles still being fought in Europe, and that life would go on serenely forever.

Skye looked at the housekeeper in annoyance, knowing that if it had been Birdie or Nurse Jenkins interrupting them, it would have been on account of her grandmother. But if it was just some domestic upset, then Mrs Arden should deal with it herself, even though it was obvious that she was agitated.

"What is it?" Skye said impatiently.

"Mrs Norwood – Ma'am – there's folk come visiting."

"At this time of night?" Philip exclaimed angrily. "What kind of folk come calling at such an hour? Go and tell them Mrs Wainwright is sleeping, and to come back tomorrow."

"I'm not to say who 'tis, Ma'am, but 'tis you they'm asking for, and 'tis certain sure you'll be wantin' to see 'em," the housekeeper said, ignoring Philip completely.

Skye realised now that she wasn't simply agitated. She was tense with excitement and brimming with her own knowledge. Her eyes glittered, and her face was flushed. And since she was normally so calm and unflustered, it must be very important folk, folk who specially wanted to see *her* . . .

Skye's heart was suddenly beating very fast, and she leapt

up from her chair, all the pulses pounding in her veins as the wildest imagining of all took hold of her. For surely, it could only be . . . it had to be . . . but it *couldn't* be . . .

The shapes in the doorway behind Mrs Arden moved into the light, and with a cry of pure joy Skye had flown across the space between them, and into her mother's arms.

"Oh Mom, I can't believe it's really you!" she gasped out, and all the pent-up emotions she had held so desperately in check recently burst out in a torrent. "And Daddy too. Oh, it's just too much. I'll never mock Cornish intuition again, if it brought you here when I needed you most!"

She raved on incoherently, laughing and crying as the three of them held each other, while Philip looked on, the outsider for the moment, and more than happy to be so.

Only he knew what a terrible strain Skye had been under all these weeks, keeping up her spirits for the old lady upstairs, and only letting her guard down in the bitter, weeping hours of the night when he had held her close.

He could see the ghost of her beauty in her mother, and the strength she had inherited in her father's jaw . . . and when the pair of them could get a word in through their daughter's babbling, he heard Primmy Tremayne laugh ruefully.

"It had nothing to do with intuition this time, honey. It was that companion of Mammie's that decided us that we'd best come and see her while there was still time. And war or no war, with Sinclair's influence in high places, we managed to get a passage on a ship right away."

"*Birdie* got you here? But how?" Skye said. "And why on earth didn't you let us know you were coming! It's too bad of you, Mom, to give me such a fright!"

Primmy gave a short laugh at this mild censure. "I know it. But I was always the unpredictable one in the family, honey, and when Birdie wrote to me, telling us just how bad Mammie was, it seemed like the best idea for us just to up sticks and travel."

251

Albie would have said it was so – so *Primmy*, thought Skye, bringing him unexpectedly to mind. How would Albie take this sudden appearance of his adored sister? How could any of them take it, except with pleasure?

"So you've seen no one else yet?" she said quickly.

"My Lord, no we haven't," her father said. "All your Mom wanted to do was to get here to see Morwen's condition for herself. And yours too, honey," he added.

"And I must say you're looking fine and dandy, Skye," Primmy said softly, and for the first time she looked to where Philip was still standing politely. "And this must be Philip."

Skye started, having almost forgotten him in the shock of her parents' arrival. But now she drew him towards them, bringing him into their circle, her happiness complete at having the three people she loved best in the world all together.

"Mom, Dad – this is my husband," she said, almost shyly.

It was a long while before any of them thought about going to bed and sleeping. Mrs Arden brought them tea and sandwiches, and arranged for a room to be prepared for the travellers, who were anxious to know everything about Morwen's condition.

"There's so little to tell," Skye said. "She simply goes on from day to day, but you'll see for yourselves in the morning."

"But I think you should prepare her, darling," Philip put in. "It will be a shock to her to see your parents, even if it's the very best of surprises."

"You'll be shocked to see her too, Mom," Skye said slowly. "She's not the way you remember her."

As if Primmy couldn't bear any more of such talk, she began asking brightly about the rest of the family. Those near enough for them to come calling, and those far away.

"Uncle Freddie and Bradley visited once and went away again," Skye said, trying not to sound too scathing. "We never hear from Uncle Jack now. Emma comes when she can, but the farm keeps her fully occupied. Charlotte's more of a regular, and sometimes her girls come here as well – I told you how well I got along with Vera when we met up in the hospital in France, didn't I? Cousin Theo is here quite a lot, and his wife brings the baby – and I *know* I've told you a few things about the delectable Sebastian!"

She paused for breath, all the family names jangling in her head, and then Primmy said the one name she realised she had been studiously avoiding.

"And Albie? Does Albie come to visit?"

By now Philip had poured the two men a glass of brandy, and Skye saw Cresswell's eyes meet his wife's above the rim of his glass. Primmy's face was tinged with pink, and in an instant Skye knew that her father had always been perfectly aware of the relationship between brother and sister.

Just how deep or incestuous that relationship had ever gone, Skye didn't know, and never wanted to find out.

"Albie doesn't visit too often. Aunt Rose is ailing, and he doesn't like to leave her. But he'll be so happy to see you and Daddy, Mom," she said carefully, including them both.

"I'll telephone him in the morning, once I've seen Mammie," Primmy said.

It was the early hours of the morning before they all went to bed, but Skye found it difficult to sleep. Wrapped in Philip's arms, she thought how simple her own life was in comparison to others. There had never been another love in her life before him, and she was sure there could never be anyone to take his place. But even as she thought it, a cold shiver ran through her.

From all she had learned about the fiery young Morwen Tremayne, her grandmother had once thought like that. Morwen's love for Ben Killigrew had been just as intense as hers for Philip, but it had waned, and she had found a second love in Randall Wainwright that was just as passionate, just as fulfilling.

Love wasn't the all-consuming, exclusive emotion everybody thought it was. There was always the capacity for more, for love to die and to grow again. Her own husband had proved that.

She moaned softly without realising it, remembering Philip's
ex-fiancée, Ruth, who had loved him long before Skye came
on the scene, and had confidently expected to marry him. How
wicked did that make her, for stealing another woman's man?

"Come here," Philip said gently, holding her closer in his
arms. "I don't know what's worrying you now, but your parents
are here, so be happy, sweetheart."

"I can't help it," she whispered into his shoulder. "Now
that Mom's here, I think maybe it's time for Gran to go. I
can't explain my fears – but this time of night was always a
bad time for allowing demons into my head, and there's no
stopping them."

She could feel his breath on her cheek, and the touch of his
hands was warm and comforting on her body.

"There are no demons in this old house, Skye, only love. And
if there are, then it's time to banish them for good. I don't think
Morwen would begrudge two people who want each other so
desperately for fulfilling that love, do you?"

She responded at once. Loving him, and needing him, and
knowing in her soul that there had been a time when Morwen
herself would have responded in exactly the same way to her
lover, wantonly and passionately . . . and totally against doctor's
orders, with the bulge of the baby between them.

Morwen took the arrival of her daughter and son-in-law far
more calmly than any of them had expected. It was just as if she
knew they would come, Skye told Emma on the telephone.

"She allus had an instinct for such things," Emma said without
any surprise in her voice. "I'll try to get over to see them if I can,
lamb, but 'tis never easy on a farm. You'll be letting t'others
know, I daresay?"

"Of course – except for Albie. Mom especially wants to tell
him herself."

"That's to be expected. They were allus as close as two halves
of the same coin."

But in the end, Primmy couldn't bear to speak to Albie on the telephone for more than a few minutes. Skye heard her choke out his name, feeling like an eavesdropper, and suddenly wanting to protect her father from whatever closeness had once existed between these two.

"Do you want to take a walk outside?" she asked Cress quickly. "Mom's going to be on the 'phone for ages."

He agreed at once, and she linked her arm in his as they strolled round the grounds of the lovely old house that had seen such turmoil in its history.

"It's so tranquil here, isn't it, Daddy? It's almost impossible to believe there's a war still raging in Europe, and that some of our boys will never come back. It was terrible to lose a whole generation of our own clayworkers."

"You love this place, don't you?" he commented. "I never realised quite how much, but now I get the feeling that you're never coming home to us, Skye."

"I *am* home. Philip and I have made our home here, and our baby will be born here. You have to go where your heart is, don't you? You and Mom knew that."

And Skye knew very well that Primmy's extra reason for wanting to live in America was to escape any hint of scandal surrounding herself and her brother, however ill-founded.

"Mom always loved you, Daddy," Skye went on, going as far as she dared. "She'd have followed you anywhere."

"I know that. We had a shaky start, but I won her in the end. And that's enough about us oldies. I want to know if my girl's truly happy."

Skye laughed. "Isn't it obvious! Philip and I adore each other. I couldn't ask for more."

And thankfully, the demons that had plagued her in the still of the night had gone. Love truly conquered everything, she thought, filing away the thought in her mind for future reference, in case it should ever be needed.

And who was being second-sighted *now*! She hugged her

father, suggesting they went inside, as it was getting cold. And if she stood for too long the baby pressed ever more uncomfortably inside her these days.

Primmy was flushed when they rejoined her.

"Albie sounded totally stunned when he heard my voice," she told them. "He wanted to come here right away, but I told him how much I wanted to see the studio again. When Mammie's settled for the afternoon, I'd like to go over there, Cress."

Skye would dearly have liked to take her, but the doctor had forbidden her to drive in the last months of pregnancy. Now that the birth was imminent, she was more than happy to take his advice, especially as she could hardly fit behind the wheel of the car any more.

What a sketch she looked, she sometimes thought, eyeing her bulge in the long mirror of their bedroom. And what an angel she looked to him, Philip always retorted.

"I'll take you into Truro whenever you're ready, Primmy," Cress said now. "You can spend some time at the studio while I reacquaint myself with the town."

"But you'll want to see Albie too, won't you?"

"Later. The two of you will have plenty to talk about."

Skye avoided looking at either of them. Whatever had happened in the past was long over, and she sensed that there was perfect trust between her parents. But she had also sensed the depth of Albert Tremayne's love for her mother, and felt its unhealthy transference to her.

She shivered, thankful to her soul that she had such an uncomplicated relationship with Philip, and in the small silence she said quickly that she'd be happy to spend time with Morwen that afternoon, to counteract the excitement of Primmy's coming home. So far nobody had dared ask how long she and Cress intended to stay.

"We must take a drive up to the moors sometime too, and take a look at the clayworks," Cress went on sociably. "It must have changed a good deal over the years."

The women looked at him, each lost in thoughts of their own. Primmy spoke slowly.

"Maybe that's not such a bad idea, Cress. I could lay a few ghosts at the same time. I never did truly forgive my own mother and father for dying on me—"

"*Mom*, how can you say such a thing!"

"Quite easily, love. Oh, I know that Morwen and Ben Killigrew became the best of parents to Walter, Albie and me, and we loved them for it. But finding out that we weren't really their children still felt like the worst betrayal any youngsters could know. And maybe because I was a girl, I felt it more than the others."

"Or it could have been because you were a particularly precocious child, honey," Cress said mildly. "And I was the one who unknowingly shattered all those illusions."

Primmy gave him a swift smile, her hand reaching out for his. "I more than forgave you, dar, in case you haven't been aware of it all these years."

Skye turned away, glad to see their obvious love for each other, and feeling guilty for wanting to register it so badly. Until coming to Cornwall she had never doubted it – and she didn't doubt it now. And she certainly wouldn't want to be a fly on the wall to see Primmy and Albie meet again.

Cress deposited his wife outside the artist's studio in Truro, kissing her lightly on the cheek as he left.

"I'll be back for you in an hour or so," he told her.

Primmy hardly saw him go. For a few wild, wonderful moments she simply stood outside the door of the studio, drinking in the atmosphere, no longer a matronly woman with two grown-up children, soon to be a grandmother herself.

No longer the wife of a successful American businessman, and an equally successful pianist invited to soirées and luncheons at all the best houses in New Jersey.

No longer anyone but the flamboyant and beautiful bohemian

257

Primmy Tremayne she had once been, dressing in outrageous, flowing skirts, and wearing beads in her hair, and mixing with all Albie's arty friends as if they were all soul-mates. Entering into their dark, forbidden world, and tasting all its freedoms and its pleasures . . .

The studio door opened, and a middle-aged man appeared. A man who had once been her life, as she had once been his beloved.

"Primmy," he said in a choked voice, holding out his arms to her. "My Primmy."

She went into his embrace as if in a dream, recognising him instantly, yet no longer knowing him.

"It's really me," she said shakily, when he seemed loath to let her go. "So – are you going to invite me inside, or do we stand on the doorstep inviting comments from the townsfolk who don't realise we're brother and sister?"

The words were out of her mouth before she had time to think, and with them she separated the past from the present.

"When did you ever wait for an invitation?" Albie said, recovering himself quickly. "It's so good to see you, Prim, and I hardly thought this day would ever come."

"Well, it has, and it took the saddest reason for it," she reminded him. "I fear that Mammie won't be with us for much longer."

"But whatever happens, you'll stay to see your grandchild born, won't you?" he said.

"Of course."

They climbed the stairs that Primmy remembered so well, to the rooms above that she and Albie had once shared so decorously, and where Rose would be waiting for them now.

"Skye's a lovely girl," Albie said abruptly. "She's the image of you, Prim."

"Of what I *was*, you mean," Primmy said ruefully.

"That's exactly what I mean," he said.

Before she could think of a suitable reply, Rose had come

out of the sitting room to greet her, plunging them all into her closet world of symptoms and treatments, of temperature charts and doctor's visits, and linctuses and pills.

"My goodness, Rose, do you have time to think about anything else?" Primmy exclaimed.

"She does not," Albie said dryly. "Nor me, neither. It's a full-time job for Rose, being ill."

"But you still have your work? Your painting?" Primmy asked him. "Nothing could take you away from that for very long in the past, Albie."

Only the wild parties they used to have right here in these rooms, and the potent drinks they drank, and the illicit substances they smoked . . . For a moment her thoughts spun out of control, as if she was seeing another world, one that she had once known, that could never be as familiar to her again. Thank God, she thought fervently, that the madness of those days had had no lasting effect on either one of them.

"Rose often sits with me while I paint," he said. "She likes to watch me work, and I like the company."

Dear Lord, but how stuffy that sounded, thought Primmy sorrowfully. Albie had always been so flamboyant, drawing a bohemian crowd to him like a moth to a flame, and it was so sad to see the staid figure he had become.

Almost appalled to realise it, she found herself wishing the time away until Cresswell came to collect her. All her life she had longed to see Albie again, loving him in the purest way, as if he was the other half of her. She still loved him, but it wasn't the same. Nothing ever was.

"We won't linger," she told her brother, once he and Cress and Rose had greeted one another. "I want to get back to Mammie, and I'd like to look in on Charlotte before we go back to New World. And I believe Theo's coming to dinner tonight."

She was speaking too quickly, knowing they had avoided too much mention of Walter, but knowing it had to come.

259

"You'll be missing Walter," Albie said, reading her mind. "It was a terrible shock to us all, him doing what he did."

Primmy nodded, not wanting to hear any accusation in his voice. Not wanting to think of how the sadness of losing Walter hurt them all so badly. First Walter's son, Jordan, fighting for his country, and then Walter himself, throwing himself into the sea. And having to hear about it all over again from Albie . . .

"Is everything all right?" Cress asked her, when she had said nothing for fully ten minutes as they drove away.

"Yes, except for Rose's tactlessness. Fancy telling me that the next time we met would probably be at Mammie's burying! She was always selfish, and far too possessive over Albie, and she certainly hasn't improved with age."

"He doesn't seem to mind. Do you?"

"Of course not. They suit one another very well, just like we do, dar."

She was rewarded by his quick smile and a squeeze of her hand. "Are you sure you want to call on Charlotte?" he asked.

She did, though they had never been very close. And when they met, they hugged one another, exclaiming that neither had changed a bit, which they both knew was a blatant lie.

"Your daughter was a bit of a dark horse, wasn't she, Prim?" Charlotte said. "Springing a wedding and a baby on us almost at the same time, I mean."

"It wasn't quite like that!" Primmy protested.

"Oh, I know, but you must admit it could have thrown a few cats among the pigeons if it hadn't been for the lovely way she wrote in the newspaper about it. She certainly has a gift for words," she added generously. "By the way, did you know the Germans are appealing for an Armistice now? They know when they're beaten, thank the Lord. It's all in the latest edition of *The Informer*."

"I didn't know any of it," Primmy murmured. "I've been rather too busy worrying about Mammie since we arrived to bother looking at newspapers."

"Well, of course you have," Charlotte said, eyeing her thoughtfully. "And I reckon I know *exactly* now, why she's been hanging on."

"What's that supposed to mean?"

Charlotte gave an uneasy and half-resentful laugh. "It's something I've only just remembered. I asked Birdie what she could possibly be hanging on for, when she was obviously ready to die – and I'm not apologising for being so blunt, neither. You haven't seen the state of her all summer the way the rest of us have. But now I know. She was waiting for you, Primmy."

"Don't say such things! It makes me feel creepy. And anyway, she couldn't possibly have known that Cress and I were coming. We didn't decide until the last minute, and then we didn't let anyone know, since we didn't want any fuss."

She was agitated now, not wanting to think about any kind of psychic involvement into why she was here, and why Morwen was still hanging on to life by a thread. And she was angry with Charlotte for putting the notion into her head.

"Well, I'm sorry, but that's how it seemed to me. You were always her favourite, the one who was most like her."

"Mammie didn't have favourites, and if she did, then it was always Walter," Primmy said, as the name of her loved brother stuck in her throat.

They were two middle-aged women, acting like opposing sides on a battlefield, and what did it matter anyway? Yet Primmy still felt a ludicrous need to defend herself.

"But Walter was a boy," Charlotte snapped, "and you were her best girl. Oh, I'm not condemning you for it, just stating facts. And I still say she was hanging on for you."

"Then I'd better get back to her and give her all the time that I have," Primmy said.

"God, I'd forgotten how insufferable Charlotte could be," she exclaimed, once she and Cress were on their way back to New World. "It comes from marrying up in the world, of course. Vincent Pollard's family were always a cut above ours – or thought they were!"

She was talking too quickly to cover her very real feelings of premonition that if they didn't hurry back to New World, Morwen would already have expired, and she would be too late to say goodbye.

Damn Charlotte, she thought savagely, for putting such ideas into her head, and making her feel responsible for her own mother's life expectancy.

"You don't think there's anything in it, do you, dar?" she said at last. "What Charlotte said, I mean. It doesn't happen like that, does it?" She gave a shaky laugh. "Oh, she makes me so mad! But if she *was* right, perhaps we should have stayed away, and Mammie would have gone on forever."

But she hid a sob in her throat as she said it, because it was a futile remark. Nobody lived forever.

"I think she was right about one thing, honey," Cress said gently. "Morwen is ready to die, and when the time comes we'll all have to be glad for her."

"And that's the daftest thing anybody could say," Primmy said viciously.

But she went straight to her mother's room when they returned, relieved to see that Morwen was the same as ever, dozing fitfully, breathing with difficulty, but still there. Skye was sitting beside the bed, holding her grandmother's hand and now she reached for her mother's hand too.

They didn't speak, but a great calmness seemed to settle in that silent room, as if the linked hands of the three women and the presence of the unborn child underlined the strongest bonds of all, Primmy thought, wishing it could always be so.

It was in the early hours of the morning, the time Skye hated the most, when she heard the tapping on her bedroom door and Nurse Jenkins' urgent voice. She roused Philip at once, knowing what the call meant.

Primmy and Cress were already in Morwen's room, together with Birdie, and they circled the bed where the dying woman fought to stay with them a little longer.

Just a little longer, Morwen begged the hovering angel . . . there was still so much to say, but the words were all in her head and wouldn't reach her mouth any more. And she was getting so tired and so muddled. She was drifting into a sweetly floating plane, filled with pastel colours, and faces that she knew and remembered were smiling and welcoming her . . .

"She's leaving us," Birdie said, choking, almost staggering away from the bed. "I can't bear it!"

Primmy gently stroked her mother's forehead, and closed the once-bright eyes. There was such a powerful sensation inside her that Morwen was already glimpsing things beyond their earthly imagination, and for the moment she couldn't even be sad for her.

"But she's happy," Primmy whispered. "Wherever she is now, she's happy."

Chapter Seventeen

"So it's over."

Luke Tremayne stared at his flag-stoned floor as he received the message over the telephone.

Philip cleared his throat. "And peacefully so. The womenfolk are with her now, and the doctor is on his way, so I volunteered to inform the rest of the family."

"Yes, yes. Good of you."

For once Luke couldn't find the obligatory right words to say. Having buried so many of his flock over the years, pontificating that the natural order of things was inevitable and God's will, the news still hit him like a violent punch in the stomach. It wasn't manly to weep, and there would be plenty of folk who had high regard for the family to do that, but this was his mother.

"I'll be there right away," he said abruptly now.

"I don't think there's any need. Tomorrow—"

But by now Philip was talking to himself, and the connection was lost. Besides, who was he to determine who came and when? It wasn't his place. He was just the man who had married the granddaughter.

But he had known Morwen long enough to respect and love her, and he wouldn't be ashamed to weep for her. When you had seen men scream in agony on the battlefield, shared their pain and wept with them, you disregarded any thought of shame.

Skye came down the stairs slowly while he was making the last of the telephone calls. The baby sat heavily and awkwardly

265

inside her now, with only a few weeks of her pregnancy left, and she looked tired and lifeless.

"The doctor's arrived, and he and Nurse Jenkins are seeing to the things that have to be done," she said, more composed than he had expected her to be.

He drew her into his arms, but aware that he was holding her too tightly as he felt the intrusion of the baby between them. He made to pull away slightly, but she held him fast and shook her head.

"No, just hold me. You won't harm him. In fact, it was the strangest thing . . ."

"What was, darling?" he said gently, as she faltered.

"Moments after Granny Morwen had gone, I was leaning over to kiss her goodbye. The baby went rigid and then kicked furiously, right against Gran's body, and just for a second I thought . . ." she swallowed hard, "I thought she was the one who moved, that she hadn't died at all, and it was all a hideous mistake. Isn't that absolutely *stupid* and *terrible*?"

She suddenly went limp and then she was sobbing in his arms. "Oh God, I'm going to miss her so! And don't start telling me she's at peace now, because I know all that. *She's* at peace all right, but the rest of us aren't! We all have to go on without her."

"But not without her legacy, sweetheart, and I'm not being insensitive or facetious. Her legacy is in the family she left, and in the clayworks she fought so hard to keep going against all the odds. There are a great many people who have cause to thank God for the life of Morwen Wainwright. And not the least of them are the men who had the good fortune to marry the Tremayne women."

Skye's mouth shook at the words, said with such simplicity, and accepting that his logical mind could put everything into such beautiful perspective, however temporary the relief of it all.

"Have I ever told you I adore you?" she whispered.

"Frequently, but I never tire of hearing it," he told her. "Now let's sit down quietly while I tell you who's likely to come to the funeral, and who sends their regrets."

"Jack and Annie won't come," Skye said, her thoughts diverted at once to the practicalities, as he intended. "Freddie and Bradley should, if they're not too busy. All the others will come, and thank God Mom and Daddy are here. I couldn't have borne it without them. But it's sad that Grandpop Matt couldn't travel from California in time, even if he was well enough, and Gran will miss him sorely—"

Her eyes widened in distress, realising she had been referring to Morwen at that moment. Philip kissed her cheek.

"So she will, but she'll also understand," he said.

"Then you really think she'll *know*?"

Philip hedged. "I don't think this is the time for a theological discussion, Skye. I simply think we each have to believe what our heart tells us to believe."

Primmy and Cress came into the room before she could probe any further. Her mother's eyes were red with weeping now, but she was still calm. And a short while later Luke arrived, pressing everyone's hands in turn.

Skye presumed it was his normal way of dealing with bereavement. Cold fish, she thought. Even now.

"I'll just go and see Mother, and then we'll start discussing the arrangements," he said, as if this was an ordinary visit and an everyday business occurrence. And so it was, as far as he was concerned, Skye conceded.

The funeral was as large and well-attended as anyone could wish for, Charlotte said with satisfaction after the event. Clayworkers had turned up from every pit in the vicinity, young and old, and a few of the older ones could still sigh over the vivacious girl that Morwen Tremayne had once been.

Some had memories of the lovely young bride of Ben Killigrew, and the way the couple had selflessly taken in the three children of Morwen's dead brother Sam; others recalled the strong-willed wife of Ran Wainwright who had stood by her man and defied the threat of a flashily-dressed

267

woman clay boss wanting to take over the works, and the husband as well.

Tributes had poured into the house on Morwen's account until New World began to smell like a floral hot-house, and was quickly starting to make Skye feel nauseous. But she knew they couldn't remove any of the flowers until after the family feast and the will-reading that followed the burial.

"It has to be done, and folk will be wanting to get back to their own affairs," Theo had said shortly, when Skye exclaimed that the arrangements seemed to be happening with indecent haste. "Life goes on for the rest of us, and your own folks will be wanting to book a passage home, I daresay."

"They will not!" Skye snapped, hating his insensitivity. "They'll stay to see their grandchild born."

"Oh ah, I suppose they will. It's a good thing it's hanging on until we get this performance over, anyway."

"I hate him!" Skye raged to Philip later. "Uncle Walter was always brusque, but he was a fair man, and never as horrible as Theo."

"He's right, all the same. How would you feel, my love, if the baby had started to arrive before Morwen was buried, and you'd been confined to bed all this time? You would have been more upset than ever. You'd have been embarrassed at the joy of seeing our baby come into the world, and you'd have been upset at not being able to grieve with the rest of them."

"Oh, you're always so damn logical, aren't you!" she raged again. And knowing that he was right, and read her thoughts too well, didn't help a bit.

But something else was plaguing her that she couldn't even tell Philip about. She shivered, knowing she was giving too much credence to something she had once read, but unable to stop herself. The belief that putting fears into words brought them too much into the light, giving them shape and form and possibility. Pagan belief.

Someone with a logical mind – like Philip's – would scoff

and say that bringing fears into the open and sharing them was the best means of dispelling them. But in her dark mood, she still couldn't tell him what she feared the most.

Ever since the day Morwen died, when she had felt the baby kick so vigorously inside her, she had felt nothing. There was no movement at all, no sudden, heart-stopping lurchings to remind her that he was anxious to be born . . . and she was too terrified of what the inactivity might mean to confide in anyone.

The will-reading held no surprises at first. The lawyer intoned all the monetary bequests to the family members, with no favouritism. All Morwen's children and grandchildren received handsome bequests. The bulk of her shares in Killigrew Clay were left to Theo, as expected, now that Walter was gone, with minor proportions for her brothers Matt, Freddie and Jack.

In her own words, she stated that although they had little interest in the clayworks now, they should still share in the profits, and there were murmurs of assent in the well-filled drawing room. There was a handsome bequest for Birdie, her stalwart companion, who snuffled her way through the entire day.

'To my granddaughter, Skye," the lawyer went on, "I leave the house known as New World, in the belief that she will care for it as I did. This will come as no surprise to the rest of the family, and I wish them all to show her goodwill. But one last bequest to Skye is an equal share in the pottery venture with my grandson Theo, since no one else has shown the slightest interest. I also leave her my diaries, to do with them what she will.'

Skye gasped, resisting the urge to glance at Philip with a great effort. Morwen had once told her about the diaries, but she hadn't thought about them for years. In an instant, she remembered Philip's idle comment that one day she should write a novel based on her family's fortunes. Distressed, she pushed the thought away at once, because this wasn't the time to be thinking of such matters. She didn't know if she could even bear to open the diaries at all. Certainly not yet, while she was still grieving for Morwen, if ever . . .

When the will-reading came to an end, the lawyer told Skye he would bring the diaries to the house whenever she was ready. At present they were in a safety box in his Bodmin chambers, and without a second thought, she quickly told him to leave them there.

But when he had gone, Primmy kissed her daughter, and spoke thoughtfully.

"I knew Mammie had started recording everything long ago, though she never showed any of it to us, Skye. But you're obviously the one she trusted most to have the diaries."

"Trusted?" Skye echoed. "That's an odd word to use."

Her Aunt Emma hovered near, and added her thoughts.

"No, Prim's right, Skye. There's some who would use them to their own advantage, selling bits of information or raking up old scandals."

"Careful, Aunt Em," they heard Theo's mocking voice nearby. "You're talking to a wordsmith here, so don't go putting ideas into her head!"

"You know I thought far too much of Granny Morwen to ever sell her out," Skye whipped out.

For once, his wife put in her spoke, however mildly.

"I'm sure Theo meant no such thing, Skye," Betsy protested. "But we all had great regard for your grandmother, and no one would want to see her words spilled out for folk to pick over. It's quite right too, that you should be in partnership with Theo in the pottery."

"Be quiet, Betsy," Theo said less than pleasantly, as if he thought she was putting even more ideas into Skye's head.

She wasn't sure he was as pleased about their so-called partnership as Betsy seemed to be. To her relief, no one else seemed overly concerned about her involvement in the proposed venture, though her first thought had been that her extra bequests could easily cause a major family upset.

But the very last thing she wanted was to make capital out of the diaries. She told her husband and parents so, when the rest of them had finally gone, and the interminable day was drawing to a close. She may have thought about it once, but now that the opportunity was here, she knew that everything had changed.

"It makes you wonder why she made such a point of leaving the diaries to you, though, if she *didn't* want folk to know the history of it," Cress said thoughtfully. "Why didn't she just burn them?"

"You don't burn your past," Skye said without thinking. "It would be like burning a part of you."

"So perhaps she really did intend you to use them in some way?" Cress persisted.

"And perhaps she just wanted me to read them and understand how we all came to be the way we are. Daddy, I just can't talk about it any longer. I'm tired, and I need my bed."

Philip stood up, speaking quietly to Primmy and Cress in contrast to their daughter's brittle tone. "She's had enough for one day, and we'll see you both in the morning. Everything will look different then."

But a few days later, Skye was still pale and drawn, her fears for the baby still undisclosed and preying on her mind. The one person she felt she could have confided in was gone, buried six feet in the ground and never again to offer her wise advice.

"You need some fresh air," Primmy told her. "You've been cooped up in this house for far too long, Skye."

"What do you suggest I do – run barefoot over the moors for exercise?" She bit her lip as the words rushed out.

"Hardly," Primmy said, refusing to take offence at her daughter's sarcasm. "But I do suggest that we all take a drive up there today. Your father and I want to see the old clayworks and the cottages again, and you can explain the lay-out of the new pottery at Clay Two."

271

"*Today?*" Skye said stupidly.

"Why not today? Mammie wouldn't condemn us for breathing fresh air and thinking about the future. And while we're gone Birdie can get rid of some of these flowers before they overpower us all with their scent. It will give her something else to do besides packing her clothes."

Primmy took charge, aware that her daughter was like a leaf in the wind, alternately brittle and limp, and needing someone to direct her.

"All right. If we must," Skye muttered, but knowing her mother was right. She needed something to raise her spirits, and the only time she had moved out of the house since Morwen's death had been to attend her funeral.

So later that morning the four of them drove to St Austell and up the moorland tracks to where the great sky tips soared towards heaven. It had rained during the November night, and the gleaming heaps of clay-spoil looked newly-washed and sparkling, with thin slivers of sunlight slanting on them.

Skye absolutely refused to admit the fantasy thought that it was Morwen's spirit shining down on them. She was done with omens and charms and anything else that wasn't normal and logical and easily explained . . . and if she caught a glimpse of the old witchwoman on the moors, she would simply turn her back on her.

As Philip drove the car slowly through Clay One and the clayworkers recognised the occupants, they fell silent and removed their caps respectfully. The sight of the milky green clay pool, so beautiful and so treacherous, could still tug at Primmy's heart, and Skye's too, knowing of Morwen's anguish when her friend had drowned herself there.

Primmy was glad when they had passed through, and paused outside the little row of clayworker's cottages at the top of the moors. She didn't deny that this trip was as much a rite of passage for her as to get Skye out of that sad, morbid house for a couple of hours.

"That was the Tremayne cottage," she said, pointing ahead to where a curl of grey smoke drifted skywards out of the chimney now. "Walter and Albie and I didn't live here, because by the time they adopted us Morwen had married Ben Killigrew and gone up in the world. But this is where our roots are, and people should never forget their roots."

Skye squeezed her mother's hand, feeling that she should be sharing her obvious emotion. But she was numb inside, and seemed to have no feelings left.

"Do you want to see how dismal Clay Two looks now, or have you had enough journey down Memory Lane?" she said. But she bit her lip, knowing how cynical she sounded. "I'm sorry, Mom, but I can't concentrate on anything for very long."

"It's all right, honey," Primmy said, patting her hand. "I was just the same when I was expecting you. The baby takes up all your energy, but yes, while we're here, drive us over to Clay Two, please, Philip."

He complied at once, and when they approached the burned-out buildings and the forlorn-looking site, he exclaimed angrily as they saw several more cars there.

"Oh no, not him today," he said. "Skye, if you'd rather stay in the car while your parents look around—"

"Do you think I'm incapable of dealing with my own cousin?" she said contrarily. "I'm a match for him any day, in case you hadn't noticed. Just help me out, before I get stuck in this blessed seat forever, will you?"

Theo came striding across to greet them, his eyes wary as he saw Skye, but she said briefly that it was clear that they all had the same idea that life had to go on.

"Good girl," he said, to her surprise and annoyance. "Then let me introduce you to Harrison Dean. You had to meet him soon, anyway, and we were just going over some of the finer details on the plans, as it happens, so you can give us your thoughts on it."

"I don't think Skye's in any mood to deal with business

matters in her present condition," Philip said sharply, but she brushed him aside.

"Please don't molly-coddle me, Philip. I'm having a baby, not in imminent danger of expiring from some fatal disease. And I'm perfectly capable of looking at a few plans, providing somebody finds me something to sit on."

Theo fetched a wooden cask on which she sat as elegantly as she could, considering. And only then did she take proper notice of the handsome young architect walking towards her, his arms full of blueprints.

She felt a mild shock. If she'd thought about it at all, she supposed she had expected him to be elderly and staid, like a lawyer or an accountant. She hadn't envisaged this dashing young man with a mane of dark hair, and deep brown eyes, and a mouth that seemed always about to smile.

Her own ludicrous thoughts almost made her laugh out loud. Here she was, as large as a whale, within days of giving birth – and madly in love with her husband – and she was practically registering the sight of this stranger with the predatory eye of a man-hunter!

She put such temporary insanity down to the gloom of the past weeks, and the fact that she had hardly been outside the house to see anyone but her sad-faced family. All the same, when Harrison Dean shook her hand she almost snatched hers out of his grasp, and concentrated instead on business, while he explained the plans in layman's terms for their benefit.

His accent, although still Cornish, was well-educated, and from his expertise she guessed he had been to university. She found herself wondering how anyone so young could have learned so much. He couldn't be more than in his mid-twenties, she thought, not much older than herself.

As if to offset her sudden and unwanted rush of interest, she turned her attention to the blueprints almost feverishly. Harrison Dean was making additional suggestions to the general lay-out of buildings and showrooms, including a considerable advertising campaign once the place was up and running, as he put it.

"Oh, I agree with that!" she said quickly. "Advertising can mean all the difference to the success of a new business."

"And we couldn't advertise it without a name. So have you had any ideas about it, Mrs Norwood?" he asked.

She looked away for a moment. She felt ungainly, awkward, heavy and unlovable, but there was no mistaking the admiration in the man's eyes. Considering her girth right now, it certainly did her a power of good, but it also disturbed her to feel pleasure in knowing he was attracted towards her.

After all, it was hardly becoming for someone about to give birth to be distracted by such thoughts about a man who wasn't her husband. And especially when she had just buried her grandmother, and was in mourning.

The thought sobered her at once, and to her relief the unreal feelings vanished. He was just a pleasant young man who meant nothing to her, and was never likely to do so.

"I don't think anyone has given much thought to it," Primmy answered for her. "We've had other family matters to attend to recently."

"Of course. But Mr Tremayne thought that getting the project started might be good for everyone," Harrison replied. "I'm sorry if I offended you in any way."

"You didn't," Theo said shortly. "But you'd best explain where you think we need further advice, Harry."

They all studied the blueprints again, and he ran his finger along a curving line from north to south on the original plan of the area.

"This is where the main problem could lie, where the narrow channels of water ran down to the settling tanks. It will need careful surveying to ensure there's no likelihood of subsidence as happened long ago, I believe."

Primmy spoke abruptly. "That was due to Ben Killigrew's railtracks being built over old disused tin mines. He had

275

arranged for the clayworkers to go on a day's outing to the sea, and the tracks collapsed."

"I remember reading something about it," Harry Dean said. "And that's the kind of thing we must guard against. There was one fatality, I believe?"

"My father," Primmy said.

Nobody said anything for a minute, and then the architect spoke awkwardly. "I begin to feel as though I've unwittingly stirred up a hornet's nest, Mrs Tremayne, and perhaps this is best left for another day after all."

"No. Please go on, Mr Dean," Skye said quickly. "You didn't know we were coming here today, and you and my cousin had obviously planned to get some thoughts in order."

He nodded, glad of her support. "Well then, these little white rivers in themselves wouldn't do much harm, but it all depends on what's beneath them, and I'll have the report on that in a week or so."

"Why do you call them that?" Skye said curiously.

He laughed. "Just a slip of the tongue. They call the river running through St Austell the White River, on account of all the clay slurry that pours into it and out to sea, and of course it's these little channels at all the pits hereabouts that's the cause of it all."

Skye stared at him, and then at Theo, feeling a sliver of excitement in her veins.

"Couldn't that be our name, Theo? If we called it White Rivers Pottery, it would get right away from the Killigrew name, but still have a deep significance to the area."

"Maybe so. But it needs some more thinking about before we make such a hasty decision," he said.

She knew very well that if he had thought of it first, it wouldn't need thinking about at all. She also knew that her small surge of excitement and well-being was quickly fading, and her make-shift seat was becoming harder by the minute. Philip saw her discomfort, and came to a decision.

"It's time to get you home, I think. We'll leave the gentlemen to get on with the investigations, and they can report back to us when they're ready."

And if he was taking a more proprietorial interest in the business than he should, Skye was too weary to make any comment. Why shouldn't he, anyway? They were husband and wife, and that made them partners in all things. And all she wanted now was to get home and rest. She suddenly felt very old and very tired, almost as if she was taking on the mantle of Morwen Tremayne.

She shivered as Philip helped her into the car, and leaned against the back of the seat.

"Are you all right, darling?" her mother asked anxiously. "If you want us to send for the doctor when we return—"

"I'm perfectly all right, thankyou, and I don't need the doctor. In fact, I'm wondering if this baby ever intends to be born at all!"

She spoke sharply as she so often did lately, unable to control the way her moods seemed to swing so rapidly from good to bad. Whatever the reason, she didn't like it, and she knew she was becoming a trial to everyone around her.

"There's one thing you can be sure about when it comes to babies, honey," her father said amiably. "They won't stay in their cosy confinement for ever, but they won't be born until they're good and ready."

Skye swallowed. Would this child *ever* be ready to be born, and would it be well and healthy? But she still said nothing, too uneasy to put it into words that made the alternative seem all too much of a possibility.

She couldn't even explain why she felt the way she did, except that she had felt such a very real surge of magnetism between herself and Morwen when the baby had kicked. As if the two of them were saying goodbye . . .

She saw Philip glance at her as she made an involuntary sound in her throat. She should be sharing this with him. This child was a part of them both, but right now she was jealousy guarding all her fears, and she knew it was creating a small barrier between them.

To ward off any further personal questions, she made her voice brighter as Philip drove carefully back down the moorland tracks towards the road leading to New World.

"Perhaps the baby's waiting for the war to end before he makes his appearance. If all the reports in the newspapers are true, it can only be days now."

"And you wouldn't doubt what's said in *The Informer*, would you, Skye?" Philip said with a smile, knowing of her regard for David Kingsley being such a stickler for facts, and not reporting anything until it was verified.

"I would not!" she said airily. "If David's got wind that German troops are being ordered to withdraw all along the Western Front, then it must be true, and surely that means the end has got to be in sight."

"Amen to that," her father said fervently. "The sooner the better. They say that some of the battles yielded no more than yards of territory for either side, at a terrible cost in lives. It's a tragedy the world shouldn't ever forget."

"My goodness, how serious we're becoming," Primmy said nervously. "Let's look forward instead of back, shall we? We've got a happy event to look forward to, and the pottery isn't the only thing that needs a name, Skye. What have you decided on? You've been keeping it a very close secret."

"That's because we've been too superstitious to decide on anything yet," Skye said.

"You – superstitious?" Primmy said sceptically.

Philip laughed. "Your daughter's become very acclimatised since living here, Primmy. She thinks like a Cornishwoman now. She's even had a clash with an old woman who lives on the moors, and I'm not sure how much of her fairy-tales Skye actually believed."

"I wish I'd never told you any of that now," Skye said crossly. And if she truly thought like a Cornishwoman now, then she could believe anything was possible under the sun.

The days following Morwen's death were subdued ones for everyone at New World. Nurse Jenkins had gone on to other duties, and Birdie was ready to bid them all a tearful farewell, promising to let them know when she was settled in her brother's house.

"You will, won't you, Birdie?" Skye urged. "Granny Morwen would want us to know that everything was well with you."

"Aye," the woman said. "And I'll want to know when this babby's born too, so you'll be hearing from me, never fear."

They hugged one another quickly, both conscious that in the parting, they were breaking a link with the past.

And then it seemed to Skye that she was just marking time, just as the whole world was marking time. She, for the delivery of her baby, and the rest of mankind for the delivery of peace. She tried not to think that way, as if she was setting herself up as some divine mother-to-be.

And at last, in the sleepless still of the night that she hated, she found the words to confide her fears to Philip. He folded her into him, gently rubbing her back to give her some relief from her awkward lying position.

"Sometimes I'm so frightened that all may not be well with the baby," she whispered. "I haven't told you how I've been feeling lately, Philip, but if we should lose him now—"

He kissed her mouth, stopping the nervous flow of words.

"Do you think I haven't guessed? You're not the only one with intuition, my darling, and I'm sure you're not the first woman to feel this way. But you've got to keep believing that you're going to carry on what Morwen began. You're not a Tremayne for nothing."

She mumbled against his shoulder. "I know. Great-grand-mother Bess Tremayne was a strong woman, and so was Morwen. And Mom too. I've got a hell of a lot to live up

279

to, and I'm not sure I can ever read Granny Morwen's diaries after all. It will be far too painful."

"They'll come to no harm where they are, and you'll know when the time is right," he said, not pressing her.

She hugged him as close as she could, considering the bulge between them, a smile in her voice.

"Now I know why I love you so much," she said illogically, but neither of them needed logic at that moment. It was enough to need and hold each other.

Shortly before a cold and misty dawn on November 11th, a group of men were bizarrely gathered in a railway carriage in the forest of Compiegne to agree the terms and sign the armistice that signalled that four miserable years of war were at an end. At eleven that morning, all hostilities ceased, and the news was circulated around the world.

Jubilation was rife in towns and cities; toasts were drunk; the silent church bells began to ring out again; cars' hooters blared out everywhere, and people spilled out of houses and taverns in the joyous knowledge that peace had come at last. And those who had lost loved ones, wept over the waste and futility of it all.

"You'd think this babe would show its appreciation, wouldn't you?" Skye grumbled, when the momentous day had come and gone, with no sign of her labour commencing.

A couple of days later the family gathered at New World for a celebration dinner, as they had so often done in the past. Theo arrived with his family, with Betsy trying hard to stop Sebastian having one of his screaming bouts of temper; Charlotte came with her husband Vincent, and their two daughters; Emma and Will had come over from Wadebridge; Albie and Rose were there, and so was Luke.

They were all acutely conscious that Morwen was missing from their midst, but everyone was determined to be bright.

"There's to be a national Victory Day on the fifteenth, Skye,"

Vera told her, gleeful at the thought of all the young men returning from France. "Maybe the baby will arrive then."

"Well, it had better be born soon," Theo said, having drunk far too much champagne to mince his words, "before she turns into a barrage balloon."

"That's a bit near the knuckle, even in these days, isn't it, old boy?" Luke reproached him mildly.

"I thought it was more like hitting below the belt," Vera chortled, always ready to bait Luke, and uncaring what she said in these first heady days of peace, any more than any of them really did.

It was a time for celebration, and the final toast before they went home again was to Morwen, who had missed it all.

"But I'm sure she knows. Mammie always did know everything," Primmy said softly, raising her glass to Albie so surreptitiously that few were aware of it.

Skye knew that families need to be together in times of stress or happiness, but she was glad when they all left and it was just the four of them again; herself and Philip, Primmy and Cress. And if there was to be a Victory Day in two days' time, it would have to happen without her, she said fervently.

But when the day arrived, she urged her parents not to miss any of the festivities that were planned. *The Informer* had published extra issues, detailing the various events.

"There'll be street parties, and they've put bunting up all over Truro and St Austell," Philip said, reading the gigantic headlines. "There're going to be firework displays too, and flags are on sale everywhere," he reported. "All the street lights have been unmasked, and shops are ablaze with lights now without their black-out curtains. It sounds wonderful, but I bet London will really be the place to be."

He stopped, realising they were all laughing at him.

"And you sound about ten years old!" Skye said. "I wish I'd known you then. I bet you weren't half as serious as the college lecturer you turned out to be."

281

"Were *you* serious at ten years old?" he countered.

"Sinclair was," Primmy put in. "But then Sinclair was serious in the cradle. He always looked like a little old man, even when he was six months old."

At which they all convulsed, until Skye begged them to stop, insisting that she had a terrible stitch in her side that wouldn't go away.

"This could be it," Primmy said at once.

"I doubt it, but even if it is, you're not to stay at home because of me, Mom. You and Daddy go and enjoy it all with Albie and Rose, and come tell me all about it later. I'm all right, *really* I am, so please don't fuss. And Philip's not going anywhere, are you, honey? You're not planning to nip off to London or anything, are you?"

She had to make a joke of it, becase the pain was becoming more intense, and she wasn't at all sure that it was just a stitch after all. But she didn't want her folks to miss out on the fun because of her.

"I'm staying right here, love," he said, and once they had seen her parents off after many protestations, he turned to Skye. "And now do I send for the midwife?"

"Yes," she gasped. "And tell her to make it *soon!*"

"The poor maid's having a hard time of it, Sir," the midwife said to Philip some hours later. "I think 'twould be a good idea to send for the doctor, just to be on the safe side."

"What's wrong?" Skye ground out between contractions.

She asked the obligatory question, although dealing with the pain that was tearing her apart was uppermost in her mind right now. Philip gripped her hand tightly, assuring her that nothing was wrong. It was just that the midwife needed a second opinion.

"What about? That the baby is still alive?" Skye muttered with an awful fatality.

If he heard, he didn't answer, but went rushing out of the room to telephone the doctor, and praying that he wouldn't be somewhere in the midst of the day's festivities, like most of the rest of the country. It was sheer good fortune that the midwife hadn't yet left for Truro to join her son and daughter, and she'd need paying double fees for attending on this particular day, Skye had joked.

"He's not there," Philip said a few minutes later. Ashen now, he stared down at Skye's pain-distorted face. "He's gone to attend a sick patient, and his housekeeper doesn't know when he'll be back."

"Then we'll just have to manage without un, won't we?" the midwife said. "You can help, if you've the stomach for it, Sir, even though a man's work was done nine months afore, and he's best out of it, I allus say. But needs must, and this little lady's getting very tired now."

"Just tell me what I must do," Philip said quietly, and Skye had never loved him more as he obeyed the midwife's crisp instructions as that long day dragged on.

It was dusk when they saw the glare of fireworks, and heard them exploding in the sky, but by then Skye was too disorientated to care about anything but ridding herself of her burden. It was almost here, the midwife said, just a little longer, and Philip was urging her to push . . .

The sudden joyous peal of church bells in the vicinity burst through her consciousness. Celebrating victory after four long years of war, and as the sounds continued to ring out like a litany, they were also celebrating the arrival of a new child into the world.

The baby finally slid out of Skye's body, uttering a weak cry, and then a stronger, more vital one. As she heard it, tears dampened Skye's cheeks, knowing the child was alive and that all her fears had been unfounded after all.

She saw Philip's awed and delighted face as the midwife wrapped the baby in a cloth and handed it to him.

"Tain't the usual way o' things, but I reckon the father deserves some credit for today's proceedings as well, don't you, Mother?"

Mother. With one word, she was elevated into another sphere, one that she would cherish as long as she lived.

"Let me hold him," she said huskily, and Philip handed the bundle to her.

"*Him*?" the midwife hooted before he could speak. "'Tis a girl-child, Mrs Norwood, and a right little beauty she be. Now I'll leave you two to coo over her while I see to tidying up."

A girl . . . but she should have always known it would be a girl, thought Skye. A dark-haired, blue-eyed daughter, with a perfectly-shaped mouth and creamy skin. A Tremayne girl.

"Isn't she beautiful?" Skye breathed, almost afraid to take her eyes away from the baby. She reached out and held Philip's hand. "Mom will be so mad to have missed it all. But you were just wonderful, darling."

"You weren't so bad yourself," he said, "even though you did shout pretty forcefully more than once that all men should be sent to Kingdom Come."

"My Lord, did I?" she grinned. "That was worthy of Granny Morwen, I'll bet."

The church bells were still ringing out far and wide, filling the air with their sweetness, and heralding the peace that was yet to feel like a reality, but was already descending blissfully over the bedroom at New World.

"So now we really do have to think of a name, don't we?" Philip said, prosaic as ever.

Skye spoke softly. "I've already thought. The moment I knew it was a girl, the name was in my head, and please don't mock, Philip, but I think maybe someone was putting it there. I want to call her Celia. Do you approve?"

Tenderly, he gathered his family close in his arms, his brave and beautiful wife, and his beautiful child.

"I think *she* would definitely approve," he said, without elaborating. And from the reaction in Skye's bright, brimming eyes, he knew she understood perfectly.